Bartender Wanted

Bartender Wanted

A Rose Leary
Mystery

Maureen Anne Jennings

This book is a work of fiction.
Names, characters, places, and incidents are
either a product of the author's imagination or are used fictitiously.
Any resemblance to actual persons, living or dead,
is entirely coincidental.

Cover design by Randy Comer
ISBN 978-0-9852835-0-6
April 2013

To Steve,
who gave me the Village

Chapter One

Some little nobody was copying the way she killed people. Whoever it was, the wretch had taste, because this had been her best murder yet. Rose had felt more pride in how she'd killed this victim than about anything she'd done in years. Her latest murder had boasted all the best signs of a Rose Leary work.

"Olive juice, Rose."

The most disgusting part was that Rose had reveled in how the woman would die. She'd been thrilled when she'd first plotted it all out, every last gory, splattery detail, including where in the kitchen a knife could be found. At the point where a blade slipped between the victim's ribs, she'd felt torn between gagging and self-congratulatory applause.

Definitely one of the best murder scenes she'd ever written.

"Darling, you heard me say olive juice, didn't you? Remember that light green liquid with more salt than Bambi and all her cousins could have licked? Do you want me to describe the gin, too? It's the funny clear stuff that smells like hair spray."

Jimmy's farmboy features held a sweetness that undermined his world-weary attitude and erased years from his age. Tall and very thin, he held himself in a posture as straight as the perfect part in his shining nut-brown hair. She could almost see the ghosts of dry-cleaning bags fluttering behind the starched white shirts and creased black pants he wore to work. Today's cufflinks were large onyx squares.

Rose laughed. "Jimmy, what are you gibbering about now?"

"I'm not gibbering, my dear. I am simply giving you a drink order. And, since the order is almost as unusual as the creature who requested it, and since the look on your face shows that your thoughts are not centered on the task at hand, I thought I would help you along. That's how this quaint establishment has things structured.

"I, as the waiter, relay the customers' drink orders to you. You, as the bartender, then make the aforesaid drinks, with whatever ingredients necessary. Then I take the drinks back to the parched customers and everyone is happy. Now do you want me to explain how tipping the bartender works? Or will you just give me the miserable martini with the olive juice instead of vermouth and go back to your daydreaming, or sexual fantasizing, or however it is you plan on passing the time until the bar fills up? I need a dirty martini before dawn, please." His lips pursed around the word dirty.

Rose, who'd grown up in restaurants, wondered how to adequately express her gratitude for lessons in the business from a man who'd decided that a career as one of New York's bitchiest waiters logically followed twelve years of teaching fourth graders in Fresno. If only he'd learn to rave without lecturing. She kept waiting for him to ask if her hands were clean.

She'd already considered slapping his hands if it would shut his mouth. But each time his chatter threatened the limits of her patience, his monologue made her laugh enough to save both his knuckles and her temper. Laughing made her feel better than losing her patience. Jolly girls had more friends than shrews.

Rose checked the backup garnishes that Diane, the day bartender, had prepped. The plastic containers held less than a dozen lime slices and three shriveled lemon twists. She really did need to ask Diane to leave the bar better prepared. Rose decided to cut extra fruit in case tonight grew busy. Thursday nights sometimes drew crowds eager to begin their weekends early, even in traditionally slow February. After only two weeks at My World, Rose couldn't predict business as well as she thought she could predict Jimmy's antics.

Slicing through a lime with the paring knife, she remembered the thrill when she'd finally calculated at precisely what angle a butcher knife would have to enter a woman's body to kill her quickly without requiring extraordinary strength. She'd argued with herself for hours, debating whether it would be safer to leave the knife in the victim's body or clean it and return it to its drawer. She had felt particularly pleased when she'd dreamed up the part about the corpse slumping below the chef's 86 list, with the blackboard empty except for a huge arrow pointing down to the body.

It had been one of the most satisfying chapters she'd ever written and structurally far superior to the apparent robbery and stabbing that had occurred at My World last month. Leaving a corpse in the big walk-in, and on the vegetable side at that, didn't rank high on her list of creative touches. Maybe the ubiquitous suspected junkies were in a hurry, or maybe the killer had wanted to start 1986 off with a dead body.

"Penny for your thoughts. Bet you must be thinking how creepy it is to fill a dead girl's shoes or at least her job. Gimme an Amstel."

Rose smiled, gave the man his beer, and took his money. His opening lines didn't encourage witty repartee. Maybe she should explain why she liked the murder she'd written better than the one that had actually happened, then tell him how creepy it felt working as the successor to a corpse. She could describe how horrified and frightened she felt thinking about her predecessor, Susan, as a real woman with a real name who had really been cruelly killed. By a real murderer.

By then, he would probably be relieved to hear she was able to find a tiny amount of comfort by thinking about it in the abstract. The coincidences between the events she'd plotted for her novel and the end of Susan's life were not all that eerie, if you only thought about them logically. Murderers only had so many ways to kill people, after all, and the anonymous copycat had paid for his plagiarism by providing her with a new job. Death struck a blow against unemployment: one bartender killed, another hired. Simple social work.

Slow down, Ro. Don't forget the first commandment of bartending: never tell a customer you're writing a book, unless you want to hear the story he has for you, the same one he's going to get around to writing himself one day, the one that will undoubtedly boast himself as hero. Stories? He has stories. Believe it or not, just his life would—

The forest would lose all its trees.

"You're prettier than the one who died, anyway."

"Thank you," Rose said. This gent had really flunked charm school. What should she reply? Oh, then it's good she's dead? Survival of the cutest? Guess nobody misses the hag anyway?

She smiled again and tried to remember the weather forecast. Today was normal and seasonably cold for February in New York. No major storm or strong warming trend approached. If God had invented the weather to give bartenders conversational topics, He should have made it consistently worthy of discussion.

"Good, I like girls who smile a lot. Matter of fact, I like everybody who works for me to smile. Good for business. Makes the customer happy; makes the employee think she could be happy. Looks nice." Ah, common ground, at last. Maybe he'd tip her with one of those adorable little smile buttons or some turn-of-the-century coins.

"It's what restaurants sell, you know. Smiles. Food,

booze, and smiles. And sex, or at least the smell of it. Know what I mean, sweetheart?"

This was getting trickier. Rose nodded and hoped it wasn't a lead-in to a come-on as she looked at the man more carefully.

He was about six feet tall, early sixties, with thick hair graying away from dark brown. He would have been wiser to start with the lite beers a while back. She saw a glint of gold among the gray hairs on his Florida-tan chest, which both a good mirror and the calendar would have suggested he cover by at least two more buttons. He returned her look steadily. She doubted he'd ever suffer the embarrassment of dropping his eyes first. Then he stood, smiling. "You'll do fine here, kid. I'm Joe Victors. I'm your bosses' boss. Keep smiling." The ten dollars he left on the bar made the instructions easy to follow. Thank God she'd kept it up. Bad test to flunk.

Jimmy stood at the service station. "Two white wines, one red, and a rum and Diet Coke. The girls are here early tonight. How'd you like meeting God the Father?"

"Who?"

"Don't you know from whom all blessings flow? That august presence was God the Father, as we all adoringly call Joe. His son, Ben, who hired you and whom you must never, ever call by his full name of Benito, is known as the Son. Ben's brother Thomas completes the trinity as the Holy Ghost, but you'll have to wait to meet him, since he's on one of his frequent and extended vacations. I imagine the shock of finding Susan's body and having to go through all those nasty police questions inspired his little jaunt." Jimmy smoothed his collar.

"Did Joe give you the smile and smell-of-sex routine? He's not as stupid as he sounds, the only one of the trinity with any real brains. Beneficent, too, because he paid for all the expenses of flying Susan's body back to Ohio and, rumor has it, also picked up the funeral costs. Least he could do."

Jimmy lowered his voice, "He's so generous that he gave the precious sons this place, probably to keep them out of trouble. The theory of infallibility is now open to serious question, however. But you'll discover all of that yourself eventually, won't you? I'd hate to ruin any of the exciting suspense for you."

"Jimmy, you can't keep your mouth shut long enough to build up any suspense about your next word. Go check on your customers." Rose started sticking olives onto picks for the martini rush. While Jimmy charmed his customers, she could think of a good topic sentence for the essay on My World's history he might decide to assign.

Jimmy feigned insult as he walked away, maintaining the mock adversarial role he and Rose had established the first night they'd worked together.

Rose ignored his act as she considered his information. The bar she tended was the heart of an old restaurant in Manhattan's far West Village. Decades as a blue collar bar and lunch place had mellowed the joint into a sweetly seedy character since the Victors had opened it in the 1940s. Reading the writing on the wall, or at least the real estate ads in the *Times*, the owners of My World had allowed evolution to start several years ago. This wasn't just the meat market area anymore.

The restaurant had changed more gracefully than the neighborhood. Steam-table cuisine departed, but the food remained good, honest, and relatively cheap. Pastas and salads coexisted with meat and potatoes. The wine list graduated beyond bicolored but still fit on the back of the menu. Gentle prices for strong drinks and the absence of slushy tropical delights gave the bar at least the illusion of integrity.

The crowd seemed a good mix, too. Old-time Village residents who remembered the place back when came in and charmed their more recent neighbors who had just discovered My World and loved it. Folks from other neighborhoods considered it a find and swore several of their closest friends to mythical secrecy. My World succeeded because everyone thought it belonged to them.

Not even Susan's murder last month seemed to hurt business. The curious came once or twice and the regulars returned to sympathize. Some even admitted to feeling safer here now, since New York wisdom dictated that a recently robbed place might stay safe for a while. The fact that the stabbing happened during a robbery seemed to be accepted as Gospel by everyone from the press to the porter.

My World was a good place to work, if you had to work in a restaurant at all. If you wanted a goodly amount of cash and plenty of time to write, you might have to work in a restaurant. Rose had quickly spent all of the small advance her devoted agent had managed to wrangle for her second mystery novel. More slowly, she'd realized that it would be a long time before she saw, much less spent, her share of the profits from selling the Massachusetts restaurant she'd owned with her ex. Her pride in receiving any advance at all, after the ten-year lull between her first published mystery and this work-in-progress, had no buying power. So she needed cash and time.

Knowing she'd gotten this job because her predecessor died still disturbed her. Died, her writer's mind insisted, made a weakling synonym for stabbed to death.

She had a bartending job and she had a writing job. The two were not the same, and combining them would be asking for trouble she didn't need. Rose decided to try to live through the rest of the night without thinking about either the woman who died or the way she died. Imagination served her better when she wrote than when she tended bar. The service economy had its own grammar.

"Hey, beautiful, give me a double vodka on the rocks. Then let me tell you about the day I had." Mr. Distraction looked as if it had been a rough one.

Chapter Two

Four dollars for a five-minute cab ride, almost half of it a tip, and the driver still didn't wait to see her safely in the front door. Rose cursed the city where a sane woman wouldn't walk six blocks at 4:30 a.m. and whose cabdrivers all seemed to need geography lessons, usually over translator headphones. That got her up the first two flights. More invective toward the ignorant drivers who insisted no such place as the corner of Fourth and Eleventh Streets existed took her up the next flight. For the fourth and final flight, she resorted to a tired rant about the Christmas tree needles still littering the stairs two months after the holiday.

Walking up the stairs to her fifth-floor apartment was sometimes a miserable experience, however good for the calves. Anger made her climb easier this morning. Pet peeves deserved exercise too. Cheap enough therapy, and she'd have her adrenaline revved up if anyone ever lurked on a landing.

Abandoning her annoyance as she unlocked her door, Rose relaxed once she secured both locks from the inside. Home. She never walked in this door without congratulating herself on the foresight or suspicion that had caused her to sublet her apartment for the years she'd left New York. Forsaking all others didn't include leases on Manhattan apartments. Thank God she'd never put her ex's name on the lease. He would have lost the apartment along with everything else he'd squandered. Or used it for assignations with one of the many girlfriends he'd successfully denied for far too long.

She hung her purse on the doorknob, kicked her shoes in the general direction of the closet, and poured a glass of wine while she decided if she wanted a flannel-nightgown or a silk-robe night. Faded red flannel would soothe, but black silk might encourage more sophisticated mental processes.

Rose tucked her feet under the hem of the cozy nightgown and rolled back the robe's silken sleeves as she settled herself into her big chair by the living room window. Fourth Street was quiet, and the Empire State Building was still there. Everything in the big living room looked as neat as she wanted it to be, with her desk in as much order as a novel in progress allowed.

Nothing about the My World murder need concern her. The police had declared the motive robbery, and she didn't have any reason to distrust their judgment.

Nobody was copying anything. The similarity between the murder she'd written and the murder at My World was simple coincidence. Life was full of coincidences; fiction had even more. Lazy fiction had the most.

Rose did not write bad fiction, and she didn't want to live it. Three months ago, she had created a wonderful murder scene wherein an irate wife stabbed a pastry chef for seducing her husband. The victim was a fictional character with a wretched and criminal past, who was fictionally stabbed by a fictional murderer whose identity the brightest reader wouldn't ascertain until at least 100 pages after the crime.

"Unless I hint at the killer more strongly in the beginning—" Rose started at the sound of her own muttering. Talking to yourself was not a good sign. Childhood in a large family and too many adult years in marriage didn't grant any excuses for using your own voice as a substitute for the company you didn't always want. If you had that much to say, you could always hit the keys and make somebody else talk.

Writing mysteries encouraged an already suspicious mind. If she insisted on the intricacies of plotting, her manuscript waited across the room. On the wall above her desk, a big red X on the calendar marked the date her manuscript was due at her agent's office. Sophie insisted on seeing the manuscript a week before the publisher's deadline, "just in case we want to tinker, darling." Sophie called Rose too often to remind her of how many days she had left, so often that Rose had actually labeled each square on the calendar with the number of remaining work days. In black.

Today's number was fifty-seven.

Maybe her pattern of not sitting down at the desk to write after standing up for ten hours pouring drinks was not divine law. Every day counted now.

She needed to stop trying to find connections where

they didn't exist. Then she could discover how to erase her insistent suspicions about Susan's death. What she'd heard about the murder didn't match the official determination that the woman died in a sloppy robbery. She couldn't rewrite this problem.

Rose walked back to the kitchen and noticed that her neighbors across the courtyard were asleep or engaged in activities suited to the dark. Staying awake past five in a New York City morning didn't erase the memories of lying in bed enviously listening to the big kids still riding bikes in the lingering light of California summer evenings. Would she ever stop feeling that the last one up knew the most?

The refrigerator offered little in the way of late-night thrills. Only her nerves needed nourishment, anyway, and three of the chocolate truffles in the breadbox settled them. She poured another glass of wine and nudged the door closed with her left hip. Something was wrong with the refrigerator. Hers sounded fine, humming and belching along as usual.

The walk-in at My World, the small refrigerated room, that cooling coffin where Thomas found Susan's body, that big fridge was definitely wrong. No random robber could have hidden Susan in there.

"Got anything to go back to the kitchen, Rose? I noticed you backed yourself up with heavy cream for that one guy belting back the White Russians. I'd just as soon put any extra back in the walk-in. Inventory's tomorrow morning." Ben had walked up to the bar just after she'd given last call earlier tonight.

Ben was obviously Joe's son, with the same dark brown eyes under heavy brows. While heredity had fished Ben's features from his father's genetic pool, they'd landed on Ben in an arrangement that looked worried most of the time. He had darker brown hair than his father but stood about two inches shorter. His solid body looked very powerful; she'd seen him stacking cases of liquor as if they were tinker toys.

"It's okay, Ben. Let me check and then I'll run whatever I find back to the kitchen myself."

"No, hon, it doesn't work like that here. The walk-in gets locked as soon as the kitchen's down. Keeps the porters from getting tempted, right? Only Tommy and me have the keys. One of us closes it up each and every night, then Tom or me opens it up each morning. I always make sure it's locked before I count the money. I'd hate to be counting fives while someone was stealing steaks.

"Once it's locked, I don't worry. Houdini would have a hard time getting through that padlock. Friend of mine knows a guy who likes to, uh, experiment with locks. Just for kicks, we brought him in here one night. Over an hour and the poor guy couldn't get the bitch open. Made me feel better about how damned much the lock cost me in the first place. So I always, I mean always, lock it. You can bet your life."

Rose understood how Ben valued routines, especially those concerning his property. She knew he'd worked the night Susan died. He'd only left the bartender to close My World herself because he trusted the few customers lingering over their final drinks. Susan should have been able to see them all out and lock the street door behind her with no trouble. He'd told Rose when he hired her that she wouldn't have to worry about closing My World herself.

Good. Walking out of a closed restaurant alone late at night asked for more trouble than she'd even want to write about.

She didn't feel relieved at remembering Ben's speech about the lock on the walk-in.

Suddenly the murder didn't seem like such a simple robbery.

The homicide investigators had decided that the killer had jumped Susan from behind just as she locked the door. She must have fought hard. Someone had shoved her back inside the door and stabbed her only four feet into the restaurant. The cops discovered her purse and a bottle of Courvoisier missing and the cash register smashed open. They hadn't found any evidence of a search for more cash or valuables. Nothing about the crime indicated planning by a professional criminal with the experience to avoid panic, much less one sophisticated enough to grab one of the bottles of single-malt scotch three times more expensive than the cognac. The cops pronounced Susan the random victim of a random thief. She was in the wrong job in the wrong place at the wrong time.

Wrong. Random thieves do not drag a stranger's body

across a dining room and into a kitchen. Random thieves do not spend hours breaking into a locked walk-in and then more hours repairing all visible damages. Random thieves would either try to find a key or break into the office to find a safe. Random thieves don't have too many reasons to lock dead bodies in among the spinach and steaks.

Right, and the NYPD's investigation would have overlooked such crucial points. Any woman who had written one well-received mystery ten years ago, read hundreds of others in the interim, and was now trying to finish her second book would naturally need less than an hour of wine and wild speculations to discover glaring flaws in the official reasoning. The same woman would probably also wake up fabulously wealthy and six feet tall tomorrow.

The police had to have raised those questions. It would be interesting, and probably even her professional duty, to discover what answers had satisfied them. Maybe stashing a corpse in a cooler was chic among slash-and-run thieves. Maybe Ben had left his key in the door. Maybe she'd better save her imagination for her own book. She'd decided to take the job at My World for the money, not writing material.

Sleep was more important than speculation at this point. 5:30 in the morning, and she still had to wash her face, set up the coffee machine, and finish the last two chapters of *Pride and Prejudice*, again.

She didn't anticipate inordinate trouble in getting

Jimmy to talk tomorrow night. He'd be happy to tell her everything he knew about the case. At length. You had to pick your sources wisely.

Chapter Three

"Welcome to My World."

The stranger who greeted her was short, pudgy, and still attempting the downtown Eurotrash look. The shoulders on his black jacket extended a good two inches from where his own doubtless ended, while his pants' designer had probably envisioned the black leather would hang more loosely than his physique allowed. He'd sculpted his dead white hair with its harsh black roots into tight curls in another affectation. She doubted he'd intended the slightly synthetic orange cast to his tan.

"Thanks," she replied.

"Would you like a table?" Rose couldn't place his faint accent.

"No, thank you."

"Well, then, you'll discover the bar just to our right. Sit down in comfort, order a specialty cocktail, enjoy yourself like a pretty woman should."

Specialty cocktail? My World didn't make them, unless she'd missed something.

"I'd love to, but I think I'll just go behind the bar and pour a few hundred instead."

"What?"

"Hi, I'm Rose, the new bartender. Well, almost new, I started two weeks ago. What's your name?" She really shouldn't have teased this poor soul, who must have just started at My World. Good restaurant manners dictated that she be nice to this newcomer.

"I am Zorro. I am the weekend night-time floor manager. You did not get to meet me last weekend because I was on my very much deserved vacation." His accent put a man's name at the end of "deserved."

"Nice to meet you, Zorro. Where was your vacation? With such a great tan, you must have gone someplace good and warm."

Grease him with a few compliments.

"Yes, it was hot, very hot, like myself, if you take my meaning. Now I think you must go downstairs and get the bar bank from Ben. My World is always very busy on Friday nights. You will probably learn that."

She walked into the office. "Hi, Ben. I just met Zorro. Didn't know you had a manager on at nights."

"Lucky you. Some manager. You ever heard of a manager taking a month off? Not that he would have been much help when Susan was killed even if he was here. The jerk's a glorified host and everyone but him knows it." Ben handed her the cash drawer.

"Remember you get an extra hundred in tens on Friday and Saturday nights. Don't let Zorro give you any trouble. I'm the one who manages this place, and Tommy, too, of course."

Rose counted the money, did her preshift primp in the women's room, and walked upstairs. Diane, the day bartender, was cheerfully cleaning up her last-minute tips. Rose wished Diane were as dedicated to cleaning and setting up behind the bar. But Diane consistently short-changed the large percentage of her chores intended to prepare the bar for the much busier night shift. Maybe hearing ten people a day say you were a dead ringer for Grace Kelly in *Rear Window* burned out one's cleaning synapses.

Out of that Main Line mouth came the kind of Brooklyn accent that enriched voice coaches.

"Jeeze, Rose, sorry about the mess. Everything looked great and then I kind of lost it when I got so busy. Want me to stay and help you?" She lowered her voice, "Be extra nice to those two suits in the corner. They just scored big on the market and they're throwing around the dividends."

"It's fine, Diane. I can take care of it. And thanks for the tip."

Diane giggled happily at the accidental pun.

Rose surveyed the bar, which looked like the disaster area she'd come to expect.

So far, Rose hadn't gotten exasperated with Diane, who always seemed genuinely surprised at the havoc she'd produced. Genuine surprise was one of Diane's main characteristics. She was as naive as an embryo, with no dumb blond act involved. At twenty-eight, she seemed decades rather than years Rose's junior. Rose still liked her enough to clean up her messes without anger. Diane inspired uncharacteristic sympathies in everyone.

Rose bent down to straighten out the jumble of empty

liquor bottles and full juice cans under the sinks.

"Hi, Rosie, I know you're down there somewhere. Nice view."

Great. Someday she would figure out why so many people in restaurants loved adding the diminutive to everybody's name. It probably had something to do with the desire for instant intimacy. Then she would figure out how to stop it.

She stood up to greet Alan. Or should she call him Allie?

The first night she'd met him, Rose had enrolled Alan in the group of men she'd dubbed the Serious Lonely Guys Club. She considered the Serious Lonely Guys Club one of bartending's worst aspects. The club's members differed from the typical men who tested their luck by coming on to the bartender. While it might be too optimistic to call that majority normal, Rose knew how to parry their overtures without hurting or unduly encouraging them. Flirting was part of the job and not always an onerous duty.

The Serious Lonely Guys Club formed an entirely different group, with a small but intense membership. They seemed to focus on bartenders because they were afraid to try with other women. These guys found false courage in the drinks and the wooden barrier separating them from the woman serving the alcohol.

They always wanted to get to know you, really know you, and liked to think that your sole purpose in working behind any given bar was to further your relationship with them. Shy and awkward, they nonetheless offered their attentions tenaciously. They were often nice enough men, but rarely good-looking ones. She always suspected they subscribed to several skin magazines delivered in plain brown envelopes and tried to avoid speculating about the objects of their fantasies.

Club members never, ever, brought a woman into the bar but usually acted chummy with some of the male regulars. As pathetic as the worst blind date, they were lonely in their seriousness and serious in their loneliness.

"Here, flowers for the most beautiful flower in town. I was in the Corner Bistro getting a hamburger when Moms came in. I thought of you and couldn't resist. She's such a nice old lady." Alan had brought her another gift. A red rose, in the late bud stage, lay right next to his crisp twenty on the bar.

Alan could run for president of the Serious Lonely Guys Club. He'd acted too friendly to Rose her first night at My World and had adorned her bar every night since then. He had the cherubic face of a child, marred only by the lingering acne scars his forty-odd years should have banished, and wispy hair the color of a manila envelope. Heavy around the middle, his build reminded her of one of those clown toys that kids could never manage to knock down.

He worked in the bookkeeping department of one of the local meat wholesalers and also lived nearby. He offered to walk Rose home every night but never pressed when she offered him one of her repertoire of excuses. Last week, he'd given her a twelve-pound beef roast. She'd given the meat to her downstairs neighbors and refrained from telling him she'd prefer chocolate.

Serious Lonely Guys often came bearing little gifts. They'd misconstrue any encouragement of their generosity.

Rose poured Alan his usual rye and ginger and made a show of putting the flower in a collins glass with water and a little bar sugar.

It was futile. The rose had as much chance of reaching a full and beautiful bloom as did Alan's fantasies about her. None of Moms' products ever survived a night. The sweet little old lady in the Lassie's mother housedress and gray topknot peddled flowers in the bars like the Little Match Girl grown old. But, rather than trudging in the cold from place to place, her husband chauffeured her on a carefully timed route around the city.

Moms went to the bars and sold flowers; Dad sat in the Cadillac he'd parked around a corner and watched the TV plugged into the cigarette lighter. Neighborhood rumor had it that Moms got her flowers from a contact at a cemetery in Queens. Rumor also said that Moms and Pop used to own a candy store that had featured kool-aid in the soda machine. Alan probably wouldn't want to hear those stories, though.

The late cocktail hour crowd flowed into the early dinner shift, fulfilling the predictions of Zorro and any other twentieth-century North American resident that bars indeed did good business on Friday nights.

Although a compliment on Zorro's jacket made him smile at her, his officious air didn't dissipate. Trying hard to be charitable, she almost convinced herself his stilted speech stemmed from the accent she still couldn't identify. His frantic flirting didn't look as if it endeared him to any of the women he subjected to it, and his accenting the pronoun each time he welcomed customers to My World grated. He would not have been Rose's first choice as a host.

But My World wasn't hers, either. She didn't own this or any other restaurant anymore. Hosts, although fun for speculation, do not tip. Customers do. Her business here was to tend bar, and tonight offered an easy bar to tend.

Rose recognized many of the customers and pleased several by remembering their regular drinks. She made time to chat with those who wanted conversation and acknowledged the others who preferred brief pleasantries. She happily helped the three male graduate students from Boston meet the two women teachers from Brooklyn. Alan had ignored her efforts to introduce him, too shy to see that the prettier woman had smiled at him several times.

The busy bar grew busier. The crowd produced that essential buzz created only by people enjoying themselves instead of waiting for the fun to start. Full bar, fun crowd, generous tips: a good night.

Jimmy seemed her only problem. The crowd kept him and a waitress racing around the full dining room so fast

that his efficient visits to the service bar didn't allow Rose
any time to grill him. Inquiring if he wanted martinis up
or on the rocks and margaritas with or without salt didn't
satisfy any of her curiosity about Susan's murder.

She finally got a chance to ask Jimmy a question
at three, when both the dining room and the bar slowed
down.

"Hey, big guy, are you hungry? I haven't eaten
anything except these damned olives since noon. You want
to go to Chinatown after work? We should be out soon
after four, if nothing surprising shows up."

"Now, that, my dear, is an entrancing suggestion. I
even have my roommate's mother's car for the weekend.
She dragged him to Puerto Rico for a family reunion,
to which I was quite pointedly not invited. Imagine my
heartbreak at being cruelly deprived of a weekend in San
Juan with the sculpted-nails set. We did, however, manage
to convince her any sensible creature would rather go to
Siberia than long-term parking at Kennedy. Now I can at
least tool around in her little auto before I'm graciously
allowed to retrieve them from the airport."

While she'd ordinarily shudder at the idea of scheming
to loosen Jimmy's tongue, a little civilized wine with
breakfast might help her questions seem more palatable.
Rose asked Jimmy if they could swing by her apartment
to pick up a bottle of sauvignon blanc. She doubted her
refrigerator held a vintage rare enough to encourage
succinct answers.

Shortly after 4:30, she walked out My World's door with Zorro, Jimmy, and Ben. When Zorro invited her to join him for a drink at Save the Robots in the East Village, Ben shook his head and waited to hear her reply. Jimmy raised his eyebrows halfway to his hairline and glared.

With all that attention, she needed a minute to formulate a decent excuse. She didn't want to include Zorro at breakfast, but felt surprisingly wary of offending him. Ben had made it clear that Zorro had no power over her, and she didn't need to coddle him like a fussy boss. Nothing she'd seen of the "weekend night-time floor manager" in action tempted her to consider him a potential friend. Without a decent reason in the world for caring what the guy thought, she only knew that she did not want him angry at her.

The perfect excuse still eluded her.

"Rose, you said you were too tired to deal with a cab driver, so don't pretend you can muster the energy for drinking at this awful hour. Please, dear, let's go. I still have to find a parking place for that monster after I drop you." Jimmy had pointed at the green Saab with New Jersey plates on the corner.

Faking a yawn, Rose asked Zorro for a raincheck, said good night to him and Ben, then followed Jimmy down the street.

"My, my, my, little Mistress Motor Mouth at a loss for words. Whatever could have silenced the queen of the comebacks? You can tell me, dear. Was that the first time anyone ever asked you out for a drink? Somehow, I should have thought life would have been kinder to you than that. But one hears about late bloomers all the time. The usual practice, I believe, is to tell the gentleman 'no, thank you' when you've already made other and certainly more enticing plans." Jimmy opened the passenger's door and waited until she'd fastened her seatbelt before closing it.

"Jimmy, go over to Greenwich Avenue, not Street, and take a right on Eleventh. I think I really want a drink after that scene. We'll have wine with breakfast, okay?" She wondered if she'd chilled any of the good stuff.

He adjusted the rearview mirror, popped a Robert Palmer cassette into the player, and sang along to "Addicted to Love" for a few choruses before sighing and turning the music way down. "God, I love that song. But, from the sublime to the ridiculous, why is it that Zorro so often inspires queer reactions in people?

I can't imagine it's his beauty that blinds them."

Chapter Four

"Picture this. The end of a long night, you're exhausted and just want to get home and relax. The dark restaurant looks ominous when you're the only one in it. The distorted light coming up the stairs and in from the street plays tricks with you. You think for a minute that you see somebody standing at the end of the bar, but it's only a shadow. The chairs upended on the dining room tables suggest a monstrous crowd materialized when the lights dimmed. The heating system groans horrid noises you've never heard before.

"The street suddenly seems much safer than staying in this restaurant alone. You can't wait to get outside. You swear you'll never close the place by yourself again. You pray the restaurant really is empty. You snort a couple more lines off your fingernail for courage.

"You're in such a hurry to get out of here that you don't check the neighboring doorways to see if anyone's lurking. Your shoulders tighten as you fumble for the front door keys the boss gave you. The junk at the bottom of your purse makes noises that sound too loud on this quiet street. Why didn't you put the keys in your hand before you came out here? You keep fumbling in your purse, you find the key, and you try to remember if you're supposed to do the top or bottom lock first.

"Footsteps run up behind you. You start to turn

around. A horrible pain explodes in your back. You pull the door open, hoping to fall into the restaurant and lock the pain out. The pain follows you. So does someone who keeps making the pain happen in different places in your body. You hear him grunt every time he hurts you. You can't find the breath to scream. You turn around to try to fight."

Jimmy stopped talking to concentrate on squeezing the Saab into a space behind a dumpster three blocks away from their destination. He'd found the parking spot in a darkened alley. Rose jumped out of the car the minute he doused the headlights. He was right behind her. She tightened her grasp on the neck of the wine bottle.

"Jimmy, if you're trying to scare me, you're doing an excellent job. All I asked was how you thought Susan had died. I didn't expect an installment of nightmare theater, thanks. Hearing you use such clean, short sentences is almost as scary as what you said. Didn't know you had such brevity in you." He possessed frightening powers she'd never imagined.

Jimmy just laughed and asked her how to find the restaurant.

When they walked in, Mon Bo was, as always, too bright and too loud. She felt as if she were sitting in an Edward Hopper painting—on opium. A waiter gestured toward an empty table, then slammed down two menus, two teacups, and a teapot. As she did whenever she ate in Chinatown, Rose wished she could read the specials written in the beautiful characters on wall pennants.

Although Jimmy's story had almost deadened her appetite, Rose picked up the plastic-covered menu. She wanted to delay her questions until she'd shaken the cold fear Jimmy's description of Susan's attack had produced.

"What do you like, Jimmy?"

"Excellent food, fascinating conversation, and sexy waiters. I do hope two out of three won't be too much to ask. Who does cut these guys' hair?" He pushed his unopened menu to the exact center of the table, "Since you seem to know all the hidden delights of this place, why don't you select the items for our repast? Nothing sweet and sour, though. Too, too redundant at this lovely formica table."

Rose ordered clams with black bean sauce, Chinese sausage with bitter greens, and vegetable chow fun. She didn't bother to ask the waiter not to serve everything simultaneously. The only way to have food arrive in separate courses here was to order one dish at a time. She didn't want those interruptions tonight.

When she heard the table behind them ask for ketchup for their egg rolls, Rose realized she'd chosen the right restaurant. Jimmy wouldn't be distracted from their conversation by any avid interest in the other customers. People-watching in a cheap Chinese restaurant at 5:00 a.m. was a masochist's sport.

"Seriously, Jimmy, thanks for getting me out of that mess with Zorro. You thought much quicker than I did."

Jimmy pulled out his own corkscrew, opened the

wine, and poured it into the teacups he'd first dusted with his paper napkin. "Don't sound so surprised. You're bright enough to have seen through my act. Everyone in the restaurant business develops an act, don't we? You like to spice up your cheerfulness with scads of sarcastic zingers; I like to carry on."

Jimmy swirled his wine in the thick cup. "You teach parochial school for ten years in a state that's considering banning gays from all the schools and see what you feel like doing afterward. Besides, it's fun, a little innocent deception of a sort. The customers think it's cute and they tip me cute, too. But don't pretend you would have bothered to invite me for breakfast, even in this charming establishment, if you really thought I were the Flitting Nun."

"Sorry. How did you hear that? I was in the office, for God's sake." Ben had loved the line; she'd felt guilty the moment she blurted it.

"Yes, and I was in the men's room. There's a peculiar acoustical fluke downstairs. Sometimes you can hear conversation from the office in the rest rooms. Don't apologize. I spent a lot of time in the company of nuns, so maybe I'm trying to exorcise that a bit."

"I did my time too." She wondered if swirling helped the five-dollar wine.

The waiter set the three dishes down on the table. While they waited for chopsticks, Rose abandoned the temptation to indulge in trading Catholic-school horror stories.

"So, how do you like working for the Holy Trinity? Especially in a place with its own Sorrowful Mysteries, too." Jimmy arranged concentric circles of clams on their plates.

"I think I like My World." She paused at the way that sounded and struggled to grasp a slippery clam with her chopsticks. "But I can't help wondering about the murder. I don't want to ruin your meal by saying it haunts me, but something about it doesn't make sense. Did you work the night it happened?"

"Unfortunately. And I had a much larger role in the tragedy than I ever would have wanted."

The clam slipped down her throat before she could chew. "What?"

"Well, all my tables had left, and I'd finished my side work. I'd almost walked out the door when the phone rang. Thomas was calling Ben, so I dutifully scurried back to the kitchen and told Ben to come to the phone. Apparently, that was what did it."

"Did what?"

"Made Ben forget to lock the walk-in. I think the police believe that's what happened because Ben took so long to admit it was even possible. Besides, there's no other explanation.

"Only Ben and Thomas have keys, and neither of them were anywhere near the place when it happened. Ben had gone to one of his haunts downtown, and the bartender remembered Thomas had called looking for Ben there. Donny, the aforesaid bartender, asked Thomas if he planned to come by later, but Thomas said he was home for the night."

Her appetite had returned with such strength that she'd finished all but two of her clams. "They both had ulterior alibis, too. Restaurant owners may be crazy a lot of the time, but they're usually very protective of their places. I don't know Thomas, but I can't see Ben wanting to commit a crime in his own store.

"Messy, and not the most charming kind of publicity. Putting the body in the walk-in is a damn costly touch. It was a Wednesday, right? So they'd probably gotten a lot of food deliveries, and the walk-in must have been full. That's a lot of food to have to throw out."

Rose dropped her chopsticks. "They did throw everything out, didn't they, Jimmy?"

"Of course they did, dear. And Ben wasn't so broken up by the death that he didn't bitch about having to pay retail for some of the replacements. The night after she died was simply, utterly, awful."

"Not a real festive crowd, huh? Did people whisper a lot? Did the cops finish in time for dinner?"

"Not completely. Two of the guys from the afternoon came back hideously out of uniform and lurked at the bar all night drinking while they spied."

"That inconspicuous? They were probably the cover for other plainclothes guys." Rose finished her last clam.

Jimmy looked for the busy waiter, then gave up and wiped their plates with napkins from the metal dispenser. He bunched the soiled napkins and dropped them over the empty clam shells on the serving platter. Then he criss-crossed two sausages over the greens he'd draped on both their plates. "I didn't think of that. What are you, some terrible mystery fiend?"

What the hell. "Jimmy, can I swear you to secrecy? I don't want everyone at the place to know yet."

Jimmy poured Rose more wine and leaned over the table toward her. "I promise not to breathe a word."

"Well, a sort of professional curiosity makes me ask you all these questions." She paused for effect. Wrong effect. Jimmy was sitting up very straight now and looking at her with distrust.

"Relax, Jimmy, Cagney and Lacey do not have a new partner. Don't worry, I'm not a cop. I'm a writer, working on a mystery. And I don't like to talk about my work because I don't want to talk the thing out, instead of writing it down. It's an old family superstition and illogical enough to be Irish."

"Rose, that is just marvelous. What's your book about?"

"I'll tell you some other time."

"No, don't. It'll make it much more exciting for me to read it once it's published. I can't wait. I'm sure it will be terrific.

Jimmy really was wonderfully good-looking. His face

shouted intelligence. This would not be the last bottle of wine they ever shared. Who said writers were insecure and egotistical?

"Well, then, Ms. Scribe, let's talk some more about the mystery at My World. A couple of things about it bothered me. I hope the police know best, but Mamma lied about other things. Let's see what you think." Jimmy lowered his voice.

"It is simply too peculiar that Ben didn't lock that door. I mean, it only takes a second. And if he really felt so thoroughly excited at the prospect of talking to his brother Thomas that he rushed to the phone without locking it, I don't know why he didn't go back to the kitchen and do it after their no doubt scintillating call." Jimmy helped himself to the rest of the sausage when she pushed away her plate.

"Plus, he's so methodical. He sounded as if he didn't believe he could have made that mistake. He walked around muttering and triple-checking everything for a week. After all those years of teaching the youth of America, I'm a pretty good judge of character. Believe me, the man was genuinely confused."

Rose was sure Jimmy's judgment of character was almost as impressive as his talent at spotting literary genius. "Maybe he just didn't want to admit he made a mistake?"

"It was more like he couldn't believe he had made that mistake. God the Son errs. I suppose he's only human after all." Jimmy cleaned their plates again for the chow fun. She wondered if his profligate use of napkins would result in raised prices.

"Half. What was Susan like?" Rose's tight waistband fought her desire for more information. The longer they ate, the longer they'd talk. She twirled a single thick noodle and raised it to her mouth.

"She was all right, I guess. Rather hyper and much too friendly with that sleaze Zorro for my taste. The girl definitely powdered her nose too much. And cocaine just isn't a fun drug anymore, dear. Oddly, I think she was in love with Ben or certainly had a big crush on him. She mooned around him in the most disgusting way. Everyone used to laugh about it. Even he couldn't help noticing but never appeared to return any of her interest. He always acted polite, but distant. Textbook employer-employee manners. He already seems easier around you than he ever was with her."

Jimmy scoured their teacups dry and poured them both tea, wincing when the chipped spout dribbled a few drops of the light green liquid onto the table. "Did you get enough? We can always order more."

As if the restaurant would risk that many more napkins. "Better not, thanks. Don't want to go over my 3,000 calorie breakfast allowance."

"It would not be at all unattractive if you gained a little weight, my dear. Curves are in, you know." Jimmy stacked their plates on the far edge of the table, spreading yet another layer of napkins over the ones he'd dirtied.

The perfect ectomorph wanted to fatten her up? Rose did like Jimmy.

The waiter saw their stacked plates and cleared the table. He brought them a hot pot of tea, then took the napkin dispenser.

"Now that we've finished eating that unexpectedly delightful meal, you can have the juicy part for dessert. I've saved the best for last. The worst, really. I must warn you, it's not the most appetizing of topics." Jimmy savored his portentous pause as much as he'd savored the meal. Rose braced herself.

"Susan might have been raped."

Rose hoped the shiver down her spine showed enough to satisfy Jimmy's dramatic tone.

He poured them both more tea. "In the kitchen, which could explain why he dragged her back there. The creep put the meat up on the worktable and had his fun. Can you imagine? Oh dear, take that righteous look off your face. I was being precise, not sexist, when I said 'meat.' The question of whether or not Susan enjoyed it is a moot one. Can you guess why?"

"Jimmy, this isn't funny. Tell me what the hell you're talking about." She cradled her cup in both hands, chilled again.

"It seems he raped Susan after he killed her."

"Jesus."

"Don't call him into this now. The public awareness

campaign about AIDS seems to have filtered down to even the lowest levels. The monster wore a rubber."

"How do you know that?"

"Well, there was the absence of certain bodily fluids. And he left the wrapper. We don't want to speculate where the actual device ended up. But this creature had some odd quirks."

"Yes, necrophilia could be considered a slight maladjustment. It might even raise Dr. Ruth's eyebrows." She studied the banners on the walls, as if they could take her somewhere kinder.

Jimmy wagged his finger until she looked at him again. "Don't act so cool. I suppose gloves during sex are de rigueur for the criminal classes, but I never thought of that type as aspiring to fastidious neatness."

He refilled their teacups. "Well, it is odd. They found the rubber packet on the floor by the worktable. He'd folded it very precisely into quarters, with the rip completely smoothed out. Who would take the time to do that? I don't suppose he had to worry about Susan's reaction, but still. Sorry. I've never seen or heard of anyone doing that. Have you?"

"No. Something so horribly detached kind of kills the crime-of-passion angle. I've never trusted people who were too neat. How do you know all of this, anyway? And why didn't it all make the papers?" Rose didn't mention the mountain of napkins the waiter had removed.

"I eavesdropped like mad. Those cops were coffee

fiends, and I never let their cups get empty. I don't know. Maybe the newspapers didn't get all the details. Haven't I seen on television that the cops hold back information so they can filter out false confessions?"

"That must be it, or maybe someone at the precinct did the place a favor by trying to point the blame outside My World. Random thieves make good scapegoats." Rose finished her tea.

"But, Ms. Mystery, I still can't figure out why he'd haul the body into the walk-in. What could he have been thinking? Any ideas?"

"Maybe he wanted a snack and took her along to raid the refrigerator? Some guys get hungry after sex. Or maybe he knew that chilling a corpse confuses the whole time-of-death issue. Honestly, Jimmy, I wish I didn't want to know what was in this guy's mind, but I can't help myself. The more I know about real murder, the better I can write make-believe ones." She grabbed the check.

"Now I think it's time I paid the check and we went home. Don't argue: this is my treat. I always pay for my great ideas." Rose wondered if any of the ideograms on the check represented paper products.

"Well, then I get it next time. And you must allow me to tip our, uh, waiter. Much as it pains me to admit it, the food was wonderful. And even though the talk did get a smidgen grisly at times, it was fun, too. Special thanks for the wine."

"It was my pleasure," Rose sighed.

Chapter Five

Rose walked into My World Saturday night feeling guilty. Awake for hours after her tête-à-tête with Jimmy, she'd then ignored the efforts of both her clock radio and programmed coffee maker to wake her. She'd finally risen at 5:00 p.m. to cold coffee and the sense of a wasted day. Nothing like starting the day at sunset to inspire guilt.

Was curiosity one of the Seven Deadly Sins? Gluttony and pride certainly were, and she'd exhibited both last night. Add sloth to the list, too: she hadn't even looked at her manuscript today. She could just picture Sister Mary Damien in some faraway home for retired nuns, smirking with the pleasure of prophecies come true. And a barmaid, too. Dear Lord. Tsk, tsk.

"Hi, Diane, is Ben downstairs?"

"No, he had to go out for an hour. Zorro's in the office. He'll give you your bank and probably make a big deal out of counting my money, too. I just want to rush out of this dump today, but Zorro won't let that happen."

Diane had nearly snarled her final remark. She collected the last of her tips from the bar with a grim face that canceled the thanks she muttered to the customers.

Rose hurried down the stairs to the office. So Diane had a bad day. It probably wasn't tragic. Rose had her own trouble mustering enthusiasm for the evening. Counting $64.50 in change, coin by coin, because Zorro had opened all the rolls of silver in her bank drawer didn't raise her spirits. Nor did the way Zorro impatiently tapped his foot while she counted. She sacrificed her preshift primp in order to get behind the bar at exactly seven. The scratchy feeling in her right eye had better disappear unaided, since she didn't have time to rinse her contact. She pocketed a small saline bottle in case she needed it later.

Diane left the bar the minute Rose came upstairs, and she didn't even bother with a ritual apology. Rose missed her daily chance to be magnanimous.

Jimmy brought a tray of dirty champagne flutes to the waiter's station. "Rose, do you know your hair is falling down in back, perhaps a bit more dishabille than you want for this early in the evening? Enjoyed last night, but we'll have to chat later. Table Twelve must be missing their mothers. They want me every other minute."

Of course her hair was falling down in back and how thoughtful of Jimmy to spare the time to tell her so. She moved the flutes onto the crowded drainboard and ran fresh water into the sinks.

The ten or so customers sitting at the bar when she'd arrived had all left. She tried not to think they'd known she was coming.

At least she could clean up in peace and force herself into a cheerful service mode.

She could test her cheerfulness on Alan, naturally her first customer tonight. She poured his drink before he'd shrugged off his corduroy jacket.

"Rosie, what's wrong with you? You gave me club soda instead of ginger ale. How could you forget what I like to drink?" Alan's expression suffered a bigger injury than the wrong mixer.

Rose knew the positions of the buttons on the soda gun as well as she knew the location of the letters on her keyboard. She checked the ginger ale. It had no color and tasted, indeed, like soda. Time to change the tank downstairs.

She told Alan she'd be right back, told Jimmy to watch the bar and told herself that tonight sucked as she ran downstairs. Wrestling with the soda tanks would not elevate her mood.

As she passed the open office door, she told Zorro about the problem and waited a second, hoping he or Diane would volunteer to fix the tank. They continued arguing over Diane's bank, Diane insisting that it matched her register tape and that he'd have to count the money again. Neither offered to help Rose.

Rose walked back to the corner where the soda tanks lurked in a snarl of hoses. She removed the prongs from the empty tank, dragged the cylinder over to the far wall with the other empties, struggled a full tank into position, and reconnected it. The job she'd dreaded took moments. Nothing had fulfilled her fears by exploding in her face.

The office door was closed when she passed it again.

Her eye still twitched, and Jimmy's remark about her hair still nagged. She'd take another minute to duck into the bathroom.

Half-blind when she heard the shrill sound of Diane cursing, Rose almost dropped the cleaned contact she'd been raising to her eye.

"No, Goddamnit, you son of a bitch scum, there is no way. Do you hear me? No way I would do that. I'd kill myself if I needed money that bad. You have some nerve even accusing me. I don't care what the hell Susan did. Look where it got her, anyway. I'm not interested, get it? Not fucking interested. Back off, Zorro, or I'll tell Ben what you said. I still might."

The slam of the office door and the unintelligible murmur of Zorro's reply followed Diane's outburst. Rose didn't need the acoustical fluke Jimmy had described last night. Diane had shouted loud enough to pierce the Cask of Amontillado.

Rose wondered if people upstairs had heard anything as she blinked her lens back into focus and skewed the combs into her hair. She could guess Zorro's end of the conversation. He must have assumed Diane was stealing after he found a discrepancy in her cash drawer.

And she wondered how genuine Diane's indignation had been. Lots of bartenders did skim a little cash each shift. The stupidly greedy ones took too much, a practice known as raping the restaurant, but the slicker ones worked harder, ringing up higher sales to cover their self-assigned bonuses. Some owners tacitly allowed it, although none admitted it. She doubted that Ben would be so liberal or that Diane could be slick enough to escape his scrutiny.

Rose didn't steal, but she'd worked in restaurants long enough to know how it worked. She hadn't seen Diane do anything to arouse her suspicions. It wasn't her business, anyway. It wasn't Zorro's business either, and he was overstepping himself in accusing Diane. Giant steps.

Rose half hoped Diane would tell Ben. She also hoped Zorro was wrong.

Diane fidgeted at the service end when Rose returned to the bar. "Listen, sweetie, I'm sorry about the mess and the soda tank. That fucking Zorro's been torturing me for the last hour. He's crazed. Someone should take a sword to him. This ain't my fucking day."

Diane fingered the earring on her left ear, a large gold knot belonging to a pair she often wore. "Keep your eye out for my earring back there, okay? It's real gold, but I don't want to stay in this dump anymore to look for it, even if my mother did give it to me. It's either behind the bar or downstairs. I'm sure as hell not going back down there again. I'm leaving. It'll take more than one cocktail to calm me down tonight. Sorry for the bitch act. I'll see you."

"Oh, Miss, do you have a moment for some paying customers? Whenever you're finished chatting down there." The tones of Long Island carried down the bar from the two couples who'd just arrived at the far end. The women wore fur and gold galore; Rose bet herself one of them could have appraised Diane's lost earring in a second. She took their order and started making their drinks, two

Pearl Harbors and two B-52's.

Someone should tell them the war had ended. Someone should stop inventing stupid drinks. And someone should stop bitching to herself and concentrate on tending her bar.

"Why so serious looking, hon? Are you finally thinking about how bad it is to poison people every night?" Mark, wearing one of his usual tight ivy-league t-shirts, sat next to Alan. Yale was tonight's alma mater.

"Stop it, Mark. Rose just had to fix the soda for me. Little thing like her shouldn't have to lift those heavy tanks." Alan rushed to Rose's defense.

"Wish I'd gotten here earlier. I could toss those things around with no problem." Mark could probably juggle with the damned tanks, since his five-foot eight-inch body boasted the gym-sculpted muscle mass of a man at least a foot taller.

Rose poured his usual smug club soda. Mark eschewed alcohol and signaled his disapproval by tipping a single quarter for each of the sodas he nursed for an hour.

If it weren't for women, Mark would never sully his Nikes with a barroom's filth. But he insisted bars were the best places to pick up women. He persisted in his efforts despite a constant lack of success, as if reps could do for flirting what they did for muscle.

"Here's your soda, Mark. I was careful to use a clean glass so it wouldn't bother you with a boozy smell like the one last night." She wondered if a little alcohol might help his chances.

He snapped at her, "Cut it out. This is serious stuff. People who don't take care of their bodies don't deserve to live. You bartenders are all like old whores, selling bad stuff."

"Now wait a minute," Alan stood. "Don't talk that way to Rose." His hands stopped shaking when he clenched his fists.

Mark rolled his shoulders in a steroid shrug. "It's only an expression. Shit, we're all whores. Sorry, Rose."

Later in the evening, after he'd gone home to his lonely exercise mat, Mark didn't seem so bad. Rose still couldn't manage to convince herself the night was going well. She could only hope none of the customers could tell they weren't dealing with Pollyanna's alter ego. My World had lost all of its neighborhood charm tonight. It wasn't a night for familiar faces.

The crowd was a bartender's nightmare. Rose needed to check i.d. before serving every fifth customer. Each time she wasted minutes trying to match pictures to faces and calculate ages, the legitimate drinkers grew impatient. While she argued with two seventeen-year-olds that she would not take their word for it that they were twenty-one, two men at the end of the bar started whistling and wildly waving their hands in the air. Although it looked as if they were trying to flag down an emergency vehicle, they only wanted more Rolling Rocks.

The place looked like the bar had advertised in the

Bridge and Tunnel Times, a tabloid distributed only in the suburbs. People from Jersey and the outer boroughs couldn't act so rudely in their own neighborhoods, or else suburban slaughters would constantly fill the news. Tonight's customers all traveled in packs, in a collection of mini-mobs. They needed refresher courses at customer-behavior school.

A young man in a down vest kept yelling at Rose to turn up the music. His friends used a volume often heard in stadiums to ask why this fucking jukebox didn't have no heavy metal and why it kept sticking. She didn't dare tell these kids to give the machine the gentle kick it probably required. Gentle didn't seem to be one of their big words. She had no desire to explain a shattered jukebox to either her bosses or the machine's owners, guys who knew a Jersey Springsteen hadn't glorified.

Too many customers at the bar waited twice the usual time for their tables. The food came out of the kitchen at half its usual speed. Ben circulated around the dining room, trying to appease his hungry patrons by ordering an extraordinary number of drinks on the house. He marched in and out of the kitchen every few minutes, but the food still dawdled. The restaurant's rhythm dragged. The whole place needed a good kick.

Zorro remained by the front door, welcoming people and promising he would seat them within ten to fifteen minutes. Since Rose couldn't see any tables who'd even received their entrees yet, she wondered why he persisted making false predictions.

By eleven o'clock, Rose wanted help. She called Zorro over and explained she was having problems carding so many kids. She asked if he could please check some i.d. at the door. He flatly refused, telling her that was not his job. When she then suggested he at least give the customers more realistic waiting times, he laughed and sauntered back to the front door.

Two more regulars walked in, assessed the crush at the bar, and left.

Five minutes later, Zorro returned to the bar. He stepped in front of Jimmy at the service station.

"Rose, I can offer you some assistance. I have a little something in my pocket I would be more than generous to share with you to help you with your sad problems tonight. You would need to excuse yourself from the bar for a minute, however. You can meet me in the storeroom."

Rose stared at him as she finished making Jimmy's drink order. Diane was right: the man was crazy. How could he expect her to leave a bar three-deep in customers to join him downstairs? And why did he assume she would want some of the cocaine he offered so blatantly? Didn't he care that Jimmy couldn't miss hearing his offer?

"No thanks, Zorro. I think Ben wants you in the dining room."

Zorro's offer confirmed her suspicions about his numerous trips downstairs, trips he didn't always make alone. It might also explain why several people had seemed very disappointed at his absence last weekend, as well as the four groups who had asked for him tonight after walking right past him at the front door.

The man had a gift for making her offers she had to refuse. Rose had enjoyed coke for a brief period in the early '80s. Cocaine had seemed the perfect drug for people in the restaurant business. Coke quickened conversations while it pleasantly distanced you from the strangers you served. It became very easy to convince yourself coke would help you through a long shift. Gradually, quick nightcaps after those long shifts stretched into more and more long hours filled with more empty chatter about things you didn't care about. Rose finally realized that, whenever she did coke, she wanted to do more. The first line was always the easiest one to refuse. The second, and the tenth, lines were harder. She'd be a richer woman today if her darling ex had learned that too. A frightening percentage of the profits from their restaurant had snuck up his patrician nose. She'd taken far too long to realize that his overnight shopping trips to Boston had patronized suppliers not licensed for wholesale. The little bags he brought home weren't filled with saffron.

Rose still didn't care if Zorro wanted to indulge. But she didn't like suspecting he might be dealing in the restaurant. She wondered if the owners knew and if they cared. The notion of a dumb dealer manning the door did nothing to raise her spirits.

"Give me the double Stoly straight up, before I kill someone in the kitchen. Don't bother to chill it." The chef had pushed his way through the crowd. Ward's plummy English accent didn't sound dignified at the moment. He looked like hell and as if he were ready to send the first person who argued with him to suffer her own eternal damnation. Seeing the usually reserved and proper Englishman stalk through the dining room and push his way up to the crowded bar in his soiled whites confirmed the kitchen's troubles tonight.

It was too bad Ben had insisted that she'd have to uphold his absolute rule that no employees could drink on the job. He'd fire her if she gave alcohol to anyone on the staff still on duty. No exceptions. He ran a tight ship here.

She couldn't argue restaurant policy now. "I'm sorry, Ward, but Ben says no."

She regretted refusing him; the man obviously wanted a drink badly. But Ben had seen Ward at the bar and vehemently signaled his 'no' to Rose. She wished he'd come and explain it himself to the infuriated chef.

"You miserable twat. You bitches are all alike. Getting your wretched little thrills from being in control up here. The way you all prance around behind the bar makes me sick. And then the idiot owners go on and on about the profits from the bar. Does it make you feel good to handle all this money for them? Well, I handle the food. Just remember that my food is what makes My World the blasted success it is. My food. This place lives and dies because of what I do in the kitchen. No one here even has the intelligence to understand what I do."

He spoke quietly, hissing his invective into her face, "The fool prep cook probably spent all of his time mooning over the blonde thing up here today instead of actually working. You twats do anything you can to turn a decent restaurant into a fucking pub, and then you're too tight-assed to give me a drink? Wretched bitch."

Ward stormed back into the kitchen.

One of the New Jersey groups had demanded blended screwdrivers. They'd ordered their fourth round of five drinks when the blender's motor blew. She wished she'd broken it intentionally. The hellish scent of burned rubber added a brilliant touch to tonight's scene.

She and Jimmy tried to cheer each other through the rest of the shift. Tonight couldn't last forever, no matter how long the time until closing loomed.

Last call was a blessed event.

On his way out the door, Ward muttered an apology. He was sure she'd understand. The pressure back there was too much sometimes. Righto.

Maybe tomorrow she'd ask him to show her the FOOD IS LIFE he was reputed to have tattooed on his belly.

Before he drove her home in the borrowed Saab, Jimmy stopped at the all-night deli on her corner so she could get the Sunday *Times* and a Toblerone.

Rose didn't plan on leaving the apartment until she went to work at My World Sunday night. She'd read the *Times* all morning and write her own immortal prose all afternoon. She wouldn't even think about My World.

While tonight's tough shift had resembled eternity, the fifty-five days remaining before her deadline threatened to turn into a nanosecond. She needed to reserve her speculative powers for her own novel. The plot she'd written didn't require any new villains.

What she wrote couldn't hurt her.

Chapter Six

Unable to sleep again after a neighbor practicing arias woke her before eight, Rose had finished half of *Arts and Leisure* when the phone rang at noon Sunday. She'd lingered over the paper and coffee, distracted by the heavy snow falling outside her windows. She admired the snow again while she waited to hear the caller's identity from her answering machine, once more blessing call-screening as one of the twentieth century's best inventions. By the fourth ring, she realized she hadn't remembered to turn the wonderful device on.

She couldn't let the phone ring unanswered. This might be Mr. McMahon calling with an early sweepstakes announcement. More likely, it was a friend wanting to wallow in a cozy, isn't-this-snow-something-and-aren't-we-both-lucky-to-be-snug-at-home, chat. Such pleasant prospects aside, she'd have picked up the phone even if she knew Charlie Manson waited on the line. People who could let a phone ring without discovering a caller's identity were as mysterious to her as people who never read novels. Curiosity might not be a sin, but indulging it was irresistible.

"Rose?" She didn't recognize the man's voice when she picked up the phone.

"Hi, this is Thomas Victors from My World. We haven't met yet, but I hear you're doing a marvelous job.

I just got back into town awfully late last night. Ben said it was a rough one. You must have worked terribly hard to end with such high sales. Listen, I'm only disturbing your Sunday because I hope you can help me with something. Sorry to bother you so early."

His voice lilted every sentence into a question. She asked what sort of help he needed.

"It's Diane. She didn't come in at ten this morning. She's been late on Sundays before but never anything near this badly. I know she likes to, um, party a little on Saturday nights. So maybe she's overslept. But she must be sleeping like the dead, because she isn't answering the phone. I let it ring forever. Perhaps she's unplugged it."

Rose wished she'd let her own phone ring forever.

"Ben's home with the flu and sounds terrible. But he says you live right by Diane. She's on Eleventh, too, over by Washington. I thought maybe you could do me an enormous favor and walk over and wake her. I'd go myself, but I'm watching the bar now. Would it be too much trouble for you? You'd have to be careful to bundle up."

Rose liked the way Thomas sounded. Relieved he wasn't asking her to cover the shift, she agreed to check on Diane. She scribbled the address on the top of the *Sports* section and ripped it off the page. Rose checked that her longest coat covered her nightgown's hem and hid her hair under her biggest woolen hat. She could wake Diane and return home in plenty of time to start the chapter she'd vowed to write today. Getting out into the snow might even be inspiring, or at least invigorating.

The walk to Diane's apartment was not a Currier and Ives stroll. A strong wind howled in from the Hudson River, blowing the snow almost laterally. Rose bowed her head and trudged west, trying to remember the tune of *Lara's Song*. After two blocks, the bitter cold mocked her for not taking the time to change out of her nightgown. She felt too miserable even to peek into the White Horse once she'd decided her outfit eliminated the temptation to pop in for a quick coffee after rousing Diane. Only another two blocks to go. The wind would scream behind her on the way back. She bribed herself into walking faster by planning a detour for a pain au chocolat from Annabel's on her way home.

Diane lived in one of the old tenements that landlords now touted as having "real Village charm." The poor immigrants who'd originally crowded the places would have laughed to hear they'd lived in such desirable splendor. Rose knew the floor plan of Diane's apartment before she rang the buzzer.

And rang and rang and rang Diane's buzzer until she finally admitted Diane didn't seem inclined to answer. Then Rose started ringing the buzzers belonging to apartments on the top floor. Despite New Yorkers' fear of crime, tenants on the higher floors of buildings without intercoms often sacrificed security to sloth. Apartment 5D had no qualms about the safety of his neighbors and buzzed Rose into the building. Maybe he was expecting someone.

Rose trudged up stairs. When she reached the third floor, she spotted Diane's apartment at the front of the building. She hurried toward the door, eager to finish this stupid mission and return home to her own warm apartment.

Walking into the wind and waiting for admission had chilled her into numb wonder at her willingness to run Thomas' errand. She was so cold she hurt. Her face stung as if she'd been slapped for an hour, and her feet and hands ached as if the cold had scorched them.

The pounding she expected it would take to rouse Diane might warm at least one hand. She'd give the doorbell a count of ten and then resort to banging. She'd reached three when she felt the door itself responding, giving gradually under the pressure of her finger. She increased the pressure. The door edged open.

Rose took a deep breath, tried to ignore the horrible scenarios her imagination proffered, and pushed the door wide open. She knocked the last of the slush off her boots and crossed the threshold, automatically locking the door behind her. Diane's coat hung from a hook on the back of the door. The radio blared the Beastie Boys at a level that Rose's neighbors would have protested immediately. She needed a long, nervous minute before she could distinguish the sound of a shower running behind a door. The relief she felt at hearing the shower acknowledged just how scared she'd felt a minute before.

Nobody described Diane as a mental giant, but Rose

couldn't believe the woman could be stupid enough to leave her door unlocked. She remembered what Thomas had said about Diane liking to celebrate Saturday nights but couldn't imagine her drinking so much she forgot to lock her door. Drunk or not, some things were reflexes.

Rose called Diane's name and tried to decide what to do. No woman who had ever seen *Psycho* wanted to startle another woman in her shower. She called Diane a few more times, envying the shower's terrific water pressure. She'd have to wait until Diane finished. It wasn't right to walk into someone's apartment, listen to her shower, and then walk out. Most people could sense when a stranger had invaded their places. Rose didn't want to add any more worries to Diane's day than arriving at work two hours late already guaranteed.

The brief scare at the door had chilled Rose more than she'd thought. She followed the sound of a banging radiator down the hall and sat at a green formica table in the kitchen, gratefully absorbing the over-heated apartment's warmth. The room was done in a cheerful '50s diner style, down to period appliances and the plates and glasses on the open shelves. Diane must have seen the '50s on t.v.

While the half-empty bottle of Cuervo Gold and two sparkling shot glasses on the kitchen table violated the retro theme, they might explain Diane's late start today. Rose wondered whom Diane had entertained last night and how late they'd celebrated. Maybe they'd toasted Diane's finding her lost earring. Both gold knots gleamed from a Fiestaware candy dish on the windowsill behind the table.

She called Diane's name again, then worried the music might be drowning out her voice. She walked into the living room and turned down the radio. The living room opened into the bedroom, and Rose was surprised to see the bed neatly made. She could never call Diane a slob again—anyone two hours late for work and most likely hungover who carefully made her bed showed a stronger commitment to neatness than Rose could boast. The entire apartment surprised her with its cleanliness; even the kitchen floor looked freshly scrubbed and those shot glasses glittered as if newly polished.

Rose called Diane again and knocked on the bathroom door. She'd waited over ten minutes already. It was after 12:45. If Diane didn't get into work soon, she might not have a job to be late for. Thomas hadn't sounded angry when he called, but this long shower might push his patience. If she left right now, Diane still wouldn't arrive at My World by one o'clock.

Rose pounded on the bathroom door and yelled Diane's name. Nothing but the sound of the shower answered her. She'd have to risk scaring Diane and walk into the bathroom to end this oddly leisurely shower. The paper would peel off the walls if Diane didn't turn off the water soon.

"Diane, it's Rose. You have to get into work right away. My God, have you been taking a cold shower all this time?"

Another chill hit her when she opened the bathroom door. No steam hung in the bathroom's air. The mirror was perfectly clear, with no condensation to blur the reflection of the lines that worry had drawn between her eyes.

She tried to make her voice sound cheerful instead of worried, "Diane? Sorry to barge in on you, but your front door wasn't locked. Thomas sent me over. He didn't sound mad. If you hurry into work, you'll be okay. Diane?"

No reply. The sound of the shower didn't seem loud enough to muffle her voice. Only an opaque plastic curtain separated her and Diane. The shower sounded strange from this close to the tub. The water didn't sound as if it were hitting a porcelain floor but was somehow muffled.

Rose cursed herself as a total idiot. Diane could have slipped and been lying in there unconscious the whole time Rose's mind scribbled different scenarios. She'd wasted too much time thinking already. Terrified of what she might see, she yanked the shower curtain open. Suppressed memories of high school horror movies pushed her hand.

Diane stared back with wide eyes.

Diane lay on her back in the tub, with her legs propped up onto the wall below the faucets, away from the drain. A piece of bright red fabric that looked like the silk scarf she often wore gagged her mouth. A long t-shirt that had once been white bunched up around her waist in graceless folds. Gashes in the fabric all over her chest stuck to the deep wounds underneath them. Someone had slashed a big hole out of her blue bikini underpants. The severed piece of fabric rested on Diane's chin like a hideous blue beard.

The shower still attacked Diane. Cold water pounded down onto her sad body. The stream flattened her hair, dulling and darkening all of its beautiful blonde color. Faint stains of mascara dribbled down the sides of her face. Her savaged clothes clung to her body. Diane didn't look as if her suffering had stopped.

Rose knew she shouldn't turn the shower off and that she shouldn't touch Diane's phone. God only knew what evidence she'd already stupidly disturbed. Her writer's mind tried to retrace her movements as she ran to the front door and struggled to open the locks. She stayed too scared to scream until she escaped into the empty hallway.

Chapter Seven

The door across the hall opened. A woman walked up to Rose and slapped her face. She was in her seventies, wearing a bright floral housecoat, furry pink slippers, and a look of concern.

"Stop now. Your shrieking does no good. I can't help you if you don't tell your trouble." The woman looked at Rose expectantly.

"I need your phone. Please. I have to call the police."

"Come in, then, and use it."

Rose headed straight for the phone she saw sitting on an end table in the living room. She stared at the handmade doily under the phone as she dialed 741-4811 for the Sixth Precinct. It was too late for 911. She gave the officer who answered the phone her name, the address, and a brief description of what she'd found. Diane's neighbor stood in the doorway to the kitchen, listening to every word. She closed her eyes and crossed herself, then turned back into the kitchen and lit the burner under a kettle. Her voice carried in to Rose, who sat memorizing the doily's pattern.

"Jesus, Mary, and Joseph. The poor girl. The animals run everywhere these days. God have mercy on her soul." She pulled two fragile Belleek cups and saucers from a cabinet above the sink.

"I'll not speak ill of the dead, but I told her many's the time to take more care with her friends. You wouldn't believe some of the creatures calling themselves men would come up those stairs. And Diane such a sweet and pretty girl. Never a nasty day that she'd go to the store without checking and I wanted something."

Rose heard the slight clatter of china as a cup of tea appeared next to the phone. "I'm Annie Costello and this will stop you shaking. You needn't say a word until you want to. There'll be plenty of questions to come, God help you."

The tea tasted strong and sweet: so did the whiskey added to it. Rose smiled gratefully at Annie and looked around the room. Annie must have lived here a very long time. The polished furniture all came from an earlier era, and the photographs grouped on every available surface chronicled four or five generations of a large and happy-looking family. In one picture, six stair-step children grinned from the same couch where she now sat. Rose studied the pictures, hoping one of the happy faces would blot out her last sight of Diane.

"Forgive me. I'm Rose Leary. I worked with Diane. You're very kind. Are these pictures of your children?"

Annie took her cue and started identifying various faces in the pictures. She refilled Rose's tea, omitting the whiskey in the second cup. She chatted on bravely about her children and grandchildren, but the tears at the corners of her eyes showed the effort she made. She had no doubt known Diane better than Rose had.

Sirens slowly approached. They sounded different

when you called for them yourself. The women looked out the window at two patrol cars, their revolving lights casting kaleidoscope patterns through the heavy snow. The banshee sirens still howled after the cars had stopped. Too much noise, too late.

Rose stood when the buzzer rang.

"Sit yourself back down, girl. You'll not go in there again. They can have their look and come in here and talk to you like civilized men. There's enough torture in it for one day." Annie opened the door and called to the cops to keep climbing.

After telling them to kick the snow from their shoes, Annie ushered four men into the living room. They filled the small room. Rose stood, nervous at the way they seemed to tower over her. The one man not in uniform started to ask her something, but she cut him off, "She's across the hall. Dead. In the shower. I don't think she was killed in the shower, though. I don't know where all the blood went. I remember what I touched, I think."

"Sit down. We'll look, and then you and I talk," said the man in street clothes. He wore a blue down jacket over a grey tweed sports coat and navy wool pants. His eyes were a much darker blue than the jacket. His thick black hair looked younger than the creases on his face, and he seemed a good ten years older than the other officers.

He introduced himself as Detective Butler and named the other officers in a blur of vowels. Then he pointed to two of the uniformed officers and cocked his head toward the door. The three men started to leave the apartment.

"Officers? Can you turn off the water? Please?" Nobody answered her, but the remaining officer shook his head. He paced a path between the front door and the living room window, careful not to let the paraphernalia hanging off his belt jostle anything on Annie's cluttered tables.

Rose sat on the couch again, wanting to cover herself with one of the crocheted afghans draped over the furniture. When she asked her guard what would happen next, he told her to wait for Detective Butler. She heard heavy footsteps walking through Diane's apartment. Loud voices blared over the radio on her guard's belt. She heard curses, the Lord's name taken in vain several times, before the officer fiddled with his radio and the voices subsided.

Annie sat wearily at the kitchen table, her back to the front door. Other footsteps sounded up and down the stairs. Neighbors' questions clamored in the hall. Another superfluous siren approached.

A uniformed officer whose name Rose thought started with a G walked in and spoke to her guard, "Your turn. You ever notice how the prettiest ones always die the ugliest?"

Annie gasped and told him to show some respect for the dead. Rose hoped he'd addressed his question to her first guard, who hurried across the hall, leaving her with another stranger in uniform. Officer G— didn't say another word until Detective Butler reappeared and told him to go back into Diane's apartment.

Butler asked Annie if she'd like to rest for a while and escorted her into the bedroom, then shut the door quietly behind her. He sat in the easy chair next to the couch and studied Rose for a long moment.

She returned his stare and braced herself for the questions.

"Sorry you had to see your friend like that. Take your time and tell me everything you can remember."

Rose knew she had to speak more coherently now. No more babbling like an idiot in shock. It was time to sound intelligent and believable. She wished she could go home. She wished she'd never left her own apartment. She wished she were writing this instead of living it. She would tear up the day.

Finally warm again, she leaned back into the couch and shrugged off her long coat. Then she told him what had happened. She started with Thomas' call and interrupted herself to ask if they shouldn't call him now. Detective Butler said they'd get to that later. So Rose told him about walking over here and trying the buzzer downstairs. It was easy to remember the number next to the buzzer that had admitted her to the building.

D was for Diane. D was for dead. D had better be for dumb for wondering if she were a suspect. She told him about Diane's door opening, about the coat on the back of the door, and about the loud music. She remembered the tequila bottle and the two glasses. She bravely explained about *Psycho* and why she'd hesitated so long before going into the bathroom. She told him she hadn't touched the body and asked if she had to describe it.

When he nodded yes, she did that, too. Her voice only broke once, when she remembered that the bathroom looked as if the water hadn't been hot for hours.

She finished. He hadn't said anything since he'd told her not to worry about calling Thomas right away. She waited, wondering what his questions would be and how he'd ask them.

She didn't give him a chance to start.

"Oh my God. I think I forgot to tell you something very important. I only said my boss called this morning. I didn't tell you where I worked with Diane. It's My World. You must know what happened there last month. Susan was stabbed, too. And raped. And left in a horrible, cold place." He stared at her.

"I heard rumors that Susan was raped," she babbled. She didn't think the explanation satisfied him.

He said they'd talk about that down at the station and stood, beckoning her to stand too. He picked her coat up and held it until she turned around and shrugged her arms into its heavy wet sleeves. When she wanted to thank Annie, he told her to let the poor lady rest.

Diane's apartment sounded even more full of activity. She wanted to know what the police were discovering behind its closed door. She'd trade the days of research she'd done while writing her novels for five minutes back inside Diane's apartment.

Detective Butler seemed to clear a path through the hallways and stairs now crowded with neighbors just by the force of his glare. Rose kept her eyes down, cautiously studying the slushy mess on the cracked linoleum as if she needed to examine every step before taking it.

He settled her into the back seat of a patrol car with a solicitous formality. A totally unfounded guilt plopped down on the seat next to her. Rose fought the urge to wave at the people on the sidewalk to show them she wasn't wearing handcuffs. Even if you weren't a suspect, sitting in the back seat of a patrol car made you feel like one.

Rose wondered why the car turned up Perry instead of continuing down Washington to Tenth and directly to the station. When the driver took a left onto West Fourth, she asked where they were going.

Butler answered. "You said you live on Eleventh and Fourth, right? Which building? I'll come upstairs with you."

"What? I thought we were going to the station."

"Ms. Leary, we at the Sixth Precinct pride ourselves on our community relations. You're trying to help me; I'm gonna help you. You'd get sick if you kept your wet coat on all day. But you really want to spend the next few hours sitting around the station house in that nightgown?"

That nightgown was a pale pink silk, semitransparent in certain lights. She tried to remember how bright Annie's apartment had been. Then she tried to remember exactly how far down the lace on the nightgown's bodice went and how far forward she'd leaned while telling her story. She didn't remember the detective giving the slightest sign that she'd revealed anything more interesting than a business suit when she'd removed her coat in Annie's apartment.

Chapter Eight

Rose raced up the last flight, ignoring Butler's puffed commands to slow down. For one wild minute as she unlocked her door, she thought she might just quickly slam and relock it before he reached her landing. Then she would take off her coat and crawl back to bed in her nightgown. Then she would be asleep and she would wake up to the smell of hot chocolate and cinnamon toast. It would all be a dream, just like a nice B movie or an old Twilight Zone.

Butler wasn't the Sandman and he wasn't Rod Sterling. He wasn't a true stone-face, either; his face finally expressed something. Butler looked very annoyed. Rose waited for him to reach her door before she pushed it open. He edged into the apartment before her.

"Now what, Detective?"

"Now you find yourself something to wear and get into it. Don't worry, I won't watch you change. If it's okay with you, I'll wait in the kitchen there."

She closed the bedroom door harder than necessary. So she wasn't a suspect. He didn't think she had a revolver hidden in her lingerie drawer or that she would make a rope of pantyhose and escape out the window. And he certainly didn't seem interested in seeing anything the nightgown's lace might have partially hidden. Rose pulled on a pair of thick black leggings, then added a heavy black wool sweater with enormous shoulder pads. The big pads should make her look more imposing than she felt. She couldn't hear a sound from the kitchen and doubted her courtyard view had entranced Butler. But, when she opened the bedroom door, he stood by the kitchen window.

"Nice courtyard. Nice kitchen. Mind if I look at the rest of the place?"

She felt stupid even as she said it. "Don't you need a warrant for a search?"

"This isn't a search and you know it. I act like a gentleman and try to save you the embarrassment of getting yourself stared at in your nightie by the boys at the station. So now you're going to go all modest and not let me look at your apartment?"

"Why do you need to see my apartment?" She wanted him to hurry and find Diane's murderer. And lock him up.

"Curiosity's part of my job. Let's just say I like to see how the people I'm sworn to protect live. But I won't look around if you don't want me to. If it turns out later that I need to look around, it can be arranged. I'll get all the proper paperwork and everything. You really should try to relax now, please."

She wondered when the next time she'd really relax would be.

"Sure. I just found a woman I knew slashed to death in a cold shower. Then I had to take a ride in a police car so you could escort me upstairs and tell me to change my clothes for God knows what interrogation. And now you want to act like a reporter for *House and Garden*? Look at whatever you want to in here. Then maybe you could start to look for the bastard who did it?"

Butler still seemed unperturbed. She followed him into the living room, where he assessed the views out of her windows. He barely glanced at the papers and books on her desk, so she couldn't tell if he'd noticed the textbook on forensic pathology she'd used to research the murders in her books. Rose tried not to imagine the charming veins the textbook might introduce into their conversation.

She'd never forget buying the book. Her diffident request for help in finding the best book on what really happened to bodies when they were murdered had inspired the Barnes & Noble clerk to ask advice from three coworkers. All four had studied her intently so they would recognize her face when it was splashed over all the tabloids as a mass murderer. She still didn't know if she or the clerks were more relieved when she'd finally grown exasperated enough to explain the motives for her purchase.

That little exercise in courage had been nothing compared to actually trying to study the lavishly illustrated volume itself. The graphic photographs of dead and brutally murdered bodies had been even worse than she'd expected. Right now, she would gladly enlarge all of the pictures to poster size and plaster them all over her walls if the redecoration scheme would somehow erase the real corpse she'd just seen and the horrors that had created that corpse.

But no demented decorator's version of the ivory tower would work, for her or for poor Diane. The ever-tempting fantasy of hiding in books, even gruesome ones, was also useless. She was still alive. Diane was dead. The killer was probably still alive too.

He lingered in front of her bookshelves. Time for the next step.

"Can we go now, Detective Butler?"

"Are you stupid, Ms. Leary?"

"Obviously, Detective, since I believed you to be concerned with community relations. Or were you out catching criminals the day they gave the tact seminar?"

"I taught that part of the goddamn course. Look, Ms. Leary, I asked you that because I know you aren't a stupid woman. So far, you've acted real smart. Lots of girls, sorry, women, would have been too shook up to remember half of what you already told me. Lots of men, too. You're going to be a big help to us in this investigation. Plenty of input." He strolled into her bedroom and picked her nightgown and sodden coat off the floor where she'd dropped them.

"The other reason I think you're smart is because you've got a couple of walls full of good books which all look like they've been read, especially those four shelves of mysteries. Even the pathology one looks broken in. You enjoy reading that stuff?"

"I'm writing a mystery and I need to know what really happens. But I didn't want to find out like this. Now can you please finish your critique of my apartment and tell me why you called me stupid?" She wondered if he'd take her nightgown and coat as evidence.

"You have a very nice apartment here. You have some very nice views, which can get very expensive. I'm not talking rent, either. You have seven nice, big windows in this apartment. Not one of them has a gate. Every lock but one is a joke."

"I'm on the fifth floor, for God's sake. It would take some kind of crazed, invisible Spiderman to get up here. This is a busy corner. Someone is almost always around on the street."

"I'm not finished. You live here alone, right? You have nothing but lace curtains on your front windows and it looks like you spend a lot of time in this room. And you work nights in a public place, right?

"So why the hell should a woman who lives alone in New York City and works until all hours of the night, where people can always tell where she is, no less, worry? What kind of creep would take advantage of the fact that he can figure out for sure when an apartment will be empty or that he could break into the apartment as easy as snapping gum? Forget the Spiderman crap. There are kids in this city who grow up using fire escapes for jungle gyms. How many of those people who are always around on the street do you think are heroes? You ever heard anybody yell 'Stop, thief' outside of the movies?"

She didn't follow him into the bathroom's close

quarters. "I always leave a couple of lights and some music on when I'm out at night. This is a pretty safe neighborhood. People in the Village usually try to help if they see something wrong. And I know a lot of my neighbors." She fought the urge to ask him to open the shower curtain.

He draped her wet coat over the shower's rod. "Con Ed is very happy that you leave the lights and music on. They are very happy that so many people think that's a bright trick. Believe me, it's not a real secret strategy anymore. The word kinda got out." He carried her nightgown back into the kitchen.

"All right, the Village is better than a lot of places in the city, and I'm sure your neighbors are very nice people. But I still have a job a few blocks away, don't I? And even very nice people sleep, or stay out themselves, or maybe pay more attention to TV than to what's happening next door.

"Your friend Diane lived in the Village. She had lights, and music, and nice neighbors, and all those good things. They didn't do a hell of a lot to help her. Somebody still got in and killed her."

She interrupted, "But it didn't look like he'd broken in, unless he jimmied the lock real well. There were those two glasses on the table, so I think she must have known whoever did it. Don't most victims know their murderers? Or maybe it was somebody she just met? Or do you think somebody else could have keys to her apartment? Or what if—"

"Stop."

"Stop what?"

"Stop with the questions. That's my job, remember? Get another coat. It's time we got down to the station to go over everything. Believe me, we'll go over everything. Your questions, my questions, everybody's questions. Maybe we'll even get some answers. But we're not getting anything answered standing around here."

She knew he'd follow her to the hall closet. "But can I just ask you one more question before we go? Please? I think I really need to know the answer to this before we leave."

"One." He watched her put her trench coat on, then handed her the nightgown. She tossed it on the closet's floor.

"Was that just your normal speech about apartment security? Or," she blurted the rest before he could interrupt, "were you really trying to scare me?"

"No." Butler walked away from her. He opened the front door and stood waiting for her to join him in the hallway.

"That doesn't tell me anything. Which question does 'no' answer, Detective?"

"The one I promised to answer. Nice try, though. Let's get going. No reason for the two of us to waste our brains standing around in this hallway all day. The locks on your front door aren't too bad."

He watched as she secured both locks, "We've got a

lot to do. Maybe you'll get some good information about police procedures that will help your book. Hell, with a smart woman like you helping us, we'll solve this case in no time. We should get the guy behind bars tonight. Don't worry, everything will be fine."

Rose didn't believe him. Butler's cheery and encouraging act was one of the scariest things she'd seen all day.

Chapter Nine

The Sixth Precinct was not architecturally imposing. Built in the late 1960s, it looked like part of a sprawling suburban school that should have been surrounded by playgrounds and parking lots instead of crammed in among West Tenth Street's old buildings. Butler led her into an office that had aged rapidly. Even the frames around the portraits of Reagan and Koch that hung on the wall looked splintered.

The room's scuffed walls and scratched furniture made the building look like a National Historic Treasure.

"Can I make a phone call?" Rose saw the look on Butler's face. "Not my lawyer. But I really should call Thomas and tell him I might be late for work tonight. How long will all this take, anyway?"

"We called Thomas from Diane's apartment to corroborate why you were over there. Everything he said matched your story. They're asking him more questions right now. He knows you won't make it into work tonight. Don't worry about My World now. Why don't you call me Frank?"

"Thanks, Frank, thanks a whole lot. And I'd love it if you call me Rose. Does this new first name intimacy signify our new-found trust? I thought it was my honest face." So maybe he hadn't considered her clothes as evidence after all.

"Does Thomas have an honest face? A yes or no answer would do fine, Rose."

She explained impatiently that she'd never seen Thomas' face and wished she'd never heard his voice.

"So how was his voice? Let's take this all over again, from the minute you got the phone call. Try to picture yourself all through it. And I don't have to tell you that even the most insignificant, silly, thing might be important, right? You're a writer. Describe it all."

She only hoped she'd be able to inspire as much interest in her readers as the obvious fascination with which Frank waited for her story. He looked much better when he allowed his face to show what he was, or was pretending to be, feeling. She answered the phone and headed out into the snow in her nightgown again. He had the grace not to smirk.

"Then you walked into Mrs. Costello's and asked me what I'd seen. I don't know why I didn't remember the earring right away. Poor Diane probably left it at home in the first place and worried about it all that time for nothing."

"Jewelry doesn't matter much to the girl now. She was another one. Keeping gold on the windowsill is a real clever move. Was she always that bright, from what you saw of her at work?"

She bristled at his tone. "Jesus, Frank, control your sorrow. What else do you need to know?"

"Plenty. How well did you know Diane? Know any

of her friends? How'd she get along with people at work? Anybody around the place seem to like or dislike her too much? How was she acting the last time you saw her?" He'd quickly ticked the questions off on the fingers of his left hand and looked annoyed at reaching his thumb.

Rose fervently wished the detective would space his queries out more evenly instead of firing them in rounds. The barrage kept her aware of a slight, uncomfortable, flustered feeling that made her fear she would forget something.

She hesitated before starting to describe exactly what had happened at work yesterday. Then she saw her desire to protect Diane's reputation as pathetic. She told Butler everything she'd seen and overheard when Diane argued with Zorro.

"So what else do you know about Diane? Anything could help."

"Not that much. I mean, I've seen her for a total of ten or fifteen minutes four times a week for a couple of weeks now. Today was the first time I ever saw her apartment. I've already told you that how clean it looked surprised me." She wondered how clean her own floor had appeared during Butler's tour.

"It struck me as very strange that her kitchen floor looked so spotless when I first walked in, like it had just been scrubbed. Who the hell mops their floor while they're drinking tequila? That doesn't even happen in country and western songs."

"Sometimes people need to mop their floors after they've been drinking too much, Rose."

"Spare me the frat-house humor, please. I have some questions here too. Do you think Diane was murdered outside the shower? The white rug in the bathroom looked perfectly dry, with no bloodstains or any part that looked as if it had been scrubbed recently. Blood spurts sometimes, doesn't it? And it would have been pretty tight for the guy to do all that slashing in the tub, too awkward to make that many cuts, even if he crouched over her. Where could he have been standing? What if it wasn't Diane who mopped the floor?" Rose waited to see if Butler would offer any answers.

"How many killers you heard of who get out the Mr. Clean after a slashing session? This guy didn't go to a whole lot of other effort to hide the fact that Diane didn't die of natural causes." So much for specific answers.

"Well, he clearly had more on his mind than just killing her and leaving. I'm not sure I want to know what you find out about the hole he cut in her panties. He'd propped her legs up so that a lot of the water was hitting her right there." She stopped herself from crossing her own legs.

"Rose, I'm glad you got a good imagination and I hope it makes you rich someday. But don't get too carried away, here, okay? The city pays a lot of very good technicians to discover stuff you want to play at speculating about. They can find blood traces in a mop if they're there, a mop or all kinds of other places. Through the miracles of modern science, they can also find fingerprints." Frank leaned back in his chair. "You got to remember one thing. Killers are people too."

"What's that, a new bumper sticker?"

He'd tilted so far away that his desk chair now resembled a recliner. "Shut up. I'll give you that this guy is twisted, but don't start thinking you know how his mind works. Don't think he's going to be a completely different specimen from the people you know. How many people you know would mop a floor if they didn't have to? The fingerprints will tell us more than all these guessing games. The place should be completely dusted by now."

She wondered how he kept the chair balanced. "Sure, I suppose you're going to tell me next how you find perfectly delineated prints at every crime scene, which must be why you guys find all the murderers so quickly. I'll bet there won't be any fingerprints. The creep probably used those ugly yellow gloves that are supposed to save your hands. It looked as if someone had washed the glasses, and I didn't smell any tequila when I sat at the table. The smell of that stuff doesn't just waft delicately away into the air. You have to admit I have a trained nose when it comes to liquor. Probably like you and blood, Detective."

She continued over the squeaks his chair made when he sat upright again. "Here's something really sickening. Right now, my nose would rather smell some food than anything else. I can't believe I feel hungry, but I'd kill for some chocolate." Rose shivered. "I guess I won't be using certain of my stock expressions for a while. I often used to say I was dying for a shower. God."

Frank was surprisingly generous. He left the room briefly and returned with two Hershey bars, one plain and one with almonds. Rose wolfed half of the plain before she offered him a square. He refused, saying he'd rather watch her devour them.

She blushed as she pulled the almond bar from its brown sheath a moment later. She neatly unfolded the silver wrapper and broke off a ladylike chunk of only the first H E, careful not to tear into this bar as rabidly as she had the first. She smoothed the wrapper, flattening out its creases.

Rose dropped the candy. "Oh my God. The same guy who killed Susan killed Diane. And he didn't just kill her. He used the opening he cut in her panties. I can prove it's the same guy."

"Calm down. What in hell are you talking about?"

She tried to hand him the candy wrapper. "Listen. This paper reminded me. I saw a condom packet on Diane's stairs. I was staring at the steps while we walked down them; you know that way you stare so hard at something you almost don't see what's there? It didn't register until now. Mixed in with all the dirty slush and other trash, it was there, I think on the first flight."

He didn't take the wrapper. "Rose, what—"

"I was so shook I looked right at it, but I didn't see

it. I'm an idiot. Please, hurry. This will prove it's the same guy. Come on, we have to go find it." She stood, impatiently shoving her arms into her coat and waiting for him to move.

Butler didn't stand. "You getting high from that chocolate, or you want to sit down and tell me what you're talking about in some kind of half sensible way? What earthshaking clue did you see on those steps?"

"A rubber packet, all folded neatly into quarters. Just like the one you guys found by Susan's body. It can't be a coincidence. And he probably took his gloves off to open the rubber, so you might find prints. Do footsteps smear fingerprints?" She shuddered at thinking that she'd even stepped near the damned thing.

"Hurry, Frank, let's go."

"Sit down, and calm down too. I'll call the guys over at the scene and have them take a look. Wish you'd thought of this earlier."

"I—"

"How sure are you that it was a folded rubber package you saw?"

"Now that I think about it, I'm positive. I was just too shocked to make the connection then. I was still trying to get Diane's face out of my mind. But I saw it." She stopped herself from removing her coat. "Frank, how many rubbers have you used in your life?"

"Oh, 834. There's a permanent ridge in my wallet. Wait, maybe it was 838. I'd have to check my diary, Rose.

What kind of question is that?" Frank was leaning over the desk, but not as if he wanted to confide in her. "Your imagination putting me in there now?"

"No, of course not. But wouldn't you agree that it isn't normal? I mean, if you're opening a rubber, you usually have more pressing things on your mind than folding up the packet all nice and neat. So maybe there's more than one guy in the world with that quirk, and maybe even more than one guy in New York City. I'll survey all my girlfriends. But I know the package is the link between the two murders, and I know that I saw it. Believe me, Frank, I don't imagine things like this."

Butler shook his head. "I hope not, Rose. I really do. I'll have them look for it, but don't get your hopes up too high. A hell of a lot of people already tromped up and down those stairs today. We'll see if it's still there, but it could have been kicked anywhere by now."

He moved a stack of folders away from his phone. "Don't look so mad at yourself. At least you remembered it eventually. Trained eye, huh? As a writer, of course. It could connect the two cases, if it was really there. I've found murderers on less. Let's just hope Diane was the end of the chain. Finish your candy while I call over there."

Rose shoved the chocolate away. Her hunger for the candy had disappeared. Fear suddenly filled her stomach quite nicely. She tried hard not to let the fear into her voice, "I guess I know the answer now. I think you were trying to scare me back at my apartment. Let's talk about chains. I'm trying to see the pattern here, and I don't like what I see. From what I know, the main thing Susan and Diane had in common was that they were both women who tended bar at My World. And both of them are dead. I'll bet anything that someone they both knew killed them."

Butler raised a finger to quiet her, then told someone at the scene to search the stairs.

She rushed on the second he hung up, "Who else is a woman bartender at My World, Frank? Who else might be getting to know the same people Diane and Susan knew, happily chatting away with some killer without knowing it? Who else you think should be scared, Frank?" Rose ripped the candy wrapper into shreds as she questioned the detective. She was looking for a scrap big enough to tear again when he pulled the pile of torn paper out of her reach.

"Who's trying to do the scaring here? Relax a little. We don't know everything about Susan and Diane. My World doesn't have to be the only link between the two of them. Maybe they'd both jilted the same lunatic. The investigation could still turn up any number of connections. Shit, they were both blondes, right? Their hair color could interest this creep more than where they worked."

She stopped herself from smoothing her own hair, which she hadn't combed all day. "So my dark, raven, tresses take me out of the guy's league? Look, I've read all too many times about people being scared silly; I'm not about to be scared stupid. You want to guarantee me that staying away from the peroxide will let me live to a happy old age?"

Frank shrugged. "Guarantees are dumb. They only come true in fairy tales and manufacturers' wet dreams."

"Even the Brothers Grimm wouldn't write this guy's wet dreams. And nothing here says I'm going to live happily ever after. My World is the most logical connection between Diane and Susan." She hoped she sounded like a woman motivated more by logic than fear.

"Logic isn't always the magic key in these situations, Rose. You want to scare yourself, be my guest. But don't try to put it on me and don't expect me to help you get yourself all worked up."

"Forgive my girlish eagerness. I don't hear you saying that My World is absolutely not the connection between these two murders or suggesting any other mysterious link. There's something else you're not telling me, too. It's a glaring omission, and a scary one. For the first time in our short but fun-filled time together, you're not telling me not to worry. I'd kind of gotten used to hearing you say those sweet little words. Do you want to tell me not to worry about it now, Frank?"

"It's New York. You should always worry."

Chapter Ten

It was dark and still snowing heavily when Rose finally left the station. She'd refused Butler's offer of a ride home, unwilling to tell him she'd rather freeze than step into another squad car. She welcomed the night snow, admiring it for accomplishing the impossible. The snow hushed and cleansed the city, erasing the present's angular ugliness to hint at the past's graceful beauty for a few magical hours. The transformed neighborhood lured her into walking its newly sculpted streets. Staying outside appealed to her now.

She couldn't pick a particular route to follow so decided to wander. She wanted to avoid her usual haunts and any familiar faces who might tempt her into discussing today. She knew she'd regret it later if she hurried home. By tomorrow morning, all of this lovely white would have been trampled into hideous dirty grey.

The two cross-country skiers who almost ran her down as she crossed Grove Street mocked her with their exuberant enjoyment of tonight's pleasures. The snow fell thickly, obscuring anyone more than a few yards away. Without a destination, she started to see the nearly deserted streets as more ominous than peaceful. Every vague approaching figure seemed more likely to be Jack the Ripper than Frosty the Snowman.

Abandoning the idea of a cleansing walk, she

wondered if Butler would mind if she worried about not appreciating this snowy evening. Finally back in her own hallway, she fingered the card he'd given her. The home number he'd scrawled on the back didn't feel flattering. She turned the card over and over as she stood in front of her apartment door. She tried to ignore her reluctance to return it to her pocket in exchange for her keys.

This was not Diane's apartment. It was hers, her own shelter from the storm. The curmudgeon Butler had actually complimented these locks. Only a child could be afraid to open the door to her own apartment. The most vicious, bloodthirsty, killer, who probably didn't have her next on his victims' list anyway, wouldn't be likely to attack her tonight. Killers probably needed a day of rest, too.

Con Edison hadn't made any extra money from her today. The apartment was dark, except for the light at the windows. The snow gave the light an extra radiance, which shone ghostly into her rooms.

The eerie light didn't threaten a thing, but her fear didn't succumb to the artificial glare flooding the apartment a minute later. Rose had turned on every light in every room. She still didn't feel safe.

There was no one here. There couldn't be. She was scaring herself like a thirteen-year-old at a pajama party. In another minute, she'd start to see The Hook dangling off her fire escape.

Ten deep breaths. Ten more. Useless.

She had to know. Rose held the twenty-first breath

in as she opened the hallway closet, which contained nothing but the usual mess of coats, jackets, and hatboxes threatening to tumble down from the top shelf, with her nightgown puddled on the floor. Maybe he was hiding in the bedroom.

Stopping to think about what she'd do if she actually found someone could paralyze her into gibbering terror. Her deep breathing changed into short gasps as she raced around the apartment, checking into, above, behind, and under anything that might conceal even a mad dwarf. She peered out each window, checking that the ridges of snow on the fire escapes and ledges were undisturbed.

She'd looked everywhere except the most frightening place. Opening the bathroom door took all the courage she thought she possessed. Then she saw the shower curtain. Rationality cowered in shame behind fear. She forced herself to take the four steps across the room and held her breath again, remembering horrible nightmares when terror silenced her screams. She inched her right hand toward the curtain and slowly pulled it open. When she saw the empty tub, the porcelain gave her laugh a hollow sound.

Rose had always wondered how someone who was abashed would look. The mirror above the sink showed her.

The only immediate threat here was to her self-respect. She made tea Annie's way and sat in her chair by the front window. Quickly feeling like an actress in a bad play with harsh lighting, she retraced her illuminating flight around the apartment until the place resembled a home more than an emergency room. The paranoia revel was finished.

So here she sat, sipping tea and whiskey by the window, watching the world through lace curtains. In a minute she'd be dragging out her First Communion rosary beads and keening a few Hail Marys, draping a rusty black shawl around her shoulders for further authenticity. She could be a sweetly senile old lady, with a selective memory blotting out recent events and dwelling instead on the peacefully distant past.

Reality refused to stamp her exit visa. She was a thirty-three-year-old woman facing ugly facts and uglier fantasies.

She knew the condom packet connected the two murders and wished the major clue had impressed Butler more. Serial killers were, after all, more his game than hers. He could have them. The only murders she'd ever wanted to know about were the ones she wrote.

She'd set both her books at a small New England inn, where everybody in the little town thought they knew everyone else. The murderers she'd created always killed more men than women, and none of the victims were innocent. Her detective was a young female cop with manners far superior to Butler's. Rose liked it much better when she could pick the victims, identify the killers, and determine everybody's motives.

Butler claimed factors besides My World might link Susan and Diane, but she couldn't imagine what they might be, any more than she could imagine knowing someone who had viciously murdered two women. She also couldn't imagine how she might keep the promise she'd made to herself not to imagine the next victim's name.

Imagination was probably not the key to this situation. She had to think as dispassionately as possible and scrutinize everyone she knew at My World. It was a simple process of elimination. Fifteen employees and perhaps a thousand customers walked through the doors each week. Since this killer also raped, she could probably eliminate roughly half of the potential suspects. Then she would simply check alibis, eliminating anyone with an alibi for either night. Her conviction that the same man had murdered both women developed into a real laborsaving device.

Coordinating her bartending shifts, her writing, and such efficient sleuthing wouldn't strain her schedule at all. Even Butler had said the guy would be behind bars in no time.

Regretfully not adding any Powers whisky to her third cup of tea, Rose savored the taste of good sense. Caution counseled her to muzzle her curiosity and rein in her wild imagination. Prudence suggested she let the people who were paid to solve crimes fulfill that task. Wisdom confirmed she had told the police everything she knew.

Nothing reasonable said she had to help solve the

crime. She had done her part already.

Naturally, she'd be a little more careful in the next few days, but she didn't need to surrender to lurid fantasies of herself as either tragic victim or victorious sleuth. Enough.

The ringing of the phone wasn't a call to destiny. She waited for her answering machine to identify the caller.

"Rose? It's Jimmy."

She picked up the phone, surprised she'd neglected to check her messages earlier. Panic made a lousy social secretary.

"I'm here, Jimmy."

"Are you okay? I just heard. It must have been awful for you. I could be over in about half an hour if you want to talk to someone. I have a very convincing mother act in my repertoire, although I must say that if what I've seen today were my role model it would be Mommy Dearest all over again."

Jimmy's cough sounded as if it had started as a laugh. "I picked up my friend and his mother at the airport today, and the snow made the drive absolutely grisly. Of course, they didn't have the grace to close the airport, just let all the flights straggle in two or three hours late. So I lounged around with the great unwashed and unbaptized waiting for the flight from Puerto Rico. The bodega meets Bloomies."

"How did you hear about Diane?" Rose drained her tea and hoped Jimmy hadn't heard her gulp.

"Instead of slipping her evil way back to New Jersey,

La Madre insisted on dinner at My World, of all places. So we heard about Diane. The aging bitch got so excited she ordered a second old-fashioned. I almost hope the old lizard gets skin cancer. Bitchiness must be contagious. Listen to me rattling on, when my entire intention was to see how you were. Would it help to talk? I'll do anything I can."

"No, thanks, I've talked and thought too much already today. I'm exhausted. I think I could sleep like the dead. Jesus, I have to stop that. No, Jimmy, you're sweet to call, but I'll try to sleep soon. We can talk tomorrow." She hung up before he could argue.

Rose couldn't bear to repeat her story again. She felt too drained to talk to anyone about anything, but managed to summon the energy to listen to the messages the blinking light on her machine signaled. Maybe Sophie had miraculously extended her deadline.

Her mother was worried because the television said there was a big blizzard in New York City and what was she doing out traipsing around in such bad weather. It was sixty-eight degrees at home.

The *beep* of a hang-up.

Thomas didn't want her to worry about missing work tonight and was sorry he'd ever asked her to go over to Diane's in the first place. If she needed a couple of days off, he'd understand. He was so sorry.

Another cowardly *beep*.

Her friend Catherine had a great idea. They should

meet for a late lunch to watch the snow and drink wine. And Catherine would kill her if she was just sitting there listening to the message and not picking up the phone. Rose winced.

Beep again. Rose hated hang-ups. People could at least identify themselves if an amusing message was beyond their ability.

A very congested Ben was also sorry she'd had such a rough time of it today. The city was a jungle. He thought it only fair to pay her for tonight. Did she know anyone who'd want to pick up Diane's shifts? She should take care.

A final tongue-tied *beep* completed the day's roster of callers. Everyone could wait until tomorrow.

Her body ached for a long, hot soak in a tub full of bubbles. She started the water and poured in half a bottle of foaming lavender oil, planning on piling the bubbles at least a foot high before sinking beneath the foamy mountain into a blissfully senseless soak.

Bad idea. Bubbles wouldn't exorcise the image of Diane's tub. She wasn't ready to sink into or under anything. Five dollars' worth of oil spiraled down the drain as she canceled bath therapy for tonight.

A good night's sleep beat simmering like a prune anytime. She'd just have to go to bed dirty. The police station's stale air couldn't really have permeated all her pores. She wondered how long it would take her to qualify as one of Jimmy's great unwashed.

A good night's sleep could also be very evasive. Two

hours later, Rose felt jumpy as a jack. Normal apartment and hallway creaks announced Armageddon. The soft and gentle thud of a clump of snow falling onto the fire escape knifed her nerves.

Surrendering to the insomnia now would inevitably lead her on a forced march around the apartment until dawn. No enemy waited in ambush on the fire escapes. Sleep would, sooner or later, conquer. She would just have to outlast the siege.

The phone rang a reprieve. Talking to someone no longer seemed such a dismal prospect, and she answered before the second ring. Let her machine rest.

"Rose?" It was a strange voice, not a good omen today. A siren drowned the caller's next words. She wondered who would call from what sounded like an outdoor phone booth on a night like this.

"Rose?"

A friend must have heard what had happened and be concerned. Working public telephones were scarce, and often distorted voices.

"Yes, who is it?"

"You know me, Rose. And you will come to know me better. And I will come to know you. We will both come, Rose. We will come together at the end." The voice paused long enough to make her think he'd finished, then exhaled loudly.

"You were a naughty girl to miss work tonight. Nasty things can happen to naughty girls, Rose. Money isn't everything, you know."

She knew she should hang up.

"Red, red, Rose. You could be the flower in my night. I will see you soon, Rose. I wait for you to see me. See me in your dreams, Rose. Nighty night." The line went dead.

She'd heard nothing familiar in the caller's voice, and was sure he'd engineered that, maybe by speaking through a cloth pressed over the receiver. The words had sounded as if he'd forced them through something, exerting himself to make each word precise. He had spoken very slowly, while either exertion or excitement forced him to breathe heavily.

Nightmare, nightmare, nightmare. It's a horrible joke. First you couldn't sleep, and now you can't wake up. Rose ran into the bathroom. She struggled to remember all of the caller's horrible words as her stomach retched its own reaction.

She splashed cold water on her face and walked slowly into the living room. She should write it all down before she obeyed her mind's screams to forget it. He was a coward and a bastard and a psychotic. She would need all the information she could get to figure out his identity, because she refused to stay in this state of terror.

Statistics said obscene callers were usually too scared to graduate into more action. She had nothing to fear but the frightened himself.

He hadn't said anything specific about the murders. But he knew where she worked. Hundreds of people did.

He hadn't exactly threatened to kill her. He could be just a harmless, sadistic, opportunistic, freak. All kinds of them roamed New York.

She hadn't said a word after her first request for information. All the articles always said not to react, since any reaction was construed as encouragement. She had done the right thing, after her initial error of picking up the phone. Rose wondered if doing the right thing would save her. She tried not to think what she might need to be saved from.

Her frantic transcript of the call had taken up less than a third of the page. She filled the rest of the page with the word SAFE in capital letters. If wishes were horses and words were swords. Safe was too short a word; it needed more syllables to be more reassuring. Never trust anything that's too easy to write.

Threats often disappeared in daylight. Only the dark night let the pitiable speaker's words seem anything worse than sadly grotesque. Oh God.

She turned her chair around and faced the window. A street lamp backlit the falling snow, which shimmered in glorious patterns behind the lace. She let her tired eyes slip slightly out of focus and half-hypnotized herself with the patterns of light and form. The aesthetic exercise seemed more peaceful than thinking about how flimsy lace really was.

Chapter Eleven

She'd been unable to sleep until after dawn, as if the murky light of this grey Monday offered some sort of guard. Her dreams didn't provide any clues or explanations, but instead roiled with Classic Comics images of fearful blood and slaughter.

Promptly at nine Monday morning, Rose returned to her chair by the window to transcribe her caller's words again. The daylight didn't help his message. The morning had already turned the streets dirty, slushy, and hard to get through. She anticipated the new week would be much the same. None of the people slogging down Fourth Street looked happy. There were worse things than cold feet and ruined boots; the ringing of the phone at this hour could be one of them.

"Rose, Ben. Still sleeping, huh? How you feel?"

Rose picked up the phone, reducing Ben's voice from the blare of the answering machine to a conversational volume.

He sounded much happier to hear Rose than her recording. "Boy, you missed some night. Half the city was in here. Everybody wanted to know about Diane. News sure travels fast. People asked after you, too. I told 'em all you're a tough broad.

Little, but tough." His deep cough sounded painful.

"So, anyhow, this is the thing. Laura covered for you

last night and she's working today, like usual. I wanted her to work tonight, too. Now she doesn't think she can handle doing a double after being so busy last night. She also said she's 'stressed out' because of Diane. Right, she's always begging for more shifts, but then she's too 'stressed out' to handle them. What, I should give her time off 'cause she's crazy? I'm sick as a dog, and here I am. 'Stressed out,' my ass."

Rose waited for him to get to the point. "So, can you work? You'll probably make good money. I'll owe you one. Shit, it'll take your mind off what happened. I still don't really believe it. You must, though. I mean, you saw it and all. I ain't gonna ask you what it was like. I hate fucking ghouls. Poor kid. Diane was sweet. We just sent a wreath."

She wondered if he expected her to volunteer a description of finding Diane's body.

"Cops are right on the case. They been questioning everybody. You got any ideas? I'd like to get my hands on the bastard. So, Rose, you working for me tonight or what?"

Rose told Ben she'd work, accepted his thanks, and hung up. She hated the thought of sacrificing any writing time, especially with only fifty-three days left. But she'd realized near dawn that her own book wanted to stay shelved until this true crime story ended. Finding Diane's body had destroyed her authorial distance. She had to figure out who'd killed the women at My World, with or without Butler's blessing. As much as she loved her novel's characters and their bucolic New England setting, she couldn't immerse herself in their world until she felt safe in hers. She didn't want to be published posthumously.

Rose's agent would threaten to kill her for taking even an hour off, but Sophie's idea of death was not being recognized by a maitre d'. Maybe she didn't have to tell Sophie that she was temporarily abandoning her manuscript to concentrate on the real-life murders instead of the two more her plot demanded. Research, the next time Sophie asked how many pages she'd completed, Rose would tell her she'd discovered she needed to do a bit more research. She'd already planned on rewriting one major scene in her novel after finding Diane's body and wondered if anyone would notice her dearly acquired new verisimilitude.

In a better universe, she could just quit My World and stay safely locked in at home to write. But her landlord never struck her as a patron of the arts and finding a new job would waste even more energy. Fifty-three days was quite a bit of time, actually. Masterpieces had been written in less. By someone.

Working at My World tonight offered more chances to pick up some useful information than staring out her window. She couldn't expect the killer's name to appear in the snow on the rooftop across the street.

Just before finally falling asleep, she'd grudgingly accepted that Butler had been right about the lack of gates on her windows, at least those on the fire escapes.

Her aesthetic hatred of the ugly security contraptions succumbed to the prospect of paranoia imprisoning her more heartlessly than any metal bars across her windows. There was no point in having an unobstructed view if she were going to cower in front of it. She'd use the extra money she made tonight to help secure her apartment. She wondered if the gates that looked like scrolls cost much more.

Diane was dead, and Rose was picking out patterns. She chastised herself for sounding like Ben, who had focused more on the extra money he'd made last night than on losing Diane. She had analyzed his every word during their call, hoping for signs of guilt or some clue. It was ludicrous to think he could have killed Diane to attract more customers. The plan could have backfired too easily. Murder didn't invariably increase business.

She'd heard nothing out of character in Ben's callous tone. From what she'd seen, he wasn't given to operatic emotions and would probably sound gruff at winning the lottery. He'd also had a good alibi for the night Susan died. At least the cops had thought it good. She imagined it was harder to assess alibis for the middle of the night, with fewer people around to confirm a claim. So she probably shouldn't suspect Ben at all, although it wouldn't hurt to find out for herself where he'd been both nights.

She could suspect everyone. She could speculate for hours instead of calling the locksmith whose number Butler had forced on her last night.

The locksmith proved to be an anachronism. His kind of service no longer existed in New York. He'd arrived within fifteen minutes of her call. In the next three hours, he measured her windows, gave her an amazingly low estimate, left to get the equipment, returned, and installed it. He wouldn't even take a tip.

Artie Casey was too good to be true. She tried again to tip him.

"No, no, no. This stuff is too expensive for you already. Francis would have my hide if I took any more of your money. He was right, you're a nice young lady."

"Francis?"

"Francis Butler. The man who recommended me. He called me before you did this morning and told me to take good care of you. He's my nephew."

Casey the locksmith probably received a lot of referrals from his nephew the policeman. The familial tie answered the question of why a skilled locksmith had been so readily available on a Monday morning. She hoped it didn't also explain why the "used but still in good shape" gates which she'd bought so cheaply looked so obnoxiously shiny.

Even an enormous volume of business couldn't justify this small bill. Casey might have clung to the craftsmanship and courtliness of fifty years ago, but his prices should have changed with the times. Rose didn't like the idea of owing Butler anything.

Whatever they'd cost, her new gates and locks weren't invincible. She mustn't let them lull her into a false sense of security. Someone with enough determination could still break into her apartment, although he'd have to make a lot of noise doing it. She stretched out on her bed to see how different the sky looked through the bars. Still wondering how to interpret Butler's concern, she dozed off. She slept with her clothes on.

The slam of a neighbor's door woke Rose at six. Waking from her deep sleep felt like a resurrection. She had less than an hour to appear at work. If the mad slasher spared her, she'd probably die of cancer or depression from sunlight deprivation. Or maybe she could start a phobia clinic that specialized in the therapeutic power of hurrying. She'd been halfway through her shower before she felt uneasy. Adjusting the hot water to a degree below scalding had stopped the momentary shivers.

Rose tucked a high-necked blue blouse into a long, loose navy skirt. Blue seemed an appropriate color for sleuthing and she didn't want anything she wore to seem provocative even to a madman. The madman. Too bad she didn't have this outfit in polyester. She could go underground as a plainclothes nun.

Our Lady of the Investigative Bartenders protect her.

Chapter Twelve

Thinking of it in time could have saved her night. She should simply have typed up a succinct little essay, an abridgment of the statement she'd signed for Butler. *How I Spent My Sunday, Answers to an Interrogation by Rose Leary.* She could have xeroxed it, or, with true foresight, had the account printed on bevnaps. The napkins would have been best, because she could have distributed them indiscriminately. That approach would have satisfied the curiosity of even those few customers too polite to ask her about Diane.

"Hey, girl, what you doing here? Nice to see you and all, but I thought Diane worked tonight. I have passes to my show for her." Larry stood at the end of the bar in his habitual black leather festooned with pounds of silver spikes and chains, a menacing costume which never disguised his sweet boyish enthusiasm. Diane had called the young musician her best buddy. Rose did not want to tell him Diane was dead or how she'd died. Larry shouldn't learn about his friend's death across the bar.

Jimmy came to the rescue again. At this rate, she'd be pricing white horses soon. He took Larry to an empty table, where no one would overhear. Then she watched a tragic silent movie. Larry listened speechlessly, shaking his head and pounding his fist into his right thigh like a metronome. He returned to the bar.

"Rose, who could have done it? Why would anybody kill Di? What do the cops say?" Sobs punctuated each question.

"I don't know, honey, I don't know. But it will help the cops to talk to all of Diane's friends. They need all the information they can get." She handed him several blank bevnaps.

"Yeah. They'll love me. I don't care. I'm heading over to the copshop right now to talk to them. They gotta find this creep. Who coulda done it?" He scrubbed at his face as he walked out the door.

It was Rose's turn to stand mutely shaking her head. Larry's departure left the bar in a strange silence. No one had missed his questions or her replies. Watching Larry's reaction finally illustrated the horror of Rose's discovery. No one here would ask her about anything for a while.

She should take advantage of this shift to start her own question crusade, except that she couldn't very well lead a nonexistent conversation into topics she wanted to explore. A silent role as the object of pitying glances didn't inspire many conversational gambits. She needed to get people talking again.

"You all heard what I said to Larry. Nobody wants this nightmare to finish faster than I do. But sitting here like a convention of deaf mutes pitying me 'cause I was the one to find her doesn't help anything. At least I'm alive. So are all of you, appearances to the contrary."

Nervous laughter was better than no laughter at all.

"Well, we could all be dying of thirst in a minute. Give me another Guinness and get these guys one too. No switching to fancy stuff, though. We'll drink to Diane and then we'll drink to my selling five shots of the World Trade Center to a magazine today. The towers looked damn good at night, if I do say so myself." Owen was one of Rose's favorite regulars. The witty freelance photographer liked to talk about books and could even amuse her with his devotion to the Mets. After making his two toasts, he started pontificating on the team's chances this year. The bar splintered back into a series of conversations, none including Diane's name. Sports talk triumphed as barroom lingua franca once again.

Jimmy called a drink order. Rose leaned over the service bar when she gave him the drinks. "Jesus, it's as if they want me to show my psychic stigmata. This feels even rougher than I dreaded."

"Courage, darling. Celebrities have had their own crowns of thorns for centuries now. Notoriety might become you eventually, or at least do more for you than this Holy Madonna ensemble you're sporting tonight. It is not one of your triumphs, I'm afraid. I knew the minute I saw you how upset you must be to have dressed yourself so blindly. No one will mistake you for a rock star tonight. And you can forget about a guest slot on *Dynasty*."

Jimmy's face expressed an inordinate amount of pleasure when she laughed at his insults.

"My outfit's intentional. Protective coloration."

The protective coloration was about to feel tight.

Ward walked up to the bar, handed her an enormous slice of chocolate dacquoise, and apologized again for his outburst Saturday night. She accepted his apologies and his pastry, hoping he wasn't trying to colonize her with chocolate. She'd eat his cake and watch him too.

Ben's gloating proved true again: murder was good for business. She doubted My World usually bustled like this on a Monday night. Her speech to the quiet cocktail-hour bar must have been repeated and undoubtedly embellished. Nobody asked her any more questions, or even mentioned Diane's name within Rose's hearing. If everybody didn't stop treating her with such excruciating care, she'd develop an allergy to kid gloves soon.

Would Alan cheat on her? He walked in carrying another moribund rose, even though he shouldn't have expected her to work tonight. Maybe he courted all the bartenders.

"Rosie, I was in at lunch and Laura told me you'd be here tonight. How are you? I can't believe how good you look. Blue makes your eyes so big, just like Bambi. It's terrible about Diane, but what if it had been you? What if the guy had still been there when you walked in? We are so lucky. You must have been very scared, though. I don't know what I'd do if anything happened to you. Here." He handed her the flower as if he'd grown it himself.

She hoped her face didn't betray the distaste with which she accepted his gift. Shame on her for accusing Alan of indiscriminate affections. Shame on her for wanting to throw the rose into the garbage. Shame on everyone at the bar who avidly watched this pathetic little scene.

"Don't worry about me, Alan. Thanks for the flower. How's that new system you invented at the office working?"

Her question didn't deter him. "Rosie, you can't be too careful, with all the crazy people in this city. You need someone to protect you. I don't understand why so many men like to hurt women. I only like to love the ladies myself. You should let me take care of you."

Her imagination balked at hoisting Alan onto horseback in shining armor. Some creative impulse produced a stand-in of sorts. She told Alan that her big, strong brother was staying with her for a while. Let that little piece of fiction move along the grapevine.

Alan didn't look relieved. "When does he leave? Still, Rosie, it's not the same. Family can't take care of you the way I would. He can't be with you every minute."

"Jesus, Alan, neither could you. Give the woman a break. You trying to scare her more? Why don't you cool the melodrama and enjoy sitting next to a soon-to-be-world-famous photographer? Here, look at the photos I sold today. If you're lucky, I'll autograph the magazine for you when it comes out." Owen winked at Rose.

"Who the fuck cares about your asshole pictures? All right, show me." Rose had never heard Alan curse before. He squinted at Owen's proofs as if they pictured his worst enemy, gulped his drink, and refused a refill. Another first:

Alan always sipped his way slowly through several drinks, apparently relishing every third drink more because the house would buy his fourth. His next uncharacteristic act was the cruelest of all: he left her an insulting quarter tip. He had never tipped her less than five dollars before.

Owen laughed at the expression on her face when she picked up the coin. "Damn, Alan would have looked longer at my prints if they had price tags. At least you got the flower to remember him by. Plan to take it home and dry it? He's changing his tactics to win your heart, Rose. No more sporty tips. He's gonna play hard to get now."

Owen drained half his pint, "Look, Rose, I can understand his having a crush on you. Anybody could. But watching his awkward courtship hurts. How do you stay so nice to him? Unless you're hiding a deep, dark, passion for him in your innermost depths?"

"Yeah. Six stories down. Give me your solemn vow you won't divulge my secret. No one must know. Think this magazine will give you another assignment?"

Jimmy wanted more drinks and information. "Four Becks and two Amstels. What brother, and when can I meet this strong and manly paragon? Tell him not to hurt me if I say something mean." Jimmy wiped the rim of a sparkling pilsner glass.

"Alan's personality doesn't allow me to say he stormed out of here, so let's just say he squalled away. You must be a very cruel person to reject such a poetic soul. I think we should tell him your middle name is Daisy and see if he moves into mixed bouquets."

"Your beers are getting flat already, Jimmy. Go harass the paying customers." She tossed Alan's flower into the trashcan under the service station.

"Such a clever girl. Hurrying back to her chores just as the boss appears. Make a good first impression, now. Try to transcend your outfit." Jimmy smirked as he picked up his drink tray.

She could have identified Thomas without the warning when she saw Ben hurry to meet him at the door. The two men were unmistakably brothers. Thomas was about two inches taller and much thinner. He had purchased his clothes with more care and more money than anything she'd ever seen Ben wear. His deep eyes looked black from across the room. He'd combed his dark hair back in a style that accentuated the wings of grey at his temples. He had the look of a romantic hero who was only slightly tortured, just enough to make any sensible woman know she should be keeping her distance while she hurtled in his direction.

He caught Rose's stare and flashed a gorgeous smile, a smile which made her want to like him as much as she liked his looks. He walked over to the bar, apparently abandoning Ben in the middle of their conversation.

"You must be Rose. You're even lovelier than Ben said. I have to tell you again how sorry I am about getting you involved yesterday. Such a pity. I have some work to do down in the office now and it appears you have plenty to occupy you here. I shouldn't monopolize you. It's terrible to take a bartender away from her customers. I'm closing tonight, so we'll talk more later. I'm very happy we've finally met."

It had been a charming speech, delivered in a distinctively low-pitched voice. Thomas knew the importance of eye contact, and Rose had not minded looking into his slightly hooded eyes while he spoke. Of all the candidates tonight, he was the most aesthetically appropriate choice to ride the white charger.

He had ridden away before she'd had a chance to ask any questions. The entire encounter had been decidedly one-way, leaving her with the feeling she imagined she might have on finishing a papal audience. Thomas was definitely smooth. She hoped it was a nice smooth, and that he would be receptive to whatever questions she'd manage to phrase, much less ask. She should probably observe him for a while before she started interrogating him, anyway.

One of Jimmy's more endearing qualities was how he never made her wonder long what he thought about anything, or anyone. "So how did you like the Holy Ghost? Ready to start speaking in tongues after your visitation? Looked like you were enjoying being the beneficiary of the blessed charm. One of the most curious things about Thomas' charm is the way he always leaves you feeling you should be grateful for his kindness.

"Maybe it's the contrast to Ben. Thomas appears so much more polished and certainly more highly developed in the wardrobe department. I hope his not complimenting this particular manifestation of your wardrobe skills didn't hurt your feelings. He's much too refined to lie that baldly."

"At least I don't look like a displaced penguin. You're the only waiter I know who insists on wearing black-and-whites when the boss doesn't require them. Color choices too confusing for you, dear? Or should we take your uniform as hinting at the clerical?" She realized she'd never seen Jimmy wear any other colors.

Jimmy smoothed his cuffs. "Proper professional dignity. But let's forget clothes, momentarily. What did you think of Thomas?"

"I don't know yet. He was terribly nice, but without giving me a chance to say much of anything. He was sorry about yesterday, but really didn't want to hear about it." Rose lowered her voice. "You know how Ben always looks worried? Thomas seemed more as if he was determined not to worry. He had an air of having his mind on matters loftier than anything happening around here. I'd still expect his brow to furrow a bit after two of the people who worked for him were murdered."

"Hallelujah. She's finally going to talk about it." Jimmy clasped his hands as if in prayer.

She gave a quick look up and down the bar to make sure none of the customers needed her. "Jimmy, I do want to talk about it and I want to ask some questions. I want to know why I can't help suspecting some lunatic is trying to reinstitute Prohibition, starting with the bartenders here. I have a new meaning for the W.C.T.U. These days, it's

Women Cruelly Torn Up."

Jimmy was actually speechless for a minute.

She'd ignored her customers too long. "Damn, I came in here wanting to get some questions answered, but so far all that's happened is that I've been surrounded by everybody else's curiosity. We can't talk with the bar this crowded. Your tables are probably pining for you, too. At this rate, we'll both be killed for bad service."

"Murder. Curiosity. Look who just walked in. It's the King of Questions himself." Jimmy made his announcement with what struck Rose as an odd relief.

Butler wore yesterday's tweed jacket over a black shirt and black corduroy slacks. Rose decided not to ask him how a homicide detective could go into mourning every time someone died.

"Detective Butler. To what do I owe this unexpected pleasure?"

"Please, Rose, I'm here as a civilian. A drink on the way home will help me sleep. Let me have a glass of any red wine that doesn't come from a jug."

"You're going home now?" It was barely midnight, but Butler looked as if dawn were only seconds away.

"Restaurant people got a patent on crazy hours? I have a lot of work these days, which is not an invitation for you to start grilling me. I'm tired, Rose. So, please, give me a break and let me just have my nightcap. I wanted to see how you were doing." He loosened the black tie she hadn't noticed against his black shirt.

"Safer." She put a glass of cabernet in front of him, wondering if she should mention the crank calls with so many people around.

He pushed a twenty across the bar before he lifted his glass. "Safer? That's great. You read a book on self-defense or something?"

"No, Frank, I talked my guardian angel into going onto overtime. Actually, I want to thank you, difficult as you may make that. Your—uh—Artie Casey was wonderful. My apartment now looks like Leavenworth."

"About time. Glad to see you still have some shreds of sense." He pointed toward his money.

She didn't touch his cash. "So aren't you going to tell me what's happening? Please, just a quick update."

"Goddamn it. I knew I couldn't have a decent drink with you across the bar. It's stupid enough of me to come into a place where I've already been questioning people. Like your boss, there, who's on his way over to try to buy me this drink. Take my money now, before he gets here. Do me a favor, Rose, take my money. The guy at the end of the bar in the green sweater needs another Rolling Rock, too."

It was wonderful the way the exhausted, homeward-bound officer had managed to spot Thomas approaching from behind. Good of him to patrol her bar, too. He probably practiced surveillance in his sleep, what he got of it.

Sending Rose to the far end of the bar neatly

prevented her from eavesdropping. All she could see of their brief exchange was Thomas nodding when Butler spoke and Butler shaking his head when Thomas replied. Then Butler put his hand over his glass and seemed to end the conversation by shaking Thomas' hand.

The damned detective was even laconic in his body language.

Thomas went back downstairs, after telling Rose to buy Butler another drink if he changed his mind. Butler shook his head again.

"Frank, I won't buy you a drink if you'll tell me something. Are you making any progress? You found any good suspects?"

Butler's eyes looked almost as red as his wine. Even his voice sounded tired. "You want me to sign an affidavit swearing I did not come in here to discuss official business? You just won't give up. No great progress, Rose. No suspects who don't seem to have decent alibis.

"I've never seen so many people who could account for where they were in the middle of the night. One guy, and don't even ask me who, was actually in his insomnia group therapy for the hours in question. Jesus. Please, Rose. Enough." His wide yawn punctuated his demand.

She didn't know for a fact that anything linked last night's crank calls to the murders. My World wasn't the place to start talking about crank callers, and the end of Butler's night wasn't the time. She could always call him tomorrow.

Butler yawned again and pushed his glass away. "Good night, Rose. Take care of yourself. Don't worry so much." He tipped her two dollars. The wine only cost three.

The bar emptied early, as if no one wanted to remain at closing time. Thomas was pleasant but quiet while they counted money and closed the restaurant. He limited their conversation to the business at hand, graciously but firmly deflecting any other topics. He insisted on putting her into a cab, waiting five minutes on the windy corner until one appeared.

Walking up the stairs to her apartment, she recognized her error in hoping Thomas would prove an outstanding source of information.

She knew she had made at least two other mistakes the second she picked up the phone, which started to ring the moment she walked into her apartment.

The same voice was calling over the same phone. He sounded more rushed tonight, as if fearful she would hang up before he finished. "Even flowers have to die, Rose. Don't you hate it when flowers die, Rose? Love keeps flowers alive, Rose. Nighty night."

She shouldn't have answered the phone.

She should have told Butler about the first crank call.

Grabbing a pen to transcribe the hateful message, Rose wondered what other blunders her caller might reveal.

Chapter Thirteen

Chocolate, caffeine, and alcohol. The treats sounded like the menu for a marvelous evening, but not a smart life-plan. She hadn't consumed anything else, except fright and worry, in two days. If the killer didn't murder her, her complexion would. Stalked by sebum.

The caffeine and alcohol both formed staples of detectives' lives in the old books. Perhaps their deductive powers were only activated by cigarette smoke, an additional habit she'd rather not resume. Chocolate apparently didn't make an effective substitute.

Maybe she'd succeed better at this whole business if she fueled herself a bit more wisely. The misery she'd awakened in this morning could result from a decadent malnutrition. Anybody would feel uneasy on this fuel. And a good warm breakfast was the beginning of a successful day, and carrots would make her see around corners. Rose poured her fourth cup of coffee, carefully adding much more milk than usual. Had anything her mother called brain food been appetizing?

Thinking about food, however desperately, had as usual made her hungry. Nothing in either the fridge or cupboards seemed appropriate. God knows what would. This suddenly raving desire for something to eat might actually force her out of her apartment today. Nothing horrible could happen to her while she grocery shopped on Bleecker Street in broad daylight.

Spending her only free day of the week holed up in her apartment might damage her mind as well as her body. The phone no longer tempted her as a link to the outside world. Any delivery boy was bound to prove himself a psychopath. Rose forced herself into the shower and a safely drab marketing ensemble of pilly sweater and jeans. Her new attitude toward clothes as protective coloration wouldn't put her on any best-dressed lists. Those women probably got crank calls, too.

At least her creepy caller hadn't committed any federal offenses. Her mailbox contained nothing but a sheaf of junk mail, which she tossed directly into the trash cans outside the building. Then she crossed the street and stared back at her apartment to see how formidable her new gates looked from the outside. Even uglier from this angle, they shone in the cold sunlight like fears exposed. She felt they drew attention to her windows, advertising new insecurities. The bad guys might think she had something terribly valuable in there to protect, or they might want to challenge the metal's glittering invincibility just to prove they could.

The damned gates hadn't come with any kind of guarantee, either. The locksmith had told her they would make it much harder for anyone to break into her apartment; he hadn't said they would make it impossible. The refusal to guarantee anything must be a genetic trait in Butler and all of his miserable relatives. She fought an urge to shake her fist at her own windows.

The day was prettier than Rose's mood. The sky reveled in a splendid blue with only a few deliberate high clouds for contrast. The cold air clarified the light and should have invigorated her too. A day like this normally inspired her to go about her business with brisk efficiency, skipping blithely over the icy patches. The lack of a decent meal in the last two days must be the culprit dragging on her today. Too many stimulants were bound to make you feel that your sunglasses were suddenly twice as dark and your coat twice as heavy.

When she passed the bird store at the corner of Bank and Bleecker, the gorgeous colors feathering the cockatoo in the window screeched at Rose's drab appearance. Life might be easier on a swinging perch with wood shavings below to catch you if anything went wrong—except she'd probably feel homesick for the tropics and bitch about the lack of privacy inherent in window living. Captivity might annoy her, too. Anyone who caught herself seriously comparing her life to a bird's had better shake her head, hasten her step, and refrain from calling herself bird-brained. This walk was supposed to clear her brain, not twist it into macramé.

She started to plan her shopping list.

Someone somewhere might even have published a self-help book that could be a good source here. *The Detective's Diet*, or *Mystery Munchies*, or, most likely, *Diet or Die*. She'd have to check *Books in Print* soon.

Never give in to fear until you're sure your bibliography is complete. Grab at every little bit of comfort laughing at yourself offers.

Bleecker Street looked inviting once again. She managed to cross Tenth Street without peeking toward the precinct house. A visit to Butler wasn't on her list of nourishing items.

Reporting her phone calls seemed a hysterical over-reaction. Even this creep should get tired of hearing himself recorded with no response. She would just have to devote herself completely to the call-screening device on her machine. Maybe she should redo her own message, although she couldn't imagine any less enthusiastic tone than the one she'd already used. She'd recorded her outgoing message in a deliberately flat and anonymously unwelcoming voice. She needed a new and improved message, or maybe no message at all.

Rose couldn't think of a good enough reason to tell Butler about her calls. She didn't want her phone tapped or her number changed. What else could he do?

Trying to anticipate the joys of shopping, she crossed Seventh Avenue South and headed into the food stretch of Bleecker. She believed these blocks between Sixth and Seventh Avenues offered the most tempting food stores in the city. The yeasty smell of Zito's and the warm round of semolina she bought there helped focus her thoughts on her errands. Joking with Charlie while he made her change never hurt either.

The guys in Murray's were gregarious today, too. She tasted four cheeses before she decided on which new one to buy this time, adding the fresh ricotta to the pound of Italian pasta, two cans of roma tomatoes, jars of anchovies and capers, crock of marmalade, log of French butter, half pounds of chevre and parmesano reggiano, dozen fresh eggs, quarter pound of black olives, and rueful box of Irish breakfast tea she'd brought to the corner. Stefano scrawled the wonderfully low prices on the big brown bag she'd carry her purchases home in. If they'd only add delivery service, Murray's would be the perfect store.

All of those helpful articles her mother read on shopping tips had probably been right when they advised against shopping on an empty stomach. Forget what it did to your food budget; it simply wreaked havoc on your ability to carry the stuff home. A rich bowl of minestrone at the Italian luncheonette on Carmine gave her the strength to continue. She poured in extra cheese and ate both pieces of bread with the thick soup, fortifying herself for more than finishing her shopping and carrying her loot home.

At the only produce store with the grace not to serve miso soup left in the neighborhood, she bought enough greens for five salads, oranges and tangerines for her big glass bowl, garlic, onions, and flat-leaf parsley. She paid for these purchases with the guilty suspicion that half of them would pass their prime, age ungracefully, and venture into rot until she tossed them out.

Half of a pound of Genoa salami from Faicco's and a

small chicken with half a pound of the great bacon from Ottomanelli's pushed the load on her arms to their limit. She'd rather not push the question of why a woman who lived alone and ate dinner at her job five nights a week was shopping for a family of six. The prospect of cooking herself a good dinner and mulling everything over in her safely warm kitchen made this beast-of-burden routine almost worthwhile. At least trudging home and up five flights loaded like a mule kept her mind on the tasks at hand.

She wanted a good long talk with her sister while she cooked tonight, too. Marie would manage to help her find something in the current mess to giggle about and would probably come up with comforting answers while they laughed.

Stock your larder, talk to your family, forget the fear. She might manage to salvage the rest of this day yet.

She didn't know how she managed not to drop the bag holding the eggs when she saw the bouquet on her apartment's doorstep.

The dead red roses were limp, each brown-edged bloom drooping off its long stem as if someone had broken its fragile neck. The bouquet hinted at none of the delicate scent of dried flowers but oozed the stale broccoli smell of moldering water. A desire to enhance their beauty hadn't motivated whoever had kept these flowers past their prime. Someone had wanted them to rot. And die.

She kicked the hideous things down the stairs with

all her strength. They slithered to a stop somewhere below as she slammed herself into her apartment, holding her shopping bags like weapons. This madman knew her name, her phone number, where she lived, and how to get into her locked building. Anyone proficient with lobby locks might also master the secrets of the devices guarding her apartment. Fine. If he waited in here, he'd regret it. She felt angry enough to kill him with her bare hands but found the baseball bat she'd inherited with the apartment before starting her rampage.

"Come on, Goddamnit, come on out. Stop hiding, you sniveling bastard. I've had enough of your miserable scare tactics. Come out and I'll show you all about coming. You'll see what scared is. I'll send your wretched dead flowers to your funeral, you coward. Come on." She searched her whole apartment, too mad to be scared.

He wasn't there. No one, hopefully including the neighbors, had heard her raging. She stood alone with her anger, and the flowers stayed scattered on the landing and down the stairs. She'd looked at them closely enough to see that the creep hadn't even sent a card. He probably couldn't write his own name. She could beat the hell out of him at that game, too. And tomorrow she could joust with the Invisible Man. As long as she stayed too mad to feel the fear, she could even pretend that she felt safe behind her locked door.

Chapter Fourteen

"Detective Butler, please."

"Hold on."

"Yankov. Homicide."

"Butler. Please." If the idiot at the other end of the line was punning, she'd break his legs.

"Not here. Message?"

Rose telegraphed her name, number, and a request for Butler to return her call as soon as possible. She banged down the phone. It was only two in the afternoon, for Christ's sake. Knowing that her secret admirer had committed himself to lunacy twenty-four hours a day maddened her as much as this latest proof of his devotion.

One of the petals from the roses had stuck to the bottom of her boot. She wanted a garbage disposal, preferably one with metaphysical capabilities. Opening a window to throw the damned thing out would become a major production thanks to the useless protection Butler had scared her into. Maybe he'd suggest she move out of this nasty city next. Carmelite convents were probably quite safe. In the Midwest.

She wanted to go back outside and walk off some of her anger, but she didn't want to miss Butler's call or imagine what little surprise might welcome her home again. She paced around the apartment. Then she washed all of the salad greens and started to dry them. The top of her salad spinner couldn't twirl fast enough. She didn't give a damn if she bruised the greens.

The calls and the fear they created had been bad enough. But they'd arrived from the other end of a plastic instrument, perhaps even coming from miles away. Her hallway was too close. Dead roses were too sick. The symbolism was too stupid.

She shook with fury, the kind of anger that could force her into tears. At least she was alone. The bastard wouldn't have the satisfaction of seeing her cry.

She couldn't let him hear her, either. She snatched the phone up on the first ring, forgetting about her new devotion to call screening and barking her hello.

"Rose, it's Jimmy. You sound monstrous, but I'll still brave it and invite you to our place for dinner tonight. We can eat like swine and talk like mynas. I need to know what you've been discovering about the mysteries of My World. About eight?"

"No, thank you. No."

"What's wrong? Is the world outside My World treating you meanly or did you crawl out of bed backward today?"

"Just one of those days. I've been out shopping—groceries, nothing exciting—and I got some, uh, bad news in the mail when I got home." When this call ended, she'd make a skull-and-crossbones label for her phone receiver to remind her to defer to the machine.

"How bad? I know another murder is impossible. Tell

me what's going on. Tell Jimmy, Rose."

She couldn't muster the inspiration for creative lying. "It wasn't really bad news. More a bad present, or maybe a bad threat. Somebody left dead flowers on my doorstep. I've been getting crank calls the last few nights from someone who knows my name, my schedule, and now, obviously, where I live. Susan and Diane might have had the same secret admirer I do. I hate admitting it, but the timing seems so close it's making me crazy. Who could it be?"

"Oh, my Lord. What kind of flowers? Have you told the police? I think—" The call-holding click interrupted him.

"Hold on, Jimmy. That could be the police calling me back right now."

The other call was a wrong number. Frustrated, she banged the phone down, losing Jimmy. It rang a second later. He must have figured out what had happened.

"Rose? When you hurt me, flowers die. Beautiful things die, Rose. But you could make them live again, Rose. You could make the red bright again. Bright, bright, red. But dry red. You don't have to worry, Rose. Just let me give you beautiful things. I want to make everything beautiful for you, Rose. Help me, Rose. Beauty, Rose. You and me. Think about it, Rose. Think about everything I say." The line went dead again.

He sounded as if he called from a different place this time. She'd heard more traffic noises, but fainter, as if further away. She had listened silently with a frantic desire to hear everything, any information she could glean. Identifying him had become much more pressing now. Her life might even depend upon it.

When the phone rang again she half feared he had read her mind and was calling back to offer a stray clue or two. She shook off the suspicion that victim mentality began like this as she gingerly picked up the receiver.

"Well, you really didn't have to be so rude about it, dear. I'm not the one who's trying to terrorize you, after all. Did the police have any sensible suggestions?" Jimmy sounded worried.

"It wasn't the police. It was him."

"What did he say, Rose?"

"Too sick to repeat. Forget it." She reached wearily for her yellow pad.

"Tell me, Rose, I have to know."

"Jimmy, let it go. I don't want to repeat any of his ravings. His words in my mouth would make me sick. I want to go now and write it all down. I'll talk to you tomorrow. Maybe we can have a quick drink after work. But I don't want to stay on the phone any more now. I really don't." She wrote 2/25/86 on a fresh page.

"Ah, the eternal writer. I'll bow to your desires, dear. Does this mean you're refusing my invitation to dinner? There's no sense in stewing there all alone when you could be eating osso bucco with my friend and me. I just want you to know you can call anytime. My lines are always open to you, Rose. Keep my number right by the phone? Call if you change your mind and want company later. I'll even come get you and bring you back in a cab. I'm so sorry about all this."

"Me, too. Thanks and good-bye." Feeling as if she were filling out an assault form, Rose wrote down everything she could remember from this most recent message. She reread her notes on last night's call to see if there had been anything more than flowers dying. The guy had a regular motif going here.

She had a wild hunch. Alan always gave her flowers. She remembered the name of his company, found the number, and called to ask for him. The receptionist said he was in an all-day meeting, fussily adding that they hadn't even stopped for lunch. When Rose insisted on interrupting the meeting, Alan's voice was unmistakable. She hung up when she heard it, convinced he wasn't today's messy messenger.

It was hard to imagine Alan having the nerve to kill anybody. He'd stop and apologize the first time a victim said, "No, don't." No matter how she tried, she couldn't see Alan as the murderer. She didn't know if Butler would volunteer the info if Alan were a suspect, but flattered herself that the overly protective officer would warn her if he considered Alan even possibly dangerous. If the man ever deigned to return her call, she'd ask Butler where Alan had been those two nights anyway.

She put her transcriptions of the first two calls next

to the sheet she'd just finished. The creep was cagey. His words didn't provide much in the way of a character sketch.

Not a brilliant conversationalist, his favorite topics seemed to be coming, love, beauty, flowers, red, and death. Subtle mind this guy had. Maybe he was an aging hippy whose chromosomes had been irrevocably scrambled. Flowers, love, death: Charlie Manson would have adopted him with joy.

In some terrible travesty of nursery talk, he had wished her "nighty night" on both his nocturnal calls. He spoke in very short sentences and revoltingly savored the taste of her name. Rose stared at the pieces of paper, waiting for his name to emerge from her scribbles.

She'd looked so hard for similarities that she'd missed one big difference. He hadn't mentioned anything about death or dying in his first call, although he had chastised her for naughtily missing work. Sex and death were obviously very closely intertwined in the swamps of this guy's mind. "Nasty things" might be his kind of foreplay. She shuddered.

She was the rose and flowers had to die.

Rose wondered if he knew how chillingly clear he'd made his threats. It would be worse if he thought he sounded poetic, winning her writer's soul through his words. But he had never mentioned her writing.

Fine. She knew his motifs, his obsessions, and even saw the beginning of the plot. She still had absolutely no idea who he might be. Extrapolating everything he'd said into a psychological profile didn't help. She didn't want to know what type of madman he was; she wanted to know who he was. She wanted his name, address, and social security number. She wanted the police to have them, too. She wanted the police to have him. In jail. Forever.

She couldn't stop thinking that the man calling her had murdered Susan and Diane. She tried not to wonder how long the crank calls would last before he moved into more direct action. Twenty questions. Animal, mineral, or vegetable? Who would the winner be?

Her head ached as her frustration blurred the letters on the page.

He might be more powerful than he knew. She had to be smarter. She couldn't let him take over her life this way.

He had even kept her from her novel, far too much control to allow some cowardly bastard. She wished she could abandon these transcripts and work on her manuscript. But she knew the flow of her words would coagulate as her characters hid behind the faces she'd seen in the past two weeks. One of those faces was a blank, and she cursed him viciously. This was not writer's block; this was watching a murderer kill her book. No.

The calendar said she had only fifty-two days before her deadline. She had to get back to finishing her novel, but first she had to discover the killer's identity. Her life might depend on it. Groaning, she returned to her transcriptions of the hated calls. She studied her notes, now even more desperate for clues. When she found herself wondering if any of his speeches could be anagrams, she knew she needed a break.

Eating something decent had helped her feel better earlier today. Fish was supposed to fuel the brain, and garlic kept evil away. She sliced garlic, then chopped anchovies while the garlic cooked slowly in olive oil. Barely wincing at their bright red, she mashed tomatoes with her left hand while she stirred the anchovies into the saute pan with her right. By the time she'd added all the splattered tomatoes to the pan, the big pot of salted water for the pasta had almost boiled. The parsley received a vicious chopping, the pasta slid into the water, and the olives, capers, red pepper flakes, and battered parsley joined the tomato mixture. The sauce could simmer while the pasta boiled. Cooking had again calmed her, as it eventually always did.

She'd suffered too much already today to contemplate eating pasta without wine. She defiantly opened a bottle of pinot noir from her California cache and gave the phone a mock toast.

"Living well is the best revenge. Ever read that one, creep? Ever read anything? I'll get you before you get me. I mean it." Talk strong, be strong.

The damn thing had the nerve to ring. Rose didn't move. Let's see if this creep wanted any of his slimy words recorded for posterity. He wouldn't trick her into forgetting call screening again soon.

"Uh, Ms. Leary, this is Detective Butler. Frank, Rose. Sorry I didn't get back to you sooner, but the idiot at the desk misplaced your message until just now. What can you do, right?" She thought she heard music in the background.

"I'm heading home now. Another long day. I was in at the office at six this morning. What am I telling you all this for? Jesus. Anyway, you have my home number, so you can call me there later. Anytime, as late as you want. I might be too tired to sleep much. So don't worry about waking me if you get in late and need to reach me then. So, sorry, I rambled on like this, but you can—"

She picked up the phone. "I'm here. I was screening my calls."

"What are you, the princess of phones? Hire a social secretary." He'd sounded nicer through her machine.

"Frank, I think I should talk to you. I think I actually have something to worry about now." The water foamed thickly and hissed down the sides of the pasta pot. "Damn. Can you hold on just one second? The damned pasta's about to drown the stove." She dropped the phone and ran to adjust the lid.

"You cook? What kind of sauce you making?" He'd barely given her time to say hello again.

"Puttanesca, but that's not important."

"Whore sauce? Did you know that's what they call it? Why you making that?"

"To give you a chance to make stupid remarks. I didn't call you to discuss culinary choices. I have something I think I should tell you." She studied the red splatters surrounding the sauté pan and turned the heat down.

"Rose, have I ever stopped you from talking? What's wrong?" A recorded voice told Butler he'd have to deposit more money for more time.

"Where are you? Aren't you in your office?" Unless the city had started charging cops for calls.

"No, I'm in the Saz. You know the place? Sure, you probably know all the bars around, 'cause of your work, I mean. I spent enough time in the office today, and I'm trying to avoid going back there, or I'll get hung up for another sixteen hours. What's the problem, anyway?"

"It might be silly, at least I thought so at first, but now I think it's serious. And I think you should know about it. I mean, I guess you should. Don't worry, I can handle it, Frank, but maybe it will help you in your investigation. But I don't want to talk about it over the phone. It can wait, Frank. Give me a call from the office tomorrow. Or let's make an appointment now for me to come in and tell you about it." She did want to see his face when she told him about the calls.

"What 'it', Rose? Why can't you tell me over the phone? Somebody there with you? What the hell are you talking about? Come on, I'll go back to the office now to meet you. The chances of my keeping any appointment tomorrow are a joke."

He spoke over the clink of coins falling into a machine, "Meet me at the station in ten minutes. Maybe if I wear my dark glasses, I'll be incognito enough to get out of there again tonight. Just throw a coat on over whatever you're wearing."

If she went to the precinct house now, she'd have to walk back up the stairs alone later. Another surprise present might send her hurtling herself down the stairs instead of the gift. A long delay would ruin her sauce. Besides, Butler sounded exhausted again.

Maybe she should think the calls over more before she told the detective about them. She wasn't sure how much she wanted him intruding into her life. It could wait. He couldn't catch her mysterious fan between now and tomorrow morning.

She tried to make her voice sound congested, "Forget it, Frank. I'm probably just being paranoid. I'll catch you at the office tomorrow. I really don't want to go out tonight. I'm—um—I'm getting a cold. I'm safe and warm and alone in here tonight. Everything is fine. Go home and get some rest yourself."

"First you call me with an urgent message, then you can't talk about it over the phone, and now you don't want to walk two blocks to the station? What's going on here? You turning into a phone prankster or something?"

She gasped.

"What? Phones freak you out now? What's going on, Rose?"

"Nothing, forget about it. Just forget it, okay? Don't worry about it, as you would say. I have to go now. The water's boiling again. Sorry. Thanks. Good-bye."

She hung up before he had a chance to reply and let the machine answer when he called back a minute later.

"Goddamnit, don't play cute now. Rose? Rose? Shit," might not be the worst message her machine recorded all week.

The pasta had over-cooked so far that Gerber's could have marketed it. She threw it into the trash and turned off both burners. Another glass of wine might revive her appetite while it banished the feeling of utter foolishness following her conversation with Butler. Why did the man make her feel so silly?

She couldn't think of a sensible reason why she'd wanted to see Butler's face while she told him the newest developments. It wasn't even as if he were particularly good looking, for God's sake. His face was too goddamned quiet to be interesting, or informative.

She recognized her behavior as idiotically melodramatic but didn't see how to rectify it now. Having the detective paged at the Sazerac would only worsen things, totally convincing him that she was a hysterical broad, as he would no doubt phrase it.

Too late to worry about it now. Tomorrow she could walk to the station house in bright daylight to deliver her information and casual apologies.

The cops didn't seem to be breaking any records in solving this case. Why think that Butler could help her with this problem?

Putting more water on to boil, Rose looked forward to enjoying her pasta in peace. She scrubbed at the sauce that had bubbled onto the stove. Funny, red food had never bothered her before.

Chapter Fifteen

Loud bangs rattled the frame of her door. The nightmare was starting early tonight. He had gotten through the lobby locks again.

"Police. Open it."

She had read about this cheap trick in a magazine. Rose looked through the peephole at a distorted hand with fun-house sworls. The shaking door blurred her vision. She hooked her foot through the long extension cord and pulled the phone nearer. Maybe she could stall him long enough for the cops to actually get here. And get him.

"Who is it? I don't recognize your voice. I can't see you. Who's out there?"

"Police. Open the door. You're outnumbered. Open the door right now. Open the door or we'll come in through it."

She recognized the voice now. It didn't belong to the madman she had expected.

"Frank, what are you doing here? What the hell's going on?"

"Open the goddamned door. Get out of the way if you can, Rose. Everybody back."

"Calm down, Frank. I'm opening the door. Jesus." She undid both locks on the door and stepped just out of its opening swing.

The door slammed open with such force she was glad

she'd backed away. Butler crouched in the doorway, both hands pointing an enormous pistol straight at her. He cursed when he saw her in front of him, grabbed her, and shoved her behind him into the hallway.

"This is the police. Listen carefully. Drop your weapon. Don't even think about trying to get out. Put your hands up and slowly come into the kitchen where I can see you. Now." He panted heavily through his speech.

Rose stood gaping behind him. He pushed her back when she tried to follow him into the apartment. "Jesus, count your blessings. You looking for more cuts? Are you okay? Don't move any more than you have to. We'll get you to the hospital in a minute. Stay out of the way. Please, stay out of the way now. Let me get this guy cuffed before you start anything. Where is he?"

She spoke to his back, "Where is who, Frank? What are you doing here? I'm not cut and I don't want to get shot by some crazy cop. Do me a favor, Frank, put the gun away. There's nobody here but me. Honest. And I'm just fine. Sit down and catch your breath, please. Then tell me what you're doing here."

Butler slammed the door, locking her out of her own apartment. She heard him walking through each room inside, checking all the same hiding places she'd patrolled earlier. He unlocked the door a long minute later.

"How did he leave? All the windows are locked. Shit, I knew I took too long to get up your damned stairs. You better sit down."

"Frank, who in the world are you talking about?"

"Who in the world did that? You gonna talk cute on your deathbed, Rose?" Butler pointed to her left breast.

"Oh my God. You thought this was blood? It's tomatoes, Frank. I splattered tomatoes on myself while I cooked. Are you making arrests for sloppy cooking now?" Rose started to laugh, and Butler started to approximate the tomatoes' color.

"Your hallway has shitty lights. You sounded like you were in trouble over the phone. I figured somebody was here and not letting you talk freely. You were babbling but not saying anything, which is as close as I figure you could come to keeping your mouth shut, even in a hostage situation. Then you didn't answer my next call and I got worried. Real worried." Butler pulled her shirt away from her body, dabbed his finger in the red, and raised it to it his mouth.

"Shit, you mean I tore my ass up those stairs for nothing? I could kill you myself right now. You must be even crazier than I thought. Unfuckingbelievable. Give me your precious phone."

Butler barked a false-alarm message into the phone, canceling the backup he'd ordered. He refused to answer any of the questions the party at the other end must be asking, repeated that the whole thing was just a big fucking mistake, and dropped the phone back into its cradle.

Giddy with relief, Rose tried very hard to suppress her laughter. Butler was quickly working himself into a temper that suggested all the humor of the situation would elude him. He sounded angrier at himself than at her, but laughing at him might easily shift that balance.

"You thought he was here? You thought the killer was just taking a break while I chatted with you? You don't think I would have had the brains to signal you if he were here? You read my not wanting to talk to you as a plea for help? You ran over here alone? I mean, just you and your gun."

Nothing she said calmed Butler.

"Drop it, Rose. I made a mistake. I'm sorry I worried because I thought some bastard was puncturing your thin skin. You're right, though. I was stupid to run over here and even stupider to run up your stairs. Somebody was trying to kill you, they'd undoubtedly do it real slow so they wouldn't miss any of your entertaining comments on the action. You figure your dying words will take much longer than the average person's lifetime? Jesus. Can I have a glass of water, please? If it wouldn't interrupt your commentary too much to go to the sink." His gun had disappeared under his jacket before she could see where he put it.

"Then, if it's not too much trouble, maybe you could tell me what you wanted to tell me earlier today. I trust your message that it was important held some kernel of truth. So now you can tell me, face to face, whatever was too classified for you to reveal over the phone." He drained his water.

"This might not be the best time. It can wait. You seem a little upset." She wondered what he'd say if she offered him wine.

Butler walked to the sink and poured himself more water. "This is the only time. I am not fucking upset. I love wasting my wine and missing my dinner. It's how I keep in shape. Let's try not to make this a totally wasted trip, huh? Give me something for tearing up all those stairs."

"All right, Frank. I'll tell you. But why don't you sit down? I can even give you a glass of wine to make up for the one you left at the bar. I was having a glass anyway. Please, it'll make me feel better, and it might calm us both down."

"I am calm." His face cheered a little at his first sip of wine, and he actually looked at the label with approval. What had he been expecting, Gallo Burgundy from the bohemian writer?

She'd be better off telling him her news than convicting him for imagined prejudices. He wasn't someone you had to imagine slights from. He wasn't someone you could stall too long, either.

He positioned a chair so that it faced the door before he sat. "The wine tastes very nice, but I'd consider it even nicer if you would stop this mystery act and tell me what was on your mind. Then you could finish cooking your dinner and eat it, and I could go eat my dinner. We could both get on with our evenings or what's gonna be left of them. Let's have a little toast to it."

He raised his glass, "To Rose and her big news, and to Frank and his patience."

"There's a short toast," Rose muttered.

She found the papers she'd transcribed the calls onto and handed them to him. "Fine, Frank. I'll tell you what's been happening. But it might not seem like a major development to you. First I want you to read something, though. It'll be quicker than my repeating everything. I hope." She grabbed the papers and checked to see if she'd written the time and date above each call log.

He reached for the papers, "What is this, last-minute editing? You want me to tell you how I like your writing? Or are you checking to see if you got the police parts right?"

She dropped the pathetic sheets on the table. "Stop, Frank. I wouldn't write this bilge myself. Just read it and see what you think. Maybe you should know before you read it that this same charmer left a dozen dead red roses outside my door this afternoon. That's when I called you. Not that I want to give away the end of the story or anything."

"Dead roses?"

"Dead roses. Read, Frank."

Butler read the pages very slowly and very carefully, looking angrier by the minute. "Christ, your handwriting is worse than mine, but that isn't gonna kill anybody. You mean to tell me that you got this first call Sunday night and you didn't see fit to mention it before now? Don't even bother trying to come up with some cock-eyed explanation.

Save your energy for the memory game. Go back to the first call, pretend the phone just rang, and tell me everything."

His voice assumed a familiar rhythm. "What did he sound like? Have you ever heard his voice before? Could you get any hints about where he called from? You're good at this, Rose. Take it slow."

"Here we go again." She hated this game but, with Butler's prodding, she played it as well as she could. He took her over each call several times, until both she and the calls were exhausted.

"I'm pretty sure those are his exact words. I wrote them down right after each call."

Butler didn't sound convinced, "You're sure you didn't say anything to encourage him? You didn't try to egg him on, hoping he might give himself away? Tell the truth, Rose. It would be natural if you did react to some of this garbage."

"I didn't want to encourage him, so I didn't say a word after I first asked his name. I know it's hard for you to believe, but I didn't say anything. I thought that discouraged these creeps. At least before the flowers, when I still thought he was just a regular slimy crank caller."

"What do you think he is now, besides slimy?"

She couldn't believe he didn't get it. "Are you kidding? I think he's the killer, and I think he's trying to get me very, very upset. And once he's gotten enough kicks from that, I think he's going to come after me for the good-bye kick. Can you check to see if Susan and Diane got these calls too? Before, I mean? And it might be nice to know how far before, too. How long should I count on having before he tries to get me?"

Butler sighed. "Nobody's going to get you. It sounds bad, but we don't know for sure that it's the same guy. Could be just some other creep trying to get on the bandwagon. Don't get yourself any more scared than you have to. I'm gonna put a tap on your line. It sounds like he's been calling from public phones, but we could still get lucky."

"You mean tap like where somebody in a cheap suit listens to every phone call I get? Spies on me, and my friends, and my family? No thanks." She cradled her phone protectively.

"Why not? You want us to stop these calls or is your sense of drama enjoying them? Need new material for the book?" He tapped the papers in front of him.

"I don't like the idea. No. It's too intrusive." Desperate as she was to know her caller's identity, she couldn't stand the idea of Butler listening to all her phone calls. She could show him her transcriptions instead, illogically placing her faith in the written word once again.

"Listen to yourself. Trying to find this guy is intrusive, but I suppose letting him torture you, get you all upset and scared every night, is acceptable? How much of that wine you had already? Enough still left to spare me another glass while I keep trying to talk some sense into you?"

"Help yourself to the wine. I have to think about this. I have a few questions to ask while I think."

He poured himself more wine. "Am I supposed to look surprised at that announcement? I'm too tired to reverse roles again, Rose."

She topped off her own glass. "Will you ever tell me about people's alibis, specifically, I mean? Suppose I suspected someone, but you knew that he couldn't possibly have committed the murders, wouldn't it be better if you told me that? Just to put my mind at rest, so I wouldn't waste time up blind alleys? Would you answer questions like that?"

He grinned. "Probably not. Who do you suspect and why do you suspect him?"

"No one in particular right now. That was just a sort of 'what if' question. Or, could you tell me who you knew couldn't have done it, to put my mind more at ease? It's terrible to suspect everyone you see." She fingered the stain on her shirt.

"Tell me about it." His eyes followed her hands.

Only the faint hope that food might loosen his tongue better than the wine inspired her to ask Butler to stay for dinner. The sauce was already made, the salad greens were washed, and she had more wine. After making him miss his dinner at the Sazerac, it seemed the least she could do.

"Somebody cancel on you tonight, or what? There's enough food here to feed an army."

"I know. *The Soup Kitchen Cookbook* is my Bible. I've never quite mastered the art of cooking for one. Anyway, I like leftovers. If I end up stuck with them, I mean."

She added the last qualifier when she saw Butler reach for his third serving of pasta. He ate slowly and deliberately, complimenting her cooking and only raising an eyebrow when he bit into an olive she hadn't pitted. The pleasure he took in her food pleased her less than it should have. Tonight, she'd prefer information to culinary flattery.

Butler, however, remained resolute about not mixing business with dinner. He had deflected all her questions about the case by telling her not to ruin his meal and asking her about her life, her family, and her book. He had even volunteered a little about his childhood in return, describing the Village he'd grown up in as a sweeter place than the neighborhood he now protected. He seemed more relaxed with every bite he ate.

Chapter Sixteen

Rose fought her own relaxation, still hoping to conquer Butler's frustrating control of the conversation.

"You know what else scared me when I was a kid, Frank? Knowing that people knew things I didn't. I always thought it wasn't fair, not just unfair but actually frightening, when I'd ask questions and get told I was too young to hear the answers. I never wanted to wait until I grew up to find out what everybody else already seemed to know. Doesn't seem like I ever outgrew that one, does it?" She poured him more wine.

"For instance, I don't like the feeling that the creepy caller knows a hell of a lot more about me than I do about him. Like my name, and where I live, and when I go out. And that he knows how he got my number, and how he got into my building, but I don't. Wait, how did you get into my building tonight, anyway?"

"Sometimes the badge comes in handy, Rose. Amazing the places it can get me into. Even your building. I don't need the badge to get into the direction this conversation is headed, though. Next you're gonna ask me a whole lot more questions that I can't answer. Most of those questions, I really can't answer. Not won't—can't." He twirled the last strands of pasta on his plate into a neat bundle.

"Tell me again what you were gonna do with the bat

if the guy waited in here today. That idea scares even me. It ever occur to you that this guy might be stronger and meaner than you? Or were you gonna just threaten him with the bat while you questioned him into giving himself up?"

She waited until he'd started chewing, "I was so mad I don't know what I was going to do. Instead of scared, I suddenly felt murderously angry. Not one of my most rational moments, but I guess I thought I had a fighting chance against a real opponent. It's easier to hit back at somebody you can see than at a revolting, cowardly, disembodied voice. I do not like feeling threatened, Frank. I wanted to do something about it."

"Like putting a tap on your phone?"

"No, like trying to care of this creep myself."

"Rose, use your head. You're up against more than you know. Please, let me help you. If the guy had been here, you could have gotten yourself badly hurt or maybe even killed. Then I might have run into something worse than embarrassment and missed your good cooking and fine wine. I might even have missed your company, Rose. Me and everybody else you know, for a long, long, time." He shook his head when she offered him the bowl of pasta again.

"I'm not completely convinced the caller is the killer. We still haven't uncovered anything like it with the other women. We've talked to a lot of people, including very close friends of both of them. Women start getting calls like this, they usually mention it to a girlfriend or someone. Not everybody believes not talking about something will make it go away, you know."

"I didn't say—"

He interrupted, "You didn't have to. Listen to me, will you? There's still a very good chance your gentleman caller is a totally separate creep. These calls go on all the time; I've heard lots worse. The thing I don't like is the flowers today. You sure he didn't try to get into your apartment? No signs at all? Your regular crank callers, they usually keep their distance. The flowers today worry me."

"I didn't love them so much myself that I was going to press them in my scrapbook, Frank."

"No, and you didn't save them so we could see if there were any prints, either. Your hallway was pretty clean when I ran up, so they must be in the garbage already. It would have been a long shot, anyway. How about changing your phone number?"

He didn't seem surprised when she refused that offer, too. "So just what do you want to do?"

"I'm going to leave my machine on all the time. If he's stupid enough to record one of his little tributes, I promise to bring you the tape. I don't think he will, though. So maybe he'll get frustrated and forget about it." At least that way she could control what Butler heard without abandoning all privacy.

"You read about a lot of cases where sex offenders forget about things when they get frustrated? Frustrated isn't the best thing to get a sex perp, Rose. Not the safest, either."

"I have another idea. I'll have a man record my message. Maybe the creep will back off if he thinks a guy's living here. I already kind of started that rumor at work, anyway."

"What guy?"

"I said my brother was living with me for a while. I even said he was big and strong. Might not have been one of my proudest feminist moves, but it seemed like a good idea at the time."

Butler shook his head. "So, if the creep somehow heard this rumor, you think maybe he was leaving the flowers for your brother? Kind of a family affair? You could change your message. It might work, or it might not. I don't think it could hurt, anyway."

"So, you want to do it?" She rose from her chair.

"Some things you don't waste words on, huh, Rose?" Butler looked confused, but somehow pleased. He stood slowly. "You think now is the right time for this?"

"Sure, why not? Everybody does it all the time, anyway. I couldn't even begin to count how many times I've done it since I moved to the city. I promise it'll just take a minute. I always like them quick." She started toward the living room and her machine.

Butler followed her. "Just one more unusual quality you got, or are you trying to shock me? Why in the hell do you like it quick better than, uh, longer?"

"I think it's less boring that way. How many times a day does everybody have to suffer through these things? Aren't that many original ones anymore, either. So, short and sweet seems right to me."

"You always felt this way?" Butler was standing right in front of her, but drew back a little, staring at her face. His eyes were impressive. She saw something in them she hadn't seen before and couldn't begin to identify.

"No, I used to try to be clever about it, but now I just get right to the point. And I never use music; I hate those cute ones. If you want to hear a song, play the stereo. It's crass to ruin good music with chatter and such. I believe in keeping these things simple. So, let's go."

"Rose, I don't think we need this right now."

"Don't back off now, Frank. You aren't getting stage fright on me, are you?"

"I wouldn't call it stage fright. Why are you pushing this all of a sudden? Are you sure you want to rush into things this way?" He stepped back again.

"Frank, we could have been done by now. Let's get it over with." She beckoned him toward her impatiently.

"Talk into this." Rose pointed toward the microphone of her answering machine.

Butler still stared at her. He'd moved closer again.

"So, are you going to record the message for me, or not? You need me to write you a script? Just give the number, it's there on the phone, and ask them to leave a message. Say thank you. Try not to be too gruff. No need to have people thinking it's the Incredible Hulk sharing my apartment." He didn't move toward the machine.

"Jesus, Frank, why do you look so insulted? I don't give a damn. Record the message the way you think sounds best. We should be done with this by now."

It was Butler's turn to stifle laughter. He assumed a serious expression and recorded her message in a monotone that would do nothing to encourage anyone toward anything. He was quick about it, too.

He was just as quick about thanking her for the dinner, insisting she call him at home or the office if anything else happened, and leaving. Slightly puzzled, Rose locked the door carefully behind him. She rejected the absurd idea that she'd somehow scared him off. Instead, she measured how much of her fear he'd carried away.

She washed the dishes, changed into her oldest, most enveloping nightgown, and sat in the big chair by the window with only the street lamps lighting the room. She'd call Marie after she'd mulled everything over just once more. How much did she want to tell her sister about Butler? And wasn't it a good thing that he couldn't eavesdrop on their conversation?

Chapter Seventeen

A single day away from My World didn't provide enough relief. Rose started work Wednesday evening wishing she'd accepted Marie's offer of an escape to California. Instead, she stood behind the bar, hoping she'd make the extra money later to pay for last night's two-hour call. The call had cost extra: they'd never talked so long but laughed so little before.

Rose almost missed Diane's mess at this quiet hour. Setting up the bar took only minutes. Thomas was working tonight, but she doubted that he'd visit the bar for any nice long chats soon. He continued to act charming while avoiding any prolonged conversation, creating what seemed a deliberate distance.

Joe Victors sat down. "Hey, honey, how you feel? My sons treating you right here? You must have had a bad time last Sunday. Bastards. Least you kept your pretty smile. Cops finished with you yet? Let me have a beer, huh?"

She gave him an Amstel and asked how he was doing.

"Good memory. Could be better; could be worse. I gotta go downstairs and talk to my Thomas. Take care of yourself, now. You keep it clean, too. We don't need to lose anybody else around here."

He left her ten dollars again. Good, she'd just financed the first hour of her call to Marie. She wished she could eavesdrop on the other familial conversation occurring in the office but consoled herself with the sight of Owen settling himself onto a barstool.

"Enjoy your day off? Guinness, please. Let's see what horrors the lab has wrought now." He thanked her for the stout and started to look through three boxes of slides he took out of a large envelope.

"I took a bunch of shots of the river in winter and the storm last weekend, but the damn lab took all this time to get them developed. Idiots. My portfolio thickens as my wallet thins. Oh." He stopped his distracted chatter and stared at one of the slides.

"What's so shocking, Owen? Shoot one out of focus?"

"No, it's of Diane. I forgot all about it. She acted so cranky when I stopped in here early Saturday for a quick one that I took her picture, trying to cheer her up. Anybody who looked like she did never minded having her picture taken. She was gorgeous and loved to flirt with the camera. Shit. You can look if you want to." He pushed the slides across the bar.

"I want to look at all of them. But let me see Diane first."

Diane's familiar grin shone out from behind the same bar where Rose now stood. She looked happy in the shot; Owen's ploy had worked. Something seemed odd about the picture, though. Rose stared at it, trying to discover the grating detail.

She found two. Diane wore both large gold earrings, and the clock behind her head said ten to seven. The photo session must have occurred while Rose counted change downstairs. And Diane had lost her earring at the restaurant after all.

This didn't make sense. Rose had watched Diane leave the restaurant right after she'd complained about her missing earring. If she'd lost the earring in the restaurant, someone had found it there too. But when? Who? And how had Diane recovered it? The picture raised more questions than it answered. Rose glared at it, waiting for the answers to announce themselves.

"Oh, damn, I'm sorry. I didn't think the picture would upset you so much. Give it back, and I'll put it away. There are a couple good shots of the piers here. Look, the light on the water is terrific." Owen tried to offer her another slide.

She tightened her grip on the slide of Diane. "No, Owen, I want to look at this one. Can I have it? Can I enlarge it? Please, it's important to me."

"Yeah, sure, anything you want, long as it won't upset you too much. Keep this slide. The fools at the lab duped everything by mistake, or that was their feeble excuse for being so late. If you really want an enlargement, I'll get one made for you."

"No thanks. I can take care of it. Thanks again. It's an important picture, I think." She tried to smile reassuringly as she slipped the slide into her pocket. Pocketful of clues. Who knows the ruse?

"Show me the other slides, please. I always like your work."

Owen cheerfully launched into an exhibition, with commentary. His work was very good; Rose wished she could give it the attention it deserved.

Alan, as usual, wanted more attention than he deserved. He had positioned himself next to Owen, too close to the service station and any exchanges she might have with the waiters.

"Owen. Rose. What are you two looking so closely at? I'd love a drink, when you have the time, Rose. Thank you very much." Alan seemed nervous, perhaps embarrassed by his rudeness the other night.

"How is your brother, sweetheart? I wanted to bring you flowers tonight but didn't want to get you into trouble with him. Does he ask you a lot of questions? Sometimes big brothers can be such bullies. Mine was, but I suppose it's different for a girl. It should be, anyway. Nobody should bully girls. Right, Owen?"

"Gospel, Alan, gospel. You speak the truth, my friend." Owen winked at Rose. She tried not to acknowledge the wink, admiring Owen's generosity after Alan's insults the other night.

"Oh, Rose, might you tear yourself away from your admiring bar long enough to pour your humble waiter some warming libations? We have the U.N. of coffee drinks in the back room tonight, with some emerging nations even you might not have heard of yet." Rose grimaced as she poured the staggeringly sweet series of liqueurs Jimmy ordered into tall glass mugs which he then filled with coffee and whipped cream.

"Yes, yes, I know, dearest. Real men drink beer and real women drink dear. I don't suggest these things to these people, you know. Are we still on for that drink after work? I promise to order a beer so as not to embarrass you, since you must want to protect your reputation in the local ginmills." Jimmy added an extra half of a teaspoon of whipped cream to the Keoki coffee.

"Perhaps your brother could join us? Or would it sully your fair name if you were seen in public with two men? Does he stay up late, waiting anxiously to see you come home at a decent hour and hoping against hope you'll be alone? Please do proffer my abject apologies for forgetting to invite him to join us all for dinner last night. Can you both forgive me? We could agonize about it over drinks later. Do say yes."

"Maybe. There's a long stretch between now and closing. Let's see how the night goes, Jimmy."

Alan clanked his glass onto the bar, "Rose, I need another drink, if you're through talking to that fa—fellow. I didn't know you two were such good friends. He's got a point though; why hasn't your brother come in here? I'd think he'd want to see where his sister works. He should."

"He has been in, Alan. You just missed him Monday night. He came in right after you left. He's pretty busy while he's here. Not much time for hanging out."

Owen looked at her quizzically but had the grace to keep quiet.

Rose tried to remember if anyone even minimally likely to be her brother had been in the bar that night. She should reconsider this brother scheme, and quickly. She could live with lying about his presence but not with lying sloppily. Creating fantasy characters was supposed to be one of her best skills.

Her mental agenda was filling up nicely: determine how Diane had recovered her earring, rally some pertinent details about her brother's visit, and pump everyone she spoke to about the murders. At least she wasn't a wallflower at the Questions Ball. And she still needed to promenade through the grand waltz of discovering the identity of the killer.

Finances aside, Rose resented the busying bar that soon demanded more attention than her sleuthing program. A couple in matching crewneck sweaters insisted she describe every item on the menu to them, including which farm had grown the lettuce. A ruddy man in his sixties swore she made one of the best martinis he'd ever had and then described a score of the other proper martinis he'd enjoyed in his travels.

Alan gazed at her expectantly, finishing his drinks faster than usual so she'd return to him sooner. Mark had come in to prowl the crowd, and she had to keep an eye on him so that he wouldn't chase the five women at the bar away. Twenty-odd other people just wanted their glasses and their social needs filled. Working the bar didn't leave her much time to unravel the mystery mess.

Ellen, a waitress Rose usually enjoyed working with, seemed to be suffering from temporary amnesia. She asked the price of every other drink she ordered, interrupting Rose's conversations with customers. The slender dancer with the hacked black hair usually worked much more efficiently. Rose wondered what distracted her tonight.

Any one of a thousand things could be bothering the woman. Rose stopped herself from wondering if the crank caller had starting dialing Ellen's number, too. She couldn't ask Ellen if her phone had become a torture instrument without mentioning her own creepy caller, and she didn't want to reveal his existence in a bar packed with eavesdroppers. There could be copycat crank callers around.

Alan pointed to his empty glass, looking as if the beached ice cubes pained him. She'd studied him all night and could absolutely not imagine him with a blade bigger than a butter knife in his hands. She'd bet her life that Alan hadn't, and couldn't, kill anything livelier than an overdraft. How could she ask him where he'd been the nights Susan and Diane died without either insulting him or encouraging him to think she cared about how he spent his nights?

"What are you looking so serious about again, Rose? Something bothering you?" She couldn't look his gift opening in the mouth.

"Well, Alan, no matter how hard I try not to think about it, I just can't forget about what happened to Susan and Diane. Especially Diane. It bothers me to think I was sleeping safe at home when two women were killed. I hate thinking I slept in perfect comfort while someone else suffered such horrors. Know what I mean?" Please, God, let him take the bait instead of making forlorn comments about her sleeping safely. Get a little, risk a little.

Alan gulped half of his fresh drink. "Do I ever. I was here the night Susan died. Brought my boss over for a break, then we went back to the office and worked until ten in the morning on those damn taxes. Only a few blocks away, and no idea what was happening here. Makes you think."

Risk a little more. "What about with Diane? Didn't that bother you, too? Or did you like Susan more?"

"No, who could like Susan better than Diane? Or either one of them as much as you? Nah, I was sleeping too, or trying to, when Diane must have got it. The plumber had torn up my apartment so bad that I spent that night on my neighbor's lumpy couch. Nice of the guy to offer, but his couch was hell. So was listening to him talk in his sleep most of the night. Worst of it was, he'd wake up every hour and ask if he'd bugged me. Wanted to know what he'd said. Like I cared. Too bad I didn't stay with you instead, huh?"

Alan drained his glass. "Listen, I appreciate your asking me about it, though. Nice to know you care. Everybody needs somebody to care about them, don't we, sweetheart?"

"Can't argue with that. Excuse me, but Ellen and

Jimmy both need drinks."

And she needed a moment to examine Alan's alibis. They both sounded tight. So she'd traded a little bit of fake concern to get that question answered. Now that she felt sure she'd been right in thinking Alan couldn't kill, his fantasy life couldn't hurt her.

Alan was off her list, and the earrings in the picture had to lead somewhere. She just needed some time to assemble all the information.

She wanted to postpone the after-work drink with Jimmy so she could ponder how the earring Diane had lost in My World had traveled to her apartment before she died.

"If you won't be seen in public with me, I'll follow you home and make you talk to me through the intercom. Now, a nice quiet drink with charming conversation, or screeching squawks invading the sanctity of your home? The choice is yours, darling."

Jimmy tapped his stack of tonight's checks against the bar until the edges aligned into a perfect rectangle. "If you don't manage to muster at least a minimal amount of enthusiasm, however false, for the prospect of spending a little time in my company, I'll precede you down to the office and ask Zorro to join us. I remember how thrilled you've always been at the prospect of drinking with that adorable creature."

"What's Zorro doing here? I didn't see him come in."

"Busy as usual with your bar, sweetness? He came

in about two hours ago, headed straight downstairs to the office, and hasn't surfaced yet. He and Thomas do seem to spend a lot of time down there together. Maybe Thomas is finally teaching Zorro the seating chart. He still doesn't know any of the table numbers."

She started scrubbing the sink. "So he's going to come in on his night off to learn them, Jimmy? That does seem likely, particularly considering how driven to succeed he acts. Ulcers aren't quite imminent unless he relaxes about this job. The customers work harder around here than he does."

"Well, why don't you hurry cleaning up and scurry downstairs to ask them what they're doing? Count your money while you're questioning them so that we can get out of here sometime before Easter. I'm quite anxious to rejoin the outer world." Jimmy wiped a few sections of the bar she'd just cleaned.

Rose couldn't hear anything behind the closed office door when she walked downstairs. Balancing the heavy cash drawer on her forearm, she knocked with her free hand. She knocked twice before Thomas opened the door. He complimented her on another busy night and sat down at his desk to separate the waiters' credit card receipts.

Zorro remained seated in the room's only other chair, in front of Ben's desk, which looked remarkably clear of seating charts or any other paperwork. Rose stood awkwardly, still holding the cash drawer and wondering if she should squat on the floor to count her money. Thomas added the waiters' charge slips with a concentration more suited to *The Book of Revelation.*

"Rose, excuse me. How rude of me to stay in this chair. I have been sitting here so long that it has become overly comfortable. Please, you must sit and finish your work." Zorro finally stood.

He continued talking as Rose removed a long white silk scarf from the chair's seat. The smooth scarf looked fresh, with none of the wrinkles Zorro's sitting on it should have produced.

"Yes, we at My World all must work many hours. I came in to discuss business with Thomas, since last weekend I was too busy to resolve everything I wished to. I suppose your job is more easy, however, without all the worries of the responsibilities of a manager. Do not let me disturb you any longer. Please, count our money."

Our money? She thanked him for the chair and began counting her bank. Thomas hadn't said a word while Zorro chattered and hung the scarf over a hook on the back of the door. She wondered what responsibilities Zorro claimed to be so conscientious about. A floor manager who only worked weekends was not exactly an executive position. From what she'd seen, Zorro barely performed a host's duties.

He leaned over her shoulder to see her sales total for the night, congratulated her, and then excused himself to go to "the men's lounge." Thomas ignored both of them, continued to add up the receipts, and then counted Rose's money. He thanked her for doing a good job tonight and returned to his paperwork.

Surprised not to see Zorro when she walked back upstairs, she asked Jimmy if he'd already left. Jimmy insisted Zorro hadn't appeared upstairs yet. Rose didn't like thinking Zorro had tried to eavesdrop in the bathroom the whole time she and Thomas worked in the office. Fifteen minutes was a long time. She still couldn't figure out what Zorro had been doing in the office in the first place, since it didn't seem as if he and Thomas had been discussing business.

More curiously, she felt certain Zorro hadn't been sitting in that chair as long as he claimed: silk wrinkled.

Chapter Eighteen

"I want to have you to myself, Rose, not waste precious time waiting for Thomas and Zorro. You'd think one of them would have the grace to come upstairs and unlock the door by now." Jimmy looked at his watch for the fifth time.

He'd dismissed all her excuses for avoiding a drink. Maybe he really did remind her of a nun. Her continued blabbing could anoint him father confessor, if she could just imagine him sitting silently in a confessional. At least his mind was almost as quick as his mouth. Volleying questions with him would delay the return to her apartment and dreaded answering machine.

Zorro and Thomas finally appeared, and they all walked outside. Thomas locked the front door and turned to Jimmy, "Are you seeing Rose home again? Make sure she gets in safely. Come on, Zorro, I'll drop you off on my way to my girlfriend's apartment. Good night, Rose, Jimmy."

Thomas had effectively dismissed them, as if he wanted to avoid the possibility of chatting for even half a block. She asked Jimmy the minute the men got into a cab, "Isn't it odd Thomas knew you took me home last week? He wasn't here those nights. So how did he know?"

Jimmy waved good-bye to the cab. "Maybe Ben mentioned it to him. You know, see how well our little employees get along. Or, more likely, you think that fucking fag is finally gonna get the sense to be interested in women?"

"That's a hard one to buy, Jimmy, not really Ben's style. I can't see him rushing to the phone to tell his brother you and I left together." She raised her coat collar against the wind.

Jimmy took her arm. "Well, it didn't have to be Ben. Zorro was around the nights we left together, and he and Thomas do seem to talk rather frequently. I've always thought Zorro too self-involved to indulge in the delights of gossip, but maybe he thought it would titillate Thomas. I'm more curious about Thomas' girlfriend. I've heard him mention her a lot, but I've never seen her. You'd think she might grace his restaurant with her presence sometime."

She quickened her pace and wished Jimmy would loosen his hold. "Whoever she is, she's smart to stay out of the place. God spare us from the boss' honey. But why would Thomas want to tell us he knew we'd left together? It doesn't make sense." They reached Hudson Street and turned south.

"Rose, my child, many things in this life don't make sense. Remember the Sorrowful Mysteries."

"Yeah, we're living them these days." Pretending her collar needed adjusting again, she pulled her arm free.

"Hush. Let's go into this charming bar you chose and try to make them joyful. Unless of course you'd like to reconsider and stroll to Florents?" Jimmy looked as thrilled at the prospect of the White Horse as he had outside the restaurant in Chinatown. Good to know she'd put her trust in someone with tastes so similar to her own. She led him to a table in the back room, bypassing her usual spot at the bar.

True to his word, Jimmy ordered a wheat beer from the dozen or so choices the waitress spieled. Rose ordered a dry vermouth and soda.

"Cheer up, dearest. Sip your drink and tell me everything. Spill it, as your chum the detective would say." Jimmy looked around the old wood-paneled room as if she'd taken him to a foreign country.

"He doesn't talk that way, actually."

"Excuse me. Anything else off the point you prefer to explore? Or can we talk about those calls and the flowers? They sound dreadful." He looked quizzically at the lemon hanging off the rim of his beer mug.

She gestured that he should squeeze the lemon into his beer. "Jimmy, I don't want my business all over the bar. Let's not encourage this guy or give somebody else ideas. Can you really keep a vow of secrecy?"

"I long for vows. Just how many people at My World have inquired about your writing since you confided in me? Has your suspicious little mind gotten even the slightest glimmering that I divulged your secret? I promise you nothing you say will leave these atmospheric doors. You have to trust someone in all of this, Rose."

She sipped her drink and considered how much to

tell him. His name didn't fit on her list of suspects, but she didn't have absolute proof that he couldn't have killed the women. She hated looking for a killer's profile in every face she knew. Almost as much as she hated talking about writing more than doing it, especially fifty-one days from her deadline.

"My God, you're looking at me with that same removed expression Butler wears. Would you smirk condescendingly if someone told you he was in an insomnia group, too?"

She'd been right; Jimmy wasn't a suspect.

"That was you," she blurted.

"Is nothing sacred? Just how close are you two, anyway?"

"Not at all. So, does the insomnia group help?"

Jimmy stopped tracing the initials carved into the old wooden table. "Well, the crowd is certainly more appealing than the creatures one meets in after-hours bars these days. The plague has really killed nightlife. Five years ago, the only clubs around My World really were meat markets. I still miss the Mine Shaft and who knows if the Anvil will reopen?

"But my sleepless nights are not the issue here, darling. Why are you so sure the same person killed Susan and Diane?"

Jimmy had, after all, told her about the folded condom packet near Susan's body. He deserved to know its significance. She described seeing the other packet on Diane's stairs. Although the police had never found it, she knew she'd seen it and she knew it connected the two murders. Jimmy agreed and wanted to know if she'd discovered any other clues.

She told him about the two earrings on the windowsill, then showed him Owen's slide.

"I know she was pretty, Rose, but her future murderer's name isn't tattooed on her forehead. I see the clock, but we all know she was still alive then." He tilted the slide into a better light. "Oh, it's the earrings, isn't it? She's still wearing both of them, so the poor thing didn't lose one at home after all. And she didn't lose it until the very end of her shift."

She took the slide back. "Somebody found the missing one, Jimmy, and he must have found it at My World. Anyone who knew Diane would recognize it. Whoever found it must have called her and brought it over to her apartment. Her number's listed; I checked. She let the creep in with no problem, then must have been so happy to recover her earring that she offered him a drink. In Diane's case, drink did bring on the devil's curse. We both know the end to the story."

Jimmy flinched when five college kids squeezed into the four-top next to them. "It makes sense, but it isn't written in stone that the same person who returned the earring killed her. Someone else could have come in later."

She steadied their glasses on the table when the kids jostled it. "Then why didn't whoever delivered the earring talk about it? Any friend would want to see Diane's killer caught. The earring is important. I'm going to show this slide to Frank tomorrow."

"Frank? First names now?"

"It's not a crime, Jimmy. He's nicer than he seems."

"Not a difficult accomplishment."

"We're not here to talk about him. I want to know what you think about my calls." She told Jimmy all about them, and about yesterday's floral delivery. "I'm afraid it's the killer, trying to upset me into letting down my guard. Detective Butler says it doesn't have to be the same person, but I think the timing is too close for serendipity. What do you think?"

Jimmy glared at their new neighbors as if he still stood in front of an unruly classroom. "Why ask me if the almighty Butler has already spoken? Please, don't title him detective again on my account. Your caller and the killer could be the same guy, but why wouldn't he have called his other victims too? Susan and Diane never mentioned anything about crank calls. The calls sound terrible enough without elevating them to a death sentence, Rose."

"You think I'm anxious to scale those heights? The coincidence doesn't let me believe they're different people."

Jimmy shook his head. "Now, on to the big question. Do your clues point to anybody? Do you have any ideas who might have done it?"

"No big answer yet. But the little questions keep multiplying like the loaves and fishes."

"Wonderful. I'll be the detective's disciple, if you'll be the detective. We can't have Susan and Diane's murderer wandering the streets, strewing prophylactic packages as he roams. And I am not in the least entranced at the thought that some cretin might be tying up your phone lines with filth just when I want to exchange some decent dirt.

"How in heaven is our friendship going to develop the way it should if you're constantly distracted by fears for your life? It's screamingly obvious you're not going to relax until they catch the lunatic. Fear does not become you. It clashes with your character. Really a discordant note."

He stopped talking just long enough to eavesdrop as the next table ordered two pitchers and five liverwurst sandwiches from the waitress. Rose couldn't tell which part of their order shocked him more.

"So, Rose, why don't you let me help you? I hereby offer my services as a sleuth's assistant. Somebody has to interject a little sense into this mess."

"We need another drink, Jimmy." She wondered what sort of help he meant.

"If you insist, dear, but please have something a little more potent this round. Vermouth and soda does more for your chic rating than your blood level. Don't you like white wine anymore?"

"I don't like house wines. This place has come a longer way than you can imagine, but they still haven't reached the cruvinet stage. I need to stay in a sober state, as do you, if you really want to get involved in this mess."

"I am involved. Believe me, Rose, I'm involved." He tried to get the waitress' attention.

"You don't have to be. It's not all that much fun, unless you like feeling frustrated and dumb all the time. What can you do, anyway?"

"I think I'll just enjoy your humility while it lasts. Maybe I'll grow into a Lord Peter Wimsey role. Such a name."

"Don't forget Ms. Vane. Choose your role models carefully." She chattered along, weighing this new view of Jimmy. She believed his intentions were good, he knew the cast at My World, and he was certainly good company. His intelligence shone through his silly facade like neon through imitation Levoliers. He made an unlikely partner, but she was playing an unlikely game.

Their second drinks inspired new ways of phrasing the same questions but produced no new insights. They knew where all of the obvious suspects at My World had been when the first murder happened, thanks to Jimmy's eavesdropping.

When Jimmy started to repeat Ben's and Thomas' alibis for Susan's murder, Rose objected that Thomas wouldn't have sent her over to find Diane's body if he'd somehow returned to town in time to kill her. What would be the point of rushing that discovery?

"What about Zorro, Jimmy? He and Diane did have that big argument Saturday. I know he was on vacation when Susan got it. I guess it doesn't make sense to think that he'd kill Diane just because he thought she was stealing. Funny way to get in good with the bosses. Then again, cocaine has never been known as a great logic enhancer. And I do think he's dumb."

"So now you think he flew in from his vacation to kill Susan after a long-distance lover's spat?" Jimmy squeezed the lemon into his second beer without prompting.

"What?"

"All right. It didn't seem necessary to tell you before. Speaking ill of the dead and all. But Susan and Zorro were having an affair. Of sorts. Cocaine passion, anyway."

"How do you know?"

"They both told me. And my eavesdropping skills were quite unwillingly transformed into those of a voyeur several times. They used to fuck in the office. Loudly."

"When? During work?" She didn't want to picture this.

"Yes, dear, on our esteemed employers' time. Susan would suddenly develop an urgent need for liquor from the storeroom or a trip to the ladies'. Thomas, or sometimes yours truly, would watch the bar for her. Then Zorro would disappear downstairs, as is his wont."

He grabbed her swizzle stick and removed a lemon seed that had floated to the top of his beer. "It only happened when Thomas worked. I could never figure out if the big guys knew what was happening. By the time our beleaguered employer could go downstairs and look for one or both of them, they'd be back. These were not the couplings of the gods. No resemblance to eternity in their timing."

She struggled for an alternate explanation, "You're sure that's what they were doing?"

"Please. One doesn't have to engage in every variety of sex to recognize the universal sounds."

"I still can't believe they got away with it." She tried to remember every surface in the office that she'd ever touched.

"It wasn't a nightly event, dear. But it happened more than once. They were slick. Slick and quick."

"Okay, I understand your distaste. But why in the office?" She couldn't help picturing the office furniture.

"Maybe they both got off on being in the throne room of power, although it would take more than cocaine to make me consider that office regal." Jimmy sniffed. "Maybe it was the lock on the door."

She didn't mind changing the topic. "Enough sex. Onto drugs. Was Susan as obvious about doing coke as Zorro is?"

"Not quite. You had to look for it with her before you knew for sure. She was a lot more subtle about the business end, too. I could never actually spot her selling it, although I know she did, especially to some of the Wall Street suits. She and Zorro had worked out lots of little tricks. I always figured the cleverer ones were hers." He sniffed again when the five liverwurst sandwiches arrived at the next table.

"You mean they were partners in more than love?" She couldn't remember the last time she'd had liverwurst, but she thought it had involved a school lunch box.

"Delicately put, Rose. Yes, and now I think Zorro finds it hard to handle the sales aspect of his game all by himself."

She felt excited now. "So what if something went wrong with their dealing? And, on top of Susan's crush on Ben, it was too much for Zorro. What if he killed her?"

"No. Zorro told me once he thought her crush was cute. Said it spiced things up. Sometimes I suspected she only faked the crush, anyway, trying to flatter Ben and throw him off balance." He tapped his fingers on the table.

"This wasn't big time drug dealing, either, just grams and even half grams. They probably only made enough money to keep themselves high. I can't see it as the stuff of murder, even if Zorro had been in town, which you must remember he was not. He even showed the cops the Visa bills from his trip. They loved them."

"All right, Jimmy, so they weren't drug kingpins, which is a word I've been dying to slip into a conversation, and it wasn't a crime of passion. Why has Zorro been able to get away with dealing in the restaurant? If Ben and Thomas know about it—say even if they're getting a cut—it wouldn't be enough money to justify the risk. They could lose the place. And I haven't seen anything from either of them that makes me think they're all that interested in coke." She paused.

"You know, Jimmy, that may be one of the reasons I liked My World so much originally. It's rare to find a restaurant where cocaine isn't a silent partner these days. But that still doesn't explain why Ben and Thomas don't stop Zorro. He's pretty obvious."

"He's also cleverer than you think. He may be obvious in front of you and me, but he's a little more circumspect in front of the owners."

"Still, they should see what's happening. He practically offered it to me in skywriting." The memory of Zorro's blatant offer still bothered her.

"Don't forget Zorro only works the weekends, and those are usually Thomas' nights. So Ben's not around to see it, and Thomas never sees anything he doesn't want to."

"True, Thomas does seem too distracted by real life to bother about drugs."

Jimmy folded his coaster and tucked it into his empty beer mug. "Rose, I hate to break this up, but it's almost four."

"Sorry, you must be tired. We should both get some sleep."

"Don't be bitchy. If we leave right away, I can still catch the last session of my group. If you laugh, you will be the next victim, although of a different killer."

She let Jimmy pay the bill and walk her home. She refused his offer to check her apartment and trudged upstairs alone.

Then she counted thirty-one hang-ups on her machine. If the creep had called from pay phones, at least it had cost him. Maybe he'd run out of quarters soon.

Still wondering why Jimmy had waited this long to tell her about Zorro and Susan, Rose washed her face, changed into her nightgown, and warmed a cup of milk with honey. Then she turned off the volume on her answering machine. Any more hang-ups and she'd never sleep. Beeps and clicks had never figured in any of her favorite lullabies.

Nighty-night yourself.

Chapter Nineteen

Too many calls, too little cash, but just the right number of rationalizations. She had forty-four hang-ups on her machine by the time she left for work, $168.70 in her $200 opening bank, and at least a dozen reasons why she hadn't bothered Butler with the news about Diane's earring.

"So, Rose, back to the old routine. Guess we just have to put it all behind us. But business hasn't been too bad for February. Hell of a way to get free advertising, huh?"

"You could say that, Ben. Sorry, but this bank is more than thirty dollars short, and I'm going to have a hard time making change with all these big bills. Yesterday's petty cash receipts are still in here, too."

"Great, Zero does it again. Maybe he's also the prince who ordered the damn foie gras. Hell, not even Ward would go that far. I should make whoever signed this scribble on the delivery slip pay for that damn stuff. Then I should make Zero pay the difference in the bank. No wonder my figures were all screwed up today." Ben slammed the sheaf of papers he'd been reviewing down onto the desk, opened the safe, and handed Rose the backup change box.

"Just straighten it out, okay, Rose? This box is right, so buy what you need and leave me a slip. Cash in those receipts, too. I guess Zero didn't want to bother with them last night. Thomas better do a better job teaching him to fix the banks, or I'm gonna put a fast stop to this business of Zorro taking on more duties. I don't even—" Ben stopped talking, cleared his throat, and bent over his paperwork again.

She didn't think it was the right moment to congratulate him on the nickname she wished she'd created herself, since it perfectly matched the blankness Zorro's face so often assumed. Or to ask him why he allowed someone he clearly didn't respect to not only stay on his payroll but to climb its hierarchy. Zorro seemed a more likely candidate for firing than for promotion in Ben's eyes.

Two men ran My World. Although Ben did most of the hiring and firing, it was obviously Thomas who guaranteed Zorro's continuing employment here. But she didn't know why. She'd yet to see any signs of Thomas sharing Zorro's drug habits. Even if he did, anyone who wanted cocaine could find many other sources in the Village bars. Arguing that Zorro's work as host was good for business would challenge a champion debater. He had to have hidden talents. Very well hidden.

She could even think while she counted. "All right, Ben, I think the money's in order now. I'm going upstairs."

"Wait a minute, huh, Rose. I wouldn't usually ask you to do this, but you probably won't be too busy for the first hour, and I got some fucking mess to deal with here." He waved at the papers covering his desk.

"So, could you pick up the phone behind the bar for me for the first hour or so? Anybody except my father or

Tommy, tell them to call back. The waitrons can handle the door for a little while. Buzz me if you guys need me, but I really want to get some of this shit cleared away before it buries me. Just an hour's peace, and I might be able to see my desk instead of these piles of screwed-up papers. Thanks, hon. Appreciate it."

She would have worn something perkier if she'd known she'd be playing secretary. Tonight's exercise in defensive dressing was an old navy blue sweater with a high cowl neck. The sweater came almost to the knees of her narrow black jeans and could accommodate her Siamese twin without stretching. This new deliberate dowdiness rebelled against her usual belief that dressing well inspired better tips. Forget dressing for success; she was dressing for survival. Pick your role; choose your costume.

"Darling, this might not be a topless bar, he says gratefully, but I do think this evening's outfit goes a little far in making the case. Why don't you wrap a muffler around your throat and don gloves while you're at it? I'm not one to leer, but some slight hint of skin would be reassuring, if not flattering." Jimmy winked, picked up the drinks she'd poured for his only table, and returned to the dining room to finish his prep work. It was difficult working with someone who wanted Diana Vreeland canonized.

Rose set up her bar quickly. Her only two customers both sat engrossed in their late-edition papers and beers. She decided to put a notepad next to the phone for Ben's messages and wiggled open the drawer next to the register to find one.

She guessed that Diane must have used the drawer last, since no one else could have left such chaos. Uncapped pens, band-aids, nubby lipsticks, check pads, register tapes, mirrored sunglasses, dated price lists, an unused copy of *Mr. Boston's*, and somebody's old calculator formed only the top layer of the drawer's contents. It should occupy her for a little while.

Rose had reassembled two flashlights from scattered pieces and was straightening a pile of five dupe pads when she noticed the writing on the first page of the top pad. She recognized Diane's scrawl.

> *To Ben,*
> *There are bad things going on around here*
> *you don't know about. Some people around*
> *here think they own the place when they*
> *don't. How would you like it if committing*
> *crimes was supposedly part of a job and*
> *people told you that was the way it was?*
> *It's dangerous. Susan did some bad things*
> *but she didn't deserve to die. You*
> *could know somebody all of your life*
> *and still not know everything. Even*
> *your own brother*

Diane had stopped before finishing her accusations. None of the pages on any of the other pads contained any writing. Rose searched the drawer but didn't find any more information. She read and reread Diane's lines, trying to understand her message. Too bad she hadn't found a book of mug shots, with the killer's face circled in red ink.

She almost jumped when she heard Ben's voice behind her, asking if she were looking for anything in particular and if she needed help. "Your own brother" what?

"No thanks, just trying to see what's at the bottom of this drawer." She didn't mention reading about his "own brother."

He looked at her oddly. "Find anything interesting in there?"

"Mostly junk. Nothing to speak of." She'd crumpled the small page in her left hand when she heard his voice, and now her hand was beginning to sweat. Wonderful, her best real clue, and her nerves were about to make it illegible.

He asked for a club soda, and she dropped the paper into an empty shaker next to the ice before she poured his drink. Ben started to walk away, stopped himself, and came back. "One more thing. I called Zorro and left a message for him to get his ass in here. If he shows up, send him straight down to me. He'll probably try to weasel what's happening out of you. Don't get into it; just send him downstairs. I want to be the one to tell him what he screwed up. Don't forget, buzz me if you guys need me up here. It better pick up soon."

She agreed, then rescued the page, smoothed and

folded it, and shoved it deep in her jeans pocket. She'd study it again later.

Why couldn't Diane have written just a few more lines? Rose doubted Diane had intended to sign her little note, but wished she knew for sure. Her teachers should have told Diane to date all her correspondence, too. She tried to shake off the image of Diane, standing behind the bar and writing her message on the dupe pad. It might have been an impulsive move, but what had inspired it?

My, my, how the questions multiply.

Zorro's appearance at the bar didn't guarantee any answers. For someone who only worked weekends, he was putting in a full schedule this week. Life in the managerial echelon was rough.

"Good evening, Rose. You look very attractive tonight. There is a simple chic to your outfit. I do appreciate the understated." Zorro looked around the quiet dining room. "Where is Ben? It is difficult when I must spend even my nights off helping him. But, I knew that acting as his manager would not be a simple job. And I am happy to help."

Zorro's own understatement tonight was a black-and-yellow checkered sweater that barely covered the waistline of his habitual black leather pants. His clothes always looked as if they'd been bought with more money than taste. She couldn't understand why he never seemed to shop in stores with full-length mirrors.

She told Zorro that Ben wanted to see him in the

office and watched him stroll downstairs. Complications must be addling her brain: she'd tried to look as chic as a coal miner. In Wales.

She didn't hear any compliments on her clothes from any of the bar crowd that slowly gathered, either. It was probably the sweater, which guaranteed that none of the men at the bar could even begin to hope for a free cleavage shot. The sweater's high neckline had eliminated a modesty check tonight, making it unnecessary for her to lean over in front of her bedroom mirror to confirm she wouldn't expose too much at work. The little circles of scotch tape she sometimes used to stop a blouse from falling too far forward always irritated her skin as much as using them irritated her.

Brilliant. She should muse helplessly over bar etiquette and wardrobe selection while a note from a dead woman festered in her pocket. Perfect priorities, absolutely perfect. She probably should have been writing for *Cosmopolitan* all along.

Ben was safely downstairs, and none of the customers at the bar looked her way. She motioned Jimmy over to the service bar.

"We have another clue." She put Diane's note on the tray between them with only a slight flourish. If she wanted to curtail Jimmy's melodramatic tendencies, she'd have to confine her own. "Look at this. I found it in the chaos drawer behind the bar. Recognize Diane's handwriting?"

He read the note but didn't return it. "Peculiar. Diane

was not one to write a note on a whim, as her spelling witnesses. She certainly hints at deeper and darker goings on at My World than I've ever suspected. This is wonderful; my life seems so much more interesting since last night. What could she have meant to say about Thomas?"

"If I knew, I wouldn't need to show you the note, would I, Jimmy? This raises a lot of questions. Unless you have a Jeanne Dixon act in your repertoire, we have to start finding some of the answers ourselves. Diane was getting ready to tell Ben something that someone wouldn't want him to know. But whoever that is couldn't have known specifically about the note, or it wouldn't have been lying in the drawer all this time." She held her hand out and waited until Jimmy returned the paper. "Granted, I wouldn't suspect anyone covering his tracks to put a search for incriminating correspondence from Diane on top of his to-do list."

"We should thank God for that, anyway." Jimmy pointed downstairs.

"Right, and curse Him that she didn't write a bit more, at least finish her line about Thomas. But she didn't. So we have to discover what the cryptic 'things going on around here' are, and what 'bad things' Susan was doing." Rose checked over her shoulder to make sure her customers didn't need her.

"At first, I thought Diane meant the dealing we talked about last night. But no matter how dumb she acted, she wasn't innocent enough to be quite so melodramatic and horrified by cocaine. The only thing I do know for sure is that this note absolutely, inarguably, and without a doubt makes it obvious that the killer is connected to My World." Her own vehemence surprised her.

"But, Rose, you already knew that, even if you weren't expressing it with quite such redundant emphasis. I think Diane wanted to write mysteries, too. Maybe My World is a hotbed of hidden mystery writers, all just murdering each other off so they'll have something to write about. Clever way of weeding out the competition. Distracting other people away from finishing their work limits the field even more, so whoever thought up the nefarious scheme multiplies his or her own chances for success." Jimmy smirked.

"Thanks for your indispensable insights, Jimmy. If you won't praise me for my humble refusal to gloat about proving the killer is tied to My World, we should both get back to work. We'll brainstorm later."

She refolded the note and pushed it deep into the pocket of her jeans. The note in her pocket felt like a passport to a better place. Finding something new to read always inspired her.

Chapter Twenty

The phone behind the bar rang again. Might as well add another message to the three she'd taken already. Successful secretaries read *Cosmopolitan*.

She started writing his words as soon as she heard his distorted voice.

"Something is wrong, Rose. I don't want to talk to a machine, not when I know you're there. I like beautiful flowers, not ugly machines. What were you doing instead of talking to me, Rose?

"You should wait for my calls, Rose.

"How can you learn to love me the way I know you will if you don't hear me? Our love will not blossom in silence, Rose.

"I can always find you, Rose.

"Wait for me, Rose. Wait." He hung up.

She took very slow, very deep, breaths as she finished her transcription and shoved those pages into her pocket too. He'd called from indoors tonight. She would hate the sound of her own name soon. He eroded its single syllable each time he used it.

He had no right.

The bastard was fighting her for her own self-control. She wished she had a chance to accept the challenge. Or reject it.

She would tell Jimmy about the call later, after she'd

managed to quiet this clamoring fear. She could tend to her customers on automatic pilot. Her job was a sociable role, leaving little room for frightened contemplation or solitary thought. Garbo had never played a bartender.

Easy now. Easy now. Smile at the customers, pour their drinks, chit with their chat. Nobody would walk into a busy bar and start slashing. She could analyze the call later. She could protect herself later. Routine would do it now.

She'd known all along that the caller knew where she worked. Nothing had changed so terribly. Nothing was new. Nothing was none of her business.

Funny, she hadn't noticed Jimmy going downstairs, but he and Zorro now laughed as they climbed the last few stairs together. As Jimmy rushed off to check on his tables, Zorro plopped himself down on the last free barstool like a man who'd just received a commendation. He smiled broadly, ordered a glass of champagne, and even had the etiquette to put a twenty on the bar. Either Ben, with uncharacteristic leniency, had absolved him for the incorrect bank, or else Zorro's hide was thicker than the worst ozone layer. She wondered if he'd pull out a new silver pocket watch to show her. Engraved.

Zorro's plodding, pompous conversation would soothe her right now. She could finish composing herself while he talked at her. They'd make the perfect couple. He, as usual, would talk primarily about himself, while she listened and tried not to think about herself. Zero conflict.

Less than zero distracting interest.

"Ah, Rose, good evening. I am glad to have a chance to see you again. I think I will sit here and have a drink with you, although you of course will not be having a drink with me. Some of the rules sometimes seem ancient here, do they not?" He gestured at her to continue pouring into his glass, even though the bubbles hadn't subsided. "It is most true that one must have all of one's facilities about one while doing work as difficult as ours. Believe me that I would enjoy my champagne more if I could clink my glass with you. It is hard to toast when one drinks alone. But, please, accept that I drink my glass to you, and to our continued success here at My World." He raised his glass to her.

"Cheers, Zorro," she lifted an imaginary glass and wondered if he missed a podium.

He flicked his finger against the flute and watched the bubbles rise. "Since I see that your bar is not terribly busy, perhaps we can enjoy a little chat. Do not worry; I am sure your bar will become more busy later. Although I myself do not work on Thursday evenings, I do know that many people like to go out on Thursdays. They like to make their weekends begin early. For me, of course, the weekend starts all too soon every week. As you know, the weekend is my most busy time."

She wondered how he defined "busy," since customers already claimed every barstool.

Zorro started to lift the flute by its bowl, then

stopped and pinched his thumb and forefinger around the stem. "And that is why I am so happy to sit here and talk with you. When we are working together, we never have the opportunity to get to know each other. I think it is important that people who work together know each other. I think it is best if all coworkers are also friends. What do you think?" The flute teetered a little when he put it down on the bar.

She scrambled for an agreeable platitude. Wasted effort: Zorro didn't need her answer.

"Please. I do not want you to be shy. Just because you are a bartender and I am a manager, this does not mean we cannot also be friendly. I do not stand on ceremony. You must not worry about rank here. We all work together. Titles are not the important thing between friends."

She was a bitch for thinking he expected gratitude for his magnanimousness; he probably thought he sounded gracious. She should toss her forelock over her shoulder coyly, without tugging it first.

He leaned over the bar as if expecting secrets, "I have been wanting us to get to know each other better since you began work here, Rose. Or, since I returned from my vacation and we started working together. That is more exact. It is too bad that my responsibilities have kept us from this. Let us take advantage of this opportunity now. Tell me about yourself."

He refined his request before she'd had a chance to recall the synopsis version of her life story. "Wait. That is such a big question. I know it is a hard one to answer for most people. So let me take that back and give you a more easy and small question to begin with. What were you thinking about when I walked up to the bar? What was the thought in your head right before I sat down?"

Better not tell him you were anticipating his boring you into feeling safe. Best to try to use even this opportunity. Forget the normal flow of conversation.

"Well, Zorro, I was actually thinking about when I first started working here, too. Or, really, about why I started working here. I'm afraid I can't help thinking about the murders. I wouldn't have gotten this job if Susan hadn't died. Then thinking about Susan dying made me think about Diane's death. Their deaths are the only connection I see between them. Do you think there were any others?"

"It would not be easy for me to say. They were very different ladies, although both of them were beautiful people. Our losses have been tragic. We all miss those two girls so much. I must think about them every day. It is so sad. But we must put it all behind us, now. It is over. We must go on. Our business here is to make the customers happy. We cannot mourn forever." His speech was delivered with the sort of ersatz sincerity usually reserved for undertakers.

He gestured for her to refill his glass, but didn't release his hold on its stem. "You know, Rose, I was out of town when those horrible robbers killed Susan. It was my vacation, as I am sure you remember. It is difficult to think how I was enjoying myself when poor Susan was being killed by stupid thieves." He gestured for her to fill the flute too close to the top. "Thomas, who was at home that night, has also said to me that he does not like to think how he was happily relaxing while Susan was dying. It makes everything so hard. What can we be allowed to enjoy?"

He didn't give her time to answer. "And then, again, when Diane died, how could we have known? You and I had worked a long, hard night together. Were you not glad to get to the comfort of your home after working so hard? I was. I remember very clearly that when I arrived home shortly after four in the morning, my doorman remarked on how tired I looked. He told me I should rest in bed all the next day and he was very happy to hear when I went out for dinner late Sunday night that I had not left my house since I had entered it then, shortly after four."

She wondered how Zorro could afford a doorman building.

"And Thomas, he called me at about 5:30 that Saturday morning to discuss how things had gone at My World while he was gone. He too thought I sounded very tired. Still, we talked until after seven that morning. There was so much business to discuss." He looked up and down the bar when he mentioned business.

"Thomas had just gotten into town when he called me. I could not let my tiredness stop me from telling him the things he needed to know about My World. Long ago, I told Thomas and Ben that they could call me at any time.

Besides, five in the morning is not so late for us restaurant workers, is it? You might call it our cocktail hour. Tonight, I am drinking too early." He laughed and gestured for another refill, finally releasing his hold on the glass.

"I need happy drinks for these sad subjects. Excuse me, I must go to the men's lounge while the bubbles settle. You pour champagne very well. It is a real talent."

So was shoehorning alibis into a conversation. She hadn't even needed to attempt phrasing questions about Zorro's activities the nights of the murders. He had volunteered all the information about himself. He had also volunteered the information about Thomas' whereabouts both nights.

It didn't seem coincidental. Why should Zorro want to exonerate himself to her? Why should he include his boss in the acquittal of unpressed charges? He'd supplied much more distraction than she'd anticipated.

Jimmy stood at the bar, adding up a check. "Fine. You can't possibly sacrifice your delicate sensibilities enough to talk to me, and then I see you leaning over the bar and listening spellbound to Zorro. Really, Rose. Unless you're garnering stupendous information, your behavior is absolutely inexcusable. I suppose you'll be trotting off for late-night drinks with him next."

He pointed to Zorro's flute. "Is his drinking champagne supposed to convince you of his sophistication? How can I, a creature of humble tastes, hope to compete? You certainly ruined any chances that I'll ever be acknowledged as an urban sophisticate when you forced me to swill beer in that place last night. Please, tell me you didn't have a hidden camera on your person in that boite. I suppose you'll have me bellowing country and western tunes next."

Jimmy displayed an admirable pout. "So, what were the two of you chatting about so avidly? Are you going into the retail business next? Or is it all too personal to disclose?"

Just how good was Jimmy's hearing, anyway? She didn't want him lingering around the bar while she talked with Zorro. "I'll have a lot to tell you later. Maybe I'll put it in a song with bad rhymes. Not yet though. Zorro's coming back upstairs, and I want to talk to him while I can. It's a rare chance, as he's informed me, for the two of us to chat. You couldn't want me to waste such a golden opportunity, Jimmy. We're learning a lot here."

"Well, do forgive me if I find it difficult to feel enlightened. I'll be certain to have my notebook ready whenever you decide to divulge your information." He finished adding the check and walked away to deliver it.

When Zorro returned, he moved his drink to the stool closest to the service station. "Ah, Rose, I am sorry it took me so long downstairs. I saw Ben again and mentioned to him how much I had been enjoying chatting with you. I also mentioned to him that I thought you are doing a fine job at My World and have caught on very quickly to how things work around here. Every restaurant is the same, and yet every one is different, I feel. You should be happy to know that Ben agreed very strongly that he also thinks the job you are doing is a good one. It is always nice to know you are appreciated at your work." He smiled as if he'd just delivered a $5,000 bonus instead of a simple compliment.

"Thanks, Zorro." How reassuring to know that Ben and Zorro shared their mutual admiration of her, if nothing else. Management should present a united front to its humble employees.

It would probably be impolitic to ask Zorro what Thomas thought of her. With luck, she wouldn't need to ask. She wondered if Zorro would prove as anxious to broadcast Thomas' opinions as he'd been to announce his boss' alibis. The questions raised by what Zorro had told her so far seemed less important than the question of why he'd volunteered that information.

Zorro, either with or without Thomas' blessing, had assumed the role of information provider. Did he also assume her unflagging interest in everyone's whereabouts at the times of the murders, or did he somehow know she needed to discover the murderer's identity? Nobody else except Jimmy or Butler could have told Zorro about her voluntary, or at least unassigned, detective role. She knew she hadn't said anything, scoffed at the idea of Butler and Zorro in a tete a tete, and didn't believe Jimmy would fake indignation at being excluded from a conversation he'd engineered.

Still, Zorro didn't need to know she was playing detective to provide her with his alibis. For all she knew, he assumed everyone speculated about his whereabouts at all times. His, and Thomas'.

Zorro and Thomas must be friendlier than either she or Jimmy knew.

Thinking she might have underestimated Zorro's intelligence was troubling. Speculating he had volunteered his information with Thomas' full knowledge verged into the ominous. Suspecting Thomas had put Zorro up to broadcasting his alibis moved her right back into the realm of the frightening.

Chapter Twenty-one

The dining room filled, while drinkers and waiting diners stood two-deep at the bar. Rose didn't have time to continue talking with Zorro, now sipping his fourth flute of champagne. He made at least one trip downstairs for every glass he drank.

She wished he'd order his refills before he made his little journeys, so that customers wouldn't assume his empty glass signaled an available seat. The last time Zorro had returned to the bar, he'd hovered behind his barstool until the pregnant woman sitting there surrendered it. He'd slipped back onto the seat and handed the woman her mineral water with a wide smile, apparently untroubled by either thoughts of chivalry or the glare the woman's husband threw in his direction.

Busy as she was, Rose tried to keep an eye on Zorro. He didn't speak to anyone else at the bar. He seemed quite content to sit quietly and appeared to pay more attention to the crowd than she'd ever seen him do when ostensibly working. Rose wondered how skewed his perceptions were; champagne with cocaine didn't make a recipe for objectivity.

She wished she had the nerve to ask him where Thomas was tonight. She also wished she didn't suspect he would know. Despite Ben's clear dislike, Thomas must insist that Zorro keep his job at My World. Maybe Thomas found Zorro useful in ways his brother didn't consider part of a host's job description. She couldn't shake the feeling that Thomas would soon hear about everything going on at My World tonight, and not from Ben. But didn't most spies work better sober, mythical martinis aside?

Too many people at the bar wanted too many drinks and too much attention to let her pursue these thoughts.

Mark, tonight wearing a Yale tee shirt over spray-painted faded jeans, acted unusually friendly as he ordered a screwdriver with his club soda. Rose didn't need to see his feet to know he was wearing Nikes and didn't need to see the face of the blonde woman with him to know she had to be extraordinarily pretty, as well as promising. Mark purchased an alcoholic beverage; lust eroded principles yet again. Rose hoped the woman gulped down enough of her drink to cushion her before Mark started the lecture he couldn't resist.

Zorro called Rose to him and slipped her a folded bill. He told her again what a great job she always did and how much he'd enjoyed talking with her. Someone took his seat before he had both arms into his coat sleeves.

She waited until he'd walked halfway to the front door before looking at the bill. Twenty dollars. She had followed the house policy and charged him for every drink but the first, but he'd still only spent twelve dollars. An eight-dollar tip signaled that Zorro certainly did want to be her friend. Or maybe he just wanted her to think he was.

Mark ordered another round, with a whispered

request that she make the screwdriver very weak. His ploy was understandable: the woman's eyes would glaze soon enough from the weight of his conversation. His abhorrence of liquor might stem from simple jealousy that it could dull someone's perceptions quicker than he could.

Eventually everyone who'd wanted a table had been seated, leaving only dedicated drinkers at the bar. The kitchen functioned smoothly again, giving the dining room its own calm rhythm. The horrible delays and chaotic atmosphere of last Saturday night must have been a fluke.

Ward really was very competent: he made wonderful food and he usually ran his staff well. She liked knowing the chef could control his domain, if not always himself. His temper tantrum could have been a fluke, too.

Alan appeared later than usual tonight, complaining again about the long hours he put in at the office. He gulped his first drink before she'd had time to collect for it and asked for a second immediately. He sipped at this one a bit more temperately.

"So, what's new, Rose? Anything exciting going on in your life? Still having fun with your brother? You ashamed of us or something? It bugs me that I haven't met him. Why can't we meet him?"

Because he's 3,000 miles away and it would be a real mystery if he were to appear here.

"Alan, he's just been so busy. It's great to have him around, but he doesn't have the time to hang out at night. I know he'd like to meet all of you, too."

"I hope he isn't too busy to protect you. How much time does he spend with you, anyway?" Alan frowned.

"As much as he can. He's around the apartment a lot, you know, making business calls and such."

"Well, don't let him tie up your phone all the time. Or run up your phone bill too high, either. Even local calls can get expensive. They add up."

"He's careful, Alan. Thanks for worrying, but he knows what he's doing. To tell you the truth, I'm so glad he's here that I wouldn't mind if he called Katmandu."

Wrong thing to say to an accountant. Alan looked as horrified at that concept as if she'd told him her brother gnawed baby bones while he chatted on the phone.

"Yeah, well, he should be paying more attention to you than to his business. What's he here for, anyway? I really wish you'd let us meet him, Rose. It might put my mind at ease. You forget how much I worry about you. Or maybe you just don't care." Worry pursed Alan's lips.

"I don't know what I'd do if anything happened to you, Rose. I really don't know. It might kill me."

His melodrama annoyed her. "Alan, please. Nothing is going to happen to me, and nothing is going to happen to you. Sometimes I think you're actually trying to scare me. You don't mean to, do you?"

For a split second, Alan looked startled, but he regained his equanimity quickly. "Of course not, Rosie, of course not. It's just that I worry about you. This isn't a safe city at the best of times. This doesn't seem like the safest of restaurants lately, either. You know what I mean."

"Yes, but I think it's safer, at least for my peace of mind, not to dwell on that. The cops say the murders aren't connected, so why should we think otherwise? I just have to believe they know what they're doing and trust what they say. That's how I manage not to worry." Her nose should be growing like Pinocchio's even as she spoke. Her trust in the official version was almost as strong as her belief in the tooth fairy.

"But, Alan, what's going on at your job that keeps you there so late?"

His initial reluctance to change the subject segued into a lengthy explanation of new accounting systems. It was more than she needed to know to balance her checkbook but better than listening to him harp on threats she couldn't ignore if she tried.

Rose wished Owen would show up. The photographer had proved very good at distracting Alan from his maunderings lately. One of the biggest problems about bartending was that you couldn't choose who would visit the bar at any given time. Skilled as Rose might be at encouraging people at the bar to enjoy each other's company, she couldn't pick her raw materials. Perle Mesta might find supplying Alan with new conversational partners a challenge.

"Damnit, Rose, I forgot. I had this beautiful present for you, but I forgot it at the office. It won't keep until tomorrow, not and be as good as it should when I give it to you. Save my stool; I'll be back in a few minutes."

Alan had shrugged on his coat and rushed out the door before she'd had a chance to demur. All of her efforts to convince him to stop his gifts had been wasted. She wondered if tonight's offering had come from the florist or the cold locker at his job and reminded herself that she absolutely could not, ever, disclose how much she preferred chocolate to beef. She'd hate to start to feel real gratitude for his offerings.

A table of heavy drinkers still sat in Jimmy's station. He ordered more cocktails in a cheerful tone, then teased her about sending Alan out into the cold to get her gift. She laughed when he asked if her apartment fridge could accommodate a side of beef. Alan couldn't carry anything that heavy.

"Still, Rose, you could invite me over after work and we could hack off a couple of slabs. It might inspire us: a gift from the butcher shop while contemplating butchery. Oh dear, that sounded awful. Do accept my apologies."

"Forget about the late night meatfest, Jimmy. When this show is finally over, we'll both reread Diane's note several times. Then we'll sleep on it in our separate homes. If we start deciphering the note together tonight, we won't stop until way past dawn. I have to get up too early tomorrow."

She didn't have to be up any earlier than normal tomorrow, although an early start on the day seemed a pleasant goal. Rose just wanted to examine Diane's note without any distraction. If she focused on every word, maybe she could understand what Diane had been thinking as she wrote the note. Transforming her thought processes into Diane's would be difficult enough alone; Jimmy's company would make it impossible. Holmes had fibbed to Watson once or twice, hadn't he?

She knew Diane's note had something to tell her. Once she'd discovered what that was, maybe Jimmy could help her decide how to use the information. Whatever it was.

She knew that then she'd also have to decide how soon she would tell Butler about the note and how she could convince him of the significance she saw in the picture of Diane wearing both earrings. He'd probably be slightly interested in the persistence of her creepy caller, too. Knowing that she should have already told the detective about all of these developments nagged at her like an overdue bill.

Ben told her to give last call to the five customers still at the bar. Mark and the blonde left together. Alcohol really did impair judgment.

She didn't know what to do about Alan. He'd left more than an hour ago and, if he returned, would certainly want his nightcap. Ben would let her pour him one after she'd closed the register, but he wouldn't like it. It seemed strange that Alan hadn't returned, since his office was only a few blocks away. She would save his change and give it to him tomorrow night if he didn't reappear soon. One more day wouldn't hurt either his gift or her gratitude.

She poured the final drinks, collected the final money, and started to clean the bar. Ben always managed to close the place quickly; he'd have her counting her bank downstairs within fifteen minutes. She hurried through her clean-up.

Jimmy came up to the bar to hand over her share of his and Ellen's tips. They'd done well tonight. He asked for another look at Diane's note, promising he'd take it downstairs to the men's room to read privately. He noticed her momentary reluctance to surrender it.

"Don't worry, darling. I'll wash my hands before I read it. By the time you have your bar all nice and clean, I promise to have it back in your very own hands. And I won't get the note dirty, either. I promise to keep it clean. And you get your bar clean in the meantime."

She gave him the note and finished wiping the bar down. Something about his repetition of the word "clean" teased her, reminding her of more than the task at hand. Somebody else had told her to keep things clean recently, in a context which should have bothered her more.

She first thought that she must be connecting the word with the eerie cleanliness in Diane's apartment, but she knew that was wrong. Someone had told her to stay clean, or keep it clean, or be clean. Or something clean.

She tried to review all of tonight's conversations while she rinsed the sinks. It hadn't been tonight. It had been last night and Joe Victors had been the speaker. God the Father had told her to "keep it clean."

At the time, she had only heard a casual phrase. Now she wondered if he'd given her a more specific directive than she'd understood. Maybe he'd wanted her to keep it clean because he thought some of his other employees weren't or, more likely hadn't, been keeping it so clean. He might not have referred to hygiene, either. The Board of Health didn't pose the biggest threat to My World's reputation these days.

Something about what he'd said somehow pointed to the message in Diane's note. Rose couldn't wait to make that something and somehow specific. She wished Jimmy would hurry back upstairs with the note. She wanted to leave for home soon.

She'd cleaned her bar, she'd counted her bank, and she'd pleased her boss by finishing tonight's work quickly. Tonight's real work wouldn't start until she got home.

When Jimmy finally returned Diane's note, Rose noticed that he'd smoothed all the creases out of the paper. She rushed him into the cab they shared, promising to call him first thing in the morning. He should know that didn't mean eight o'clock.

Safely home, Rose threw off her work clothes and cinched herself into her terry robe, as if tightening the belt would transform the robe into a detective's trench coat.

She tried very hard to transform her mental processes into Diane's as she settled into her big chair. It wasn't an immediate alchemy.

Maybe the wine she sipped kept her too far out of character. She'd found a bottle of tequila on Diane's table. Diane had been a passionate fan of the distinctive liquor, once telling Rose that she'd discovered it at thirteen and hadn't wanted to drink anything else since. Rose hated knowing Diane would never have the chance to broaden her tastes, in liquor or anything else.

She knew that it was ludicrous to think she had to drink like Diane in order to think like Diane. She shouldn't turn method into madness. The next associative step would be to acknowledge she was clutching at straws and decide that meant she should call Zorro for some cocaine. She hated flailing around like this.

Rose typed Diane's note, hoping the printed word would reveal more than the scrawled. She tried to ignore the thought that copying another's lines should inspire her to write her own and didn't need to look at the calendar to know that her manuscript was due in a nice round fifty days. Finish this mess first.

If it was hard to underestimate a dead woman's warnings, it wasn't any easier to understand them.

All right. Something bad was going on at My World. It involved certain employees, including Susan, and implicated Thomas too. Somebody wanted more power than he deserved. Ben hadn't seemed to know anything about these problems, and Diane had thought it imperative to kick Ben out of his ignorant bliss. Unfortunately, her note hinted more than it explained.

Rephrasing wasn't revealing. Her last reading of Diane's note yielded only as much insight as her first. Listmaking was supposed to encourage logical thinking.

Rose had only made a little list: sex, drugs, power, deception. Common elements, not hard to recognize. Television and trash novels flourished on them. All she had to do was take these elements, assign them to the proper players, and arrange the pattern. She should find it a simple exercise.

She'd rather play Scrabble with the editors of the *O.E.D.*

The written word, read or unread, had yet to guarantee anyone's survival. The scraps of paper she'd written on bore no resemblance to an Ouija board. Concentrating on the message wouldn't make it appear. Sleeping on it offered her only hope.

She needed a safe, relaxing, distracting novel to help her fall asleep. She spent ten minutes scanning the contents of her crowded bookshelves and finally took a three-week-old copy of *The New Yorker* to bed with her. She resolved to buy Stephen King's complete oeuvre in the morning, so she'd have some pleasant escapist stuff around.

A nice hot shower wouldn't help. She never took showers at night anymore. At least she understood one thing.

Rose wondered what the killer might take from her next.

Chapter Twenty-two

Friday morning sashayed in with a false spring, boasting brilliant sun and temperatures near sixty degrees. February proved her cruelty again in assuming such blithely enticing disguise, seducing everyone into forgetting how the unlined leather jacket flirting warmly with noon would court pneumonia at six. If wildflowers bloomed through concrete, Rose would stumble over them when she walked down the block. Potholes might deliver long-stemmed roses, the live and fragrantly desirable kind.

Finishing her third cup of coffee, Rose abandoned her keyboard and unburied the phone from the stack of pillows she'd buried it under last night. The series of frustrated beeps and hang-ups on her machine didn't morse-code any useful knowledge. It seemed tantalizingly perverse to refuse messages from someone who probably had all the terrible answers to your worst questions. She had to remember that the creep hadn't called to volunteer information. An exchange of ideas was not what he had in mind.

The only thing he wanted her to know was fear. She didn't need to learn that from him. Rose erased all the non-messages and decided a long walk would do her more good than another frustrating vigil by the phone.

Writing her novel, of course, would do her even more good. Discovering Diane's body seemed to have drained her creative juices. Every time she'd wanted to work on her book since Sunday, ugly memories erased the images she hoped to describe. Her need to discover the real-life murderer dissolved the storyline she'd so carefully crafted. Fear flourished into a horrible writer's block. Soon she'd have to dodge her agent's calls the same way she avoided the creep's.

No one except a writer whose work was going well voluntarily stayed inside on a day like this. Rose headed south, to the splendid weather's source. She could always think while she walked, whereas chewing gum ruined the teeth.

In Soho, she looked at clothes she wouldn't even fantasize about buying until the sales and wandered in and out of a few galleries, wondering when it had become so hard to tell the difference between the two types of establishments. Not much fun in this neighborhood anymore: no one she knew still lived here and she was never quite sure who had replaced her artist friends. Whoever they were, they knew money better than they knew English. She couldn't even complain that West Broadway looked like Madison Avenue anymore, not since the chain restaurant featuring ribs and the rumors of Blimpies arrived.

Canal Street funked a welcome relief. She really should figure out something to do with all the tempting junk spilling onto its sidewalks. One of those electronics classes advertised on the back of matchbooks could be a start. A new, highly profitable, career should be just the ticket.

After that, she should take a course in Chinese cooking, or at least one in ingredient recognition. She admired the fish and lobsters and marveled at the shades and shapes of things one could only assume were vegetables. Window-shopping was hungry work, so she ordered dim sum and a pot of black tea at a Bowery restaurant, happily letting the empty plates pile up in front of her. There seemed a simple justice in the bill here: certain plates held dishes costing certain prices. No need for long and detailed checks; a quick count of the plates produced the bill. At any rate, she hoped it was the justice and not her outsider's trust that was simple as she paid the bill.

Rose strolled north, disturbed by how far above Chinatown she'd had to walk before recognizing Little Italy. Canal Street had stopped being the great divide between Chinatown and the Italian neighborhood several years ago, a fact she never remembered until surrounded by the proof. Stores she remembered as pizza parlors and social clubs now flaunting ideographic signs reminded her. Loyalty to old neighborhoods and their diversity lured her into a surviving coffee shop for cappuccino and rum cake, although she realized the $4.50 she contributed to the store's coffers probably didn't guarantee its outlasting the next lease. Only the knowledge that she'd already overstocked her kitchen cupboards allowed her to resist more shopping at the surviving salumeria and bakery.

She hadn't eaten this much before two in the afternoon since the last time she'd visited her mother's house. She quickened her pace crossing Houston Street, not wanting to carry all of her indulgence up the stairs. She decided to continue on up Hudson and cut across to her apartment on Eleventh Street. She didn't need to pass Bleecker Street's food stores this afternoon.

It was good she'd gotten out of the house. A long walk always helped her spirits. She'd needed distraction. Distance often lent perspective.

She should have walked further.

Two street phones had rung just as she passed them, forcing her to question both her own paranoia and the probable limits of her creep's reach as she tried to pretend she'd had a sensible reason for jumping. Even the blurred demarcation between neighborhoods seemed symbolic. Her unconscious categories and controls were wavering, too.

The clothes in Soho had shown her the look Zorro aspired to. One of the furniture stores had reminded her of the Fifties style Diane had favored. The clatter and smells of the dim sum place made her review everything Jimmy had ever told her about My World and its mysteries. The waiter at the Italian pastry shop flirted with eyes that could have been plucked out of Thomas' head.

She hesitated on the corner of Tenth and Hudson, knowing she had to tell Butler about Diane's picture, and her note, and probably even about all the new calls. But the man must work until at least five tonight. It would be absurd to turn down Tenth Street and just drop in on him at the precinct. He might be busy. He might not be there. He might make her wait. Everything she had to tell him could be communicated just as well over the phone. She would go home, compose herself, maybe jot down the salient points she needed to report. She had plenty of time to call Butler. She might even solve this whole damn mess without him if she tried hard enough.

She considered putting a procrastination class on her new post-graduate schedule, resolving to make the decision soon.

Turning her back on the precinct, Rose crossed Hudson Street. She'd forgotten to buy the books that had been one of the original impetuses for her ramble. Hudson Street Papers always had something she wanted to read, and she could squander another half hour browsing through their books and bibelots. She should probably also pick out a clever card or two, since it was always safe to assume she owed someone correspondence. After all, she hadn't sent out any Valentines this year.

The afternoon would disappear before she knew it. Her subconscious would solve everything. She would never feel fear again. Prince Charming was begging God for her phone number at this very moment. He and Sir Lancelot were clamoring for her home address, each striving to outdo the other in his claims on her affections. Both had started Money Markets in her name.

Her nerves had achieved a new calm already as she walked up Hudson Street. Only a raving paranoid thought every sound on the street was directed at her. She basked in this new calm, which allowed her complete ease in disregarding the sound of someone tapping on the Sazerac's plate-glass window as she passed. Ignoring what sounded like someone calling her name strained her composure only slightly. Hearing the calls amplified into bellows snapped her brittle serenity into sad little shards.

She hadn't recognized the voice, but Butler's face had become all too familiar. The bright sunlight cooperated with his navy sweater and did nice things to the blue of his eyes. The light, probably anticipating the amount of gratitude it would receive, was more cruel to the bags under those eyes. It etched the wrinkles radiating out from them and down his face. The man looked completely exhausted. Even Doctor Pangloss couldn't begin to construe the detective's scowl as putting a bright face on things. Maybe he'd felt embarrassed at raising his voice in public. Rose slowly retraced her steps in his direction. She should have walked on the other side of the street.

Chapter Twenty-three

"Come on. Get inside. The temp has dropped about twenty degrees in the last hour, or haven't you noticed? Stupid question, right? You must have much loftier things on your mind than the weather. Weather must be one of those practical things that are below you." Butler reached for her arm, then drew his hand back.

"Come on, Rose. I'm freezing out here. And I hate cold soup. I'll buy you a cup of coffee. Something stronger if you want it. God knows how many times I tried to call you already. I was giving it one more try before my lunch came out of the kitchen. Good timing, huh? Come inside, please."

She followed Butler to the back booth by the fireplace. It was the best seat in the restaurant, if you didn't want anybody to know where you were. She slid into the booth across from him.

"It's not that cold, not in the sun," she protested, unwilling to admit how welcome the fire's heat felt. Trust Butler to take the glow out of the day.

"Tea will be fine. With milk, please," she told the waiter. Butler's cauldron of bubbling onion soup only tempted her nose because it smelled so delicious. She couldn't even think of joining him in his late lunch after her earlier over-indulgence.

"Rose, you should order something to go with that

tea. You're gonna want to celebrate when you hear my news. I don't even know if I can bring myself to waste this great news on someone who's just gonna sit there drinking tea like some ageing harpette. Have a drink, have a sweet. Believe me, you will want to savor this moment to its fullest." Butler allowed a big, mischievous smile to sneak across his face. He looked like he loved this, whatever it was.

"What moment, Frank? The Messiah arrived with less fanfare. Just what is it you want to tell me, Frank?"

"Maybe the pecan pie. It's very good here. Maybe you should have a slice of that. Hot, with whipped cream." His smile even reached his eyes.

"I do not want anything to eat. Thank you very much. But, Frank, I would love to hear your news. What happened, Frank?"

"A pretty, young, blonde woman was murdered last night in the East Village. She was raped and then cut up. Her body was left on the rooftop of her building. Out in the cold on the rooftop." His face looked as if he'd just played Santa to a roomful of orphans.

"Wonderful. Hold on, perhaps we should order a bottle of Barry's finest champagne. Lord knows we should certainly celebrate that incident." She didn't return his smile. "Have you lost your mind, Detective? Completely, I mean? The last pathetic little shreds of humanity just disappeared? What the hell makes you think I should be happy to hear about that? And why in God's name were you so eager to make me eat something or have a drink while you told me this news?"

"With a drink, you could have celebrated. With something sweet to eat, you wouldn't have choked on the taste of humble pie." His smile disappeared.

"See, Rose, maybe you didn't notice, but I didn't tell you the girl's name. I didn't tell you her name because it wouldn't mean anything to you. This poor girl had nothing to do with My World. Far as we know, she might never have been in the place or maybe never even heard of it, if that's possible, of course. If there could be anybody in the city who doesn't know about the restaurant where you work. The restaurant meant nothing in her life. It wasn't what got her killed by the same guy who did Diane and Susan."

"How do you know the same guy did it? How do you know what got her killed?" Now she wished she had ordered a drink.

"'She was killed the same way. Raped, slashed, left in a cold place. And 'cause she knew the killer the same way that Diane and Susan did. He hasn't admitted yet that he killed them, too, but his book shows that he knew both of them, the same way he knew the woman he killed last night."

"You mean the guy was a writer? Or did he just keep a diary? Or was 'too' the key word in that sentence, and am I missing the implication that you have a confession already for the murder last night?"

"Rose, who does your hair?"

"My friend has her own salon on Spring Street. She does men, too, Frank. I'd be more than happy to give you her card. She loves a challenge. If you wanted to compliment me on the windswept look, save it for later." She clasped her hands below the table to stop their involuntary rush to smooth the hair she didn't want to imagine.

"You're going to drive me to drink yet, Frank. Please, I'll eat three desserts if you'll stop torturing me and just tell me the whole story straight out. I'm still not quite sure why this news should make me happy."

"Jesus, I really thought you were smarter than that. The news should make you happy because it means you don't have anything to worry about anymore. We got the killer, Rose. We arrested him this morning. It's just a matter of time before he confesses to the other murders. He's locked up and won't get out anytime soon. So, you're safe. It's over." Butler sat back with what she would have described as a beatific smile on anyone else.

He neatly emptied his soup bowl, finishing one of the deftest jobs of onion soup consumption she'd ever seen. Her distracted prayers for just one strand of cheese to dribble down his chin had gone as unanswered as the rest of her recent entreaties.

Butler accepted a refill of coffee and continued. "Okay, I'll go over it real slow. The woman who was killed last night, her name was Charleen Sandower. She worked on Wall Street, but she lived in the East Village, undoubtedly paying five times more than she should have in rent. Her body was found on the roof of her building.

"The guy who killed her lived in the building, too, in what he called the penthouse apartment and what I would call three shitty apartments on the top floor of a tenement combined into one bigger shitty apartment. Of course, my ex calls the big dump where she lives and paints in Brooklyn a loft, and I'm still dumb enough to call it a dump in a bad neighborhood. So what do I know, right?"

He didn't seem to want an answer. "I guess he needed all that space because he also worked there. That's how he knew Charleen, and Diane, and Susan, too. They were all his clients. He'd been cutting them for a long time."

She didn't try to keep the impatience out of her voice. "This isn't getting clearer all that quickly, Frank. The candle of illumination is barely guttering here."

"The guy was a hairdresser. He called himself Blueboy, I swear it. All three of the murder victims were his clients. Their names, their phone numbers, their addresses— he had everything in his book, one of those big, pricey, filofax numbers. I never could figure how somebody who isn't into lifting weights is supposed to haul one of those things around all day. We're talking a detective's dream. No muss, no fuss, just turn the pages. Everything written down in aqua and white. Yeah, aqua. A real artistic spirit, our boy. Consistent, too."

He waited for a moment and she wondered if she was supposed to congratulate him. "Get it now, Rose? The case is solved. You don't have to worry anymore. My World wasn't the link. It never was. You can go back to feeling as safe as you ever did in this city."

She had to know. "Did he wear a rubber like the guy who killed Susan and Diane?"

"Jesus, you're developing quite a fixation here."

"Did he?"

"How should I know? I didn't stand there and watch."

"You know, Frank. The tests would have told you. Did this Blueboy creature wear a rubber or not?"

"No, they found semen in Charleen," Butler sighed.

"So then it's not the same guy."

"Rose, lots of guys don't wear rubbers religiously. Remember, I never agreed that the thing was a major clue. Goddamn it, it is the same guy. This is one of the tightest cases in years. Everything fits—the slashes, the rapes, how he knew the women. He even admitted he hated blonde hair. Said it was too 'colorless' and 'lifeless'. Those are his exact words. What do you need, his signed confession to the three murders?"

"Yeah. Then I can write out a big statement and sign it for you. I'll confess how I made a mistake in insisting on the rubber's importance. I will also admit how right you were in maintaining that being blonde was what got the women killed. We could swap statements." She refused the waitress' offer of more hot water for her tea.

"Give it up, Rose. I might just get you a copy at that. You're too damn much. Even more stubborn than I thought. Would it kill you to act relieved, or, God forbid, grateful that this guy has been caught?"

She tried to remember how relief felt as she stood, "It might. Give me a quarter and I'll find out."

"Where's the fortune-telling machine?" He didn't reach into his pocket.

"In my apartment. Lend me a quarter, Frank. Maybe if it's your money, it'll turn out the way you want it to. I actually hope it does. Come on, you should hear this."

She took his quarter and walked toward the pay phone at the front of the restaurant. He followed her as if Bellevue's outpatient program were bound to be the recipient of her call. She dialed her own number, dropped in the quarter, and held the receiver out between them. She took only brief pleasure in watching Butler's eyes avoid hers while they listened to his voice reciting her message. Then she pressed her playback code and waited anxiously to hear who had called her since she left the house today.

Jimmy wanted her to call him right away. He thought he knew what Diane's note meant. She shushed Butler, moving the receiver a little closer to his ear. She'd tell him about the note soon enough.

A *beep*, followed by a phone slammed into its cradle.

A *beep* and a slam.

A *beep* and a slam.

The rhythm continued for eighteen calls, interrupted only twice by calls from Sophie and Marie. Neither of them tapped their feet while they listened.

Butler had stopped looking as if he wanted to arrest her for withholding Diane's note. He looked sorry for her. Pity became him as well as white became whores. She couldn't stand the softness that didn't sit well in his eyes and wanted to see them turn hard again. He shouldn't take the defeat this badly.

She didn't want to dwell on her disappointment at knowing her caller was still in fact out there. Before she'd asked about the rubber, those few brief minutes when she'd thought the cops might have arrested the My World killer had reminded her how not feeling frightened felt. But her old pal fear wasn't going anywhere just yet.

"So, Frank, I really do want to congratulate you, and the other officials of the police force, on your new liberalism. When did murder suspects get unlimited phone calls? It's really liberal and wonderful of you guys. I guess those plaques from the ACLU will cover all your wallpaper soon. Did you give Blueboy the quarters, too? Sure, Blueboy, Boys in Blue, I can see where the bond would start."

She followed him back to the booth, surprised he hadn't interrupted her yet. "I suppose making what would have been threatening phone calls if anyone had answered the phone is just part of how the poor soul expresses himself. You wouldn't want to hamper that, at least not now that you've locked him up and blamed him for lots of murders. Frank, if this guy killed Susan and Diane, why am I still getting the phone calls? Why haven't they stopped?"

"We never knew for certain that the killer made those

calls, Rose. It seemed right, but we never knew, absolutely knew, that it was. Now, I guess we have to say it wasn't. Some other lunatic must be jumping on the bandwagon."

The regret in his voice disappeared, "We'll talk about your calls some more in a minute. What note from Diane, and why is this Jimmy fellow helping you decipher it? I appreciate you trying to spare my busy schedule, but I wouldn't have minded giving you and your friend a hand. Where is the note, Rose? What did it say?"

"I think it said Blueboy may take longer than you think to confess to killing Susan and Diane, Frank. Unless you can trace him to My World during the final half hour of Diane's last shift." Wishing she had called him this morning, Rose told Butler about the note and the picture. She recited the note verbatim and described the photo.

"Ms. Leary, you have fifteen minutes to run home, find the note and the slide, and hurry yourself over to the station. I don't suppose the charge of withholding evidence has ever been explained to you, or at least not in a way you couldn't argue against." Butler looked at his watch. "No reason Blueboy didn't get the earring or maybe sneak around in My World once or twice. But it's a hell of a lot easier to ask questions when I know what I'm asking about. Not that such a disadvantage would ever stop you, of course." He stood.

"Put on your coat, or whatever you call that flimsy thing. You want to bring the transcripts of your calls along, fine. You don't have to, since they're really your property.

The note and the slide, no discussion. Leave it to you to try to ruin the prettiest bust we've had in years. Move, please, Ms. Leary. This is not a smart time to argue with me. Trust me on that."

Arguing didn't tempt Rose at all, since it would keep them together longer. She'd known all along she should have given him the note and the slide, but hadn't suspected the delay might have such serious consequences. She couldn't determine if she or his case were more at risk. Butler was not cute when he was mad. She'd already known that. Further proof was just redundant.

No wonder his ex-wife preferred any hovel, in any borough, to life with him.

Rose walked home at a brisker pace than she'd used all day, telling herself she only rushed away from Butler to keep herself warm now that the temp had indeed dropped. She didn't reduce her speed as she climbed her stairs, cursing the rude, stupid, overbearing detective all the way up. It was a familiar refrain by now. She didn't miss a beat.

Chapter Twenty-four

Returning to the Sixth Precinct was not a jolly stroll down Memory Lane. Rose opened the heavy door and felt sickened by the odors of parfum de precinct. The blend of old smoke, sour coffee, and dry heat spiced by the tense reek of fear summoned only bad memories. Sniffing at the perfume on her own wrist for the fifteen minutes it took Butler to appear and usher her into his office didn't help.

She handed him the note and the slide. "I don't know why you're acting as if I ruined your case. I'd like to see the My World murderer locked up too, you know, and I could live perfectly happily without those phone calls. The sounds of silence do not bother me. A quiet phone is a happy phone."

She made herself stop talking and waited to hear what he thought about the evidence. He just looked at her.

Rose stood in the doorway of his office, stretching her good-byes into embarrassing repetition. Butler held the slide and the note in his hands, but his eyes didn't leave her face.

If he'd look at his crucial damned evidence, she might be able to shut up and leave. It was as if all the times he'd blamed her for being too talkative had prophesied this stupid new verbosity. He said she babbled, so babble she did. God help her if he ever charged her with something really serious. She'd be signing a confession before he finished his accusations.

She couldn't confess to anything now except yearning for the relief she would have felt if the cops had really caught the right murderer.

If the killer were behind bars, criminals would lose all their menace. She would find it impossible to cower in front of any mere mugger, crack criminals would only arouse her pity, and the bogeymen and burglars might as well stay home if frightening her were their game.

She would become an instant celebrity, the New Yorker who didn't worry about daily crime. Ripley's would want to do a special issue, and medical science might want to investigate. The media would clamor for interviews, with book offers sure to follow. Elaine's would reserve a table in Rose's name every night. She might need to consider hiring a manager, or the publicity could overwhelm her. She'd have to be careful to protect her writing time. And she'd certainly need a whole new wardrobe for such a public life.

"Rose? Sit here. Now." Butler pushed her into the battered chair next to his desk. "All of a sudden there, you got very pale and your eyes went about a million miles away. Are you all right?"

"Fine, Frank. I have to go now, okay?" She hadn't meant to sit.

"Sit a minute more. I really don't like the way you look."

"Thanks, thanks so much. Next time I'll dress better

and do my face before I come into the station to talk about killers at large. If I had my purse, I'd throw on a little lipstick right now. Damn, a girl just never knows when she'll need to primp." She hadn't liked how easily he'd pushed her into the chair.

"My purse would have been safe in here, wouldn't it? Have the police at least gotten to the point where they can protect a woman and her purse if she's sitting right in the precinct house? Tell me, Frank, would my purse have been safe?"

"Depends, Rose. See, what probably would happen with your purse is that you'd insist on putting it in the riskiest spot in the precinct. Like maybe right by the front door, but at an angle where the desk man couldn't see it. And if some stupid cop suggested that you let one of us keep an eye on it, you'd refuse such an intrusion on your privacy. So, the purse might disappear, with the police, naturally, to blame." He still studied her face.

"Then, what the hell, let's take this a bit further. Maybe you'd be the one in a thousand women who gets lucky. We'd get your purse back, with everything still in it, the thing most women would pray for if their purses were unfortunately stolen. But not you, right, Rose?"

She wondered if he'd ever wait for her to answer and why she'd ever mentioned her purse.

"You wouldn't want the purse back. You'd say it was the wrong one. Maybe the money in the purse, which we were lucky enough to get back, would be arranged differently than how you keep your money. A five could be in the wallet face down, instead of facing up like all the other bills. Then, of course, you'd know it wasn't your purse, just some other purse that looked enough like yours to fool the stupid cops."

How did he know how she kept the money in her wallet?

"So I don't think I could swear your purse would be safe. There's only so much I can do. I'm not a miracle worker. Sorry about that." The edge in Butler's voice could have cut sushi.

"Why did I have to rush down here with the note and the slide if you're not going to bother to look at them, Frank? As much as I'm enjoying your poetic symbolism about the purse, I wouldn't mind hearing a little inspired prose, too. Like what you think about the note, and the slide, and the fact that my calls still continue. And why the police haven't been checking out everybody at My World more carefully. And—"

"Stop. You don't know what you're talking about. You don't know who we check out, or how. And this? This is not proof. This is not the kind of evidence juries like, Rose. Judges wouldn't be too crazy about it either. I try to anticipate judges' and juries' tastes when it comes to evidence. It makes things work better, somehow. A simple guy like me can find himself in big trouble trying to convince the D.A. to prosecute with hunches. They're picky that way." He'd finally looked at the slide.

"But the earring—"

"The earring, or the slide showing them both, is not proof. It is, I grant you, thought provoking. It could make me look at the facts in a different way. But, it's not proof and it doesn't make me want to tell Blueboy he has nothing to worry about. He should still cancel his plans for Club Med next month." He read the note quickly.

"Sorry, Rose, but same with this note. People get unhappy at work all the time. People get mad at the folks they work with, or for, all the time, too. People let their anger out different ways, and one of those ways can be to write a note putting blame on somebody else."

Great, now he wanted to be a literary critic.

"You might consider that if Diane had been really serious about the contents of this note, she might have done things differently. First, she might have written the note so it said something, instead of just hinting. Then, she might have delivered the note, instead of throwing it back into a drawer with a lot of other worthless junk. Again, nowhere in this note do I see a message telling me to set Blueboy free. His innocence is not proclaimed here." He tapped his fingers on the note.

"Now you're going to bring up your calls again, Rose. You're going to insist that, since Blueboy can't be making those calls anymore, he can't be the guy we're looking for. And I'm gonna have to tell you, again, that nothing firmly identifies your caller as the killer. Nothing. It would be neater if it was the same person, but you'd be amazed at how many murder cases are messy.

She kept picturing Diane's body while he continued his tirade.

"Of course, this could make you feel better, if you'd let it. You might feel a little easier knowing the guy making them isn't really dangerous. He's just a phone creep. Those flowers were as brave as he's gonna get. You keep your machine on long enough, he'll get the hint and drop it."

"But he called me at work when he couldn't get me at home." She wondered how carefully Butler had listened when she described the calls.

"So you figure it out so you don't take any calls at work for a while. Don't let the guy reach you for a couple of weeks, he'll give it up. Persistence isn't included in this type's profile. Or, you could still give in and let us tap your line, if you really want to get rid of him in a hurry. That idea probably makes too much sense to interest you though, right? Practical thought like that must be anathema to your free artistic spirit. Better to suffer soulfully, huh?"

She stood up and backed away from the desk. "We're not married, Frank. I'm not your wife, or your ex-wife, either. You want to compare exes? The only thing mine ever created was debt—and heartbreak. Who are you talking to here, anyway?"

"No kidding. Here I thought you were the woman I lived with for ten years, and that I knew for fifteen before that. The tall one, with the strawberry blonde hair. No wonder I confused the two of you. Good of you to pick up on it and warn me. Imagine how I could have embarrassed myself if I'd gone on. Thanks for saving me, Rose."

What did she care what his ex looked like? "You should return the favor someday, Frank, at least professionally." Brilliant.

She wondered what might happen if she continued antagonizing Butler. Instead of keeping criminals away from her, he could pass out her name, address, phone number, and daily schedule to every felon he encountered. She should ask him if a current photo would help and what he would suggest she wear or not wear for the shoot. Her phone would really come alive then. It would never stop ringing. Phone booths all over the city would carry her number. Scratched into the truncated booths' dull paint, her seven digits would glitter provocatively in the exposed metal.

She needed to get out of here before she said another stupid word. Rose's anger at knowing in her heart that Diane and Susan's killer still crept the streets was irrationally magnified by hearing that Butler, and presumably the NYPD, believed they'd stopped him.

Butler had armored himself in judicial history. She didn't know how to pierce the armor of his certitude. The connections she'd made between her clues and his case weren't sharp enough to get through to him. She'd be damned if she'd stay here uselessly any longer. Every time she and Butler were together, she seemed to drop layers of dignity she couldn't afford to lose.

He was a stubborn fool.

"So, anyhow, Detective Butler, am I safe in assuming I'm free to go? You probably don't want to bother to press charges for withholding such flimsy, irrelevant evidence. Not worth the time for the paperwork. But do rest assured that I feel suitably chastened and, if I ever find anything again that I know would waste your time and be of no use to you whatsoever, I'll rush right down here with it. God knows I wouldn't want to risk a record." She walked to the door.

"Anyway, it's such a pleasure to spend time in a place like this, especially if we can pass most of that time establishing my stupidity. No better way to spend a day, right? So now I guess I'll just leave here and walk out into a safe and sane city, with anyone who ever wanted to hurt me or anybody I know no longer a threat. I can't wait. Good-bye."

A curt nod and a wave toward the door did not constitute an answer. She hated him for not even bothering to reply. She rushed out of the precinct house before his office door stopped slamming.

Rose hurried home, furious at how cold the weather had turned and how ridiculous she was to feel that the bitter wind aimed particularly at her back. The brief warmth of the short, sunny day had been only a cruel tease. Winter was tired of pretending to be sweet. None of this weather was directed personally at her. It had been years since she'd been a romantic.

Rose walked into her apartment, closed her eyes, and threw her leather jacket over the answering machine. She wouldn't wear this jacket again for a while. She didn't need it, or the sight of all the demonic red blinks she knew her machine would flaunt.

She hoped the creep wouldn't find having his messages blunted by leather too exciting, if he'd managed to get her apartment under visual surveillance by now. He could probably camp in a stained army tent in front of a raging campfire on the roof across the street and brandish weapons in her direction before Butler and his cohorts suspected anything. And then they'd probably award him an urban-camping Eagle badge.

Nor had Butler managed to dismiss the roses to her satisfaction. He probably didn't waste a lot of his time thinking about flowers.

Slowly dressing for work, Rose chose clothes that paid homage to Butler and his prize suspect. She wore black and blue, rejecting red as her accent color.

Then she sat at her desk and wasted ten minutes failing to think of a good excuse for calling in sick tonight. She kicked her purse across the room when she realized that she couldn't miss a shift in a bar whose staff rolls kept shrinking.

Crazy as Butler had made her, she wasn't ready to call in dead.

Chapter Twenty-five

Rose pitied everyone unfortunate enough to choose her bar tonight. The absolute most they could hope for would be a good drink at a fair price, period. Anyone looking for charm or attention would do better in some other establishment. Any other establishment. Including the Automat.

 The day's beauty had gone with the sun. It had been dark out when she'd slammed out of Butler's office, and it was darker when she arrived at My World. The hallway leading to the office was dark too. Rose flipped the light switch up and down several times before accepting that both bulbs must have burned out. So let there be dark. Fine.

Thomas' expression when he opened the office door to her determined knocking was not a ray of sunshine or any other source of illumination. His dark eyes had sunk even deeper in the last few days, and the charcoal grey of his cashmere sweater exaggerated his pallor. Zorro looked revoltingly healthy in comparison as he sat at Ben's desk counting what Rose feared was her night bank. The deep gold of his soft wool shirt echoed his miraculously still-deep tan. The warmth of his enthusiastic greetings highlighted his employer's mood, as if Zorro meant to nominate Thomas for honorary president of the Undertakers of America.

After quick hellos to both men, she counted the bank Zorro ceremoniously handed her. He apologized like a courtier for what he called the slight errors of the last bank he'd prepared for her. She accepted his apologies with a peasant's finesse and indifference to matching his florid airs. She'd reserve whatever minimal charm she could rally tonight for her paying customers.

The bank was correct, with plenty of change. Rose thanked both men and asked Thomas if she could leave the bank on his desk while she visited the women's room before her shift started. She needed a minute to phrase her appeal about not answering the phone tonight.

Not paying serious attention to the mirror, she did a cursory primp, motivated more by habit than any real interest in her appearance. Rose yanked a wide comb through the snarls the wind had teased into her hair, foregoing powdering her nose or repainting her lips. She would have to do.

On second thought, maybe a brighter red lipstick would fake the smiles she didn't anticipate beaming across the bar. Rose dug into her purse, knowing that at least three differently hued tubes lurked somewhere in its depths. She was deliberating aloud between Really Red and Cherries in the Snow when a loud moan cracked her concentration.

The moan was deep and low, the sound of either terrible pain or terrific pleasure. Her own mumbling might have drowned out its start, but she heard its finish clearly. The sound hadn't lasted long enough for her to determine its source. Rose didn't know how to respond, unsure if she should rush to help or stay to envy whoever had made the maddening noise.

Nobody shared the women's room. She couldn't see anyone in the small area between the men's and women's rooms, or on the stairs leading up to the main floor. Her unanswered knock and the quick survey she gave the deserted men's room eliminated it as the sound's source.

Rose opened the door leading back to the office and storage areas, peering down the dark hallway. A line of light showed under the office door like a bad clue. In here, Stupid, the sound came from in here. She ran to the light and banged on the office door, bracing herself for the sight of possible slaughter.

Zorro opened the door quickly, then returned to the piles of singles he'd been counting at Ben's desk. Thomas sat at his own desk reading receipts. He removed the ledger he'd placed over her cash drawer without raising his eyes. Neither man acted as if they'd heard anything out of the ordinary in the last few minutes, certainly nothing odd enough to take them away from their work to investigate. The scene lacked even a hint of melodrama.

No signs of pain or passion in this office. The sound must have come from somewhere else. Perhaps the pipes had creaked. Maybe she'd moaned unconsciously at her appearance. Maybe her imagination craved ghostly moans from invisible sources haunting her maquillage. Marvelous.

Butler would love to hear this new development. Too bad she didn't have the time to call him. He might deserve at least the quarter a call would cost.

Looking at her watch, Rose realized she had barely enough time to ask Thomas to excuse her from phone duty for her next few shifts, let alone to ask him if he'd heard any strange noises lately. She still didn't know how she'd explain why she didn't want to answer the phone, no matter how busy the host was, without mentioning her crank calls. Inspiration would have to hurry now, because she had less than five minutes before her shift started.

"Excuse me, Thomas, but may I talk to you for a minute? I have a favor to ask." She took her bank and waited next to his desk

Thomas finally looked up from his papers. "Of course, Rose. All things considered, I'd say I'm already inclined to agree to any favor you ask. We owe you quite a bit after everything that's happened around here. What do you need?"

He gave her a quick smile but then waited to hear her request with another mournful look on his face. Zorro waited with a more cheerful expression. It appeared that Thomas expected to be pained, while Zorro expected to be amused.

She couldn't do anything about her boss' disposition, but she didn't want everyone in the place knowing she'd asked for special treatment.

"Well, Thomas, I'm afraid it's kind of a personal

favor." She glanced quickly at Zorro as she stressed the word personal. He looked even more eager to hear what she would say.

"That's all right, Rose. You've gone out of your way for us here, and I'd like to return the favor. Anything I can do, it's yours. I know Ben would agree with me. Anything within reason." Thomas made his speech graciously, then waited again for her to speak.

She now had two minutes before her shift started.

"Thomas, I hate to keep repeating myself, but the favor is personal."

"It's okay, Rose, go ahead."

This was impossible. Zorro's limited grasp of the language must not have extended to certain implications of personal yet. She didn't have time to keep rephrasing herself until he got the point, and Thomas didn't seem inclined to help her.

"I guess I'm trying to say I'd rather talk to you alone, Thomas. No offense, Zorro, but I think I'd feel more comfortable asking Thomas for my favor by myself. Just one of those things."

Zorro laughed merrily. "Of course I do not take offense, Rose. But, please, do not worry about my presence in the room. Perhaps I will be able to assist Thomas and Ben in granting the favor you are so cutely shy about. Please, go ahead."

She looked toward Thomas for help. He wouldn't meet her eyes.

"Do go on, Rose. There's nothing you have to say to me that Zorro can't hear. He is, after all, the general manager here. And, don't worry about confidentiality. Nothing you say will leave this room. Right, Zorro?"

"Absolutely. Yes, do go ahead, Rose. You do not want to be late for your bar on a Friday of all nights. We will try to help you."

Amazement stimulated her imagination. From weekend host to general manager was quite a jump. Trying to understand the drastic change in Zorro's status distracted her from worrying if her story about a rejected boyfriend pestering her with unwanted calls sounded plausible.

Ben hadn't mentioned the promotion last night or in any way indicated its possibility. If asked to predict, she would have put her money on Ben's firing Zorro instead of promoting him.

"Why, Rose, I do hope that all of my new responsibilities will be as simple and as full of pleasure for me to fulfill as this one is. I will tell the waiters to take care of the phone when Thomas and I are occupied otherwise. Of course you do not need to answer it tonight, or tomorrow night, or for some nights after that. It is terrible to be bothered by a lover you no longer love. I understand this. Thomas must understand this also. Even Ben, he must understand this. We will speak to him about it, yes, Thomas?"

Zorro seemed to struggle to keep a grave expression as he announced what might be his first managerial decision. Instead, he looked as if his delight in doing her a favor might inspire him to break into song at any moment. His future might not lie at the executive level after all, if this were any indication of how he would assume the dignity of his position. He looked like a child who'd just been given a charge account at FAO Schwartz. For just a second, she thought Thomas looked like the adult whose address would receive the bill.

Then Thomas agreed curtly that Rose could avoid the phone for a few days, although she thought she heard an odd tone of reluctance in his voice. She thanked them both again and started to leave the office.

Thomas didn't look at her as he spoke, "Uh, Rose, maybe you could do me a small favor in return? The official announcement of Zorro's promotion isn't until Monday, so I'd appreciate it if you didn't mention it to anyone until then. Let's do this right. Thanks."

Zorro chimed in, "Please, Rose, do keep our secret. I'd like to see everyone hear the news at once. It is better for things like this to happen in a group. Can we rely on you?"

"My lips are sealed, Zorro. I'll even hold off on my congratulations until the official announcement. Are you going to call a staff meeting or something?"

"That has yet to be decided. But you can rest assured that we will do things in the gracious and businesslike way. Won't we, Thomas?" This time it was Zorro whom Thomas didn't look at as he mumbled his assent.

She could keep the secret easily, since she didn't want to break this news to anyone she worked with. Zorro as gracious manager was not her idea of inspired casting. She couldn't imagine what would have made Ben agree to the change but felt sure the idea hadn't originated with him.

Maybe the moan she now suspected she'd imagined had come to her telepathically from the restaurant's soul, grieving over the prospect of Zorro in charge. Or Thomas might have found a mathematical error in one of the receipts. Or the mirror itself could have spoken in disgust at her drawn and harried face. The possibilities were endless.

She might have dismissed Butler's constant criticisms of her imagination too soon. As often as she'd thought the detective maddening, only now did she suspect the quality might be deliberate. She tried to see herself as the heroine in a remake of *Gaslight*, but balked at Boyer by Butler.

The blare of the jukebox wouldn't let her imagine any strange noises for the rest of the night. Tips on Friday nights were usually decent. Thomas had granted her favor. She was safe from answering the phone for the next nine hours.

Rose was counting her blessings. On one hand. With a finger to spare, which was good because she needed to save a finger anyway. She'd use it to dial the phone when she called Butler. As soon as she could prove it in terms simple enough for the bullheaded detective to understand, she'd convince him he was wrong to think he'd closed the case.

Chapter Twenty-six

The full bar delayed Laura's removing her bank from the register and herself from behind the bar. Rose sometimes missed Diane, but never during a shift change. Starting work at a clean and fully stocked bar didn't inspire grief.

Laura had even managed to leave her with a full beer cooler, no mean feat when a large group of apprentice Wall Streeters occupied more than half the bar. Rose heard them praising Reagan's budget and hoped they would only stay for the cocktail hour and not the duration.

Something about being in a group numbering more than four brought out the worst in baby yuppies, as if they wanted to substitute a mob for the fraternities they'd recently left. They would raise the bar's decibel level more than the register's total. Part of the mob act included acting drunker and talking louder than their alcohol consumption warranted. Grownups didn't raise their voices on the second round.

Three of the group ordered beers while Rose was putting her bank into the register. Yelling "Hey, honey" at the bartender's back was not the best way to insure friendly service, particularly when the bartender was at least ten years the customers' senior. Rose wondered how old they'd be before they started buying their Rolling Rocks by the round, instead of individually. If they were going to act like a group, they could at least drink like one. She wished a construction crew would come in and teach them bar etiquette by example.

Jimmy wore the same smirk he always did whenever he had a particularly obnoxious order. "Careful, careful, careful, something could happen to scare you and those scowl lines could become permanent. I have a drink order from those two at table seventeen who teethed in Brooks Brothers rompers. They'd like, and I quote, 'two mahvellous mahtinis, please. Be sure the girl doesn't bruise the vermouth and do make the glasses shivery cold.'"

"'Shivery cold', Jimmy? Do you prompt these people?" She stirred a drop of vermouth into the gin.

"Careful, Rose, don't bruise the vermouth, now."

"And to think I put Martini and Rossi in traction last week. Word must be out. Scurry off with these fragile little bevs now, poopsy, before the heat of my glare disturbs the shiveriness. Why do these people always sit at your tables, Jimmy?"

"Because they wouldn't dare sit at your bar?" He left with the drinks before she could answer.

The Wall Street brats gathered their briefcases and Burberrys. Everyone in the restaurant heard their boisterous plans to regroup at a place featuring overpriced Mexicanish food and pastel margaritas to "fuel up for Limelight."

The bar's noise level dropped drastically. Rose knew the empty seats would fill quickly now that anyone approaching the bar no longer had to worry about trespassing on a private club.

"Once there was a way to get back home," Owen flashed a big smile as he crooned the line. He smoothed a crumpled fifty on the bar like a performance prop.

"Is there a message in that tune, Owen, or was it the song on the clock radio when you woke up this morning?"

"Nah, I just thought I'd introduce a note of ominous, inaccessible, comfort into the bar and see where it went. Pretty much an irrational move, so don't bother looking for motives in a whim."

"Right. You want some sort of whimsical drink or you sticking with Guinness?"

"Guinness is fine. Don't want to ruin the macho image I'm so proud of."

Owen toasted his beer with an invitation to dinner next week. "And I promise we won't talk about this place or its horrors. Dinner doesn't have to be a biggie, Rose, so wipe that dumbfounded look off your face. I'd just like it if we talked while we were both sitting down sometime."

"Next week is bad for me, Owen. I appreciate it, but I have to get back to work on my—um—on this project. I'm really going to have to devote all my free time to that for a while. Sorry, thanks." She ignored the ringing phone.

He took her refusal with grace.

Owen was smart, talented, attractive, and funny. He also drank at the bar where she worked. They would not be dating, not while she still worked here. Thanks anyway.

Nothing worse than starting a relationship with someone who only needed a thirsty few dollars to hang around you whenever he wanted, no matter what happened. No.

Keep one rule; break another. She admired Owen's photography, and evading his questions about her project might make her excuse seem glib. Rose told him about her novel and gave him the line about superstition stopping her from discussing a work in progress. Her pride prevented her from telling him how little progress she'd actually made lately or mentioning the forty-nine days before her deadline. He accepted her explanation and offered a few of his own working superstitions. They could at least be friends.

"Good luck with it, Rose. If you ever want to talk about it, you know where I am. Damn, guess we'll have to focus on my work, huh? Pity. Look, I brought in some more slides to show you."

He waved Zorro over with the envelope holding the slides. "Zorro likes my work, too, for some reason. So we can all look at them together. A little cocktail hour viewing, eh?"

The three of them had their heads together over the slides when Thomas walked up to the bar. She'd never heard his voice so loud.

"Jesus, Rose, what's wrong with you? Ten minutes ago this bar was full, and now it's almost empty. Couldn't you keep the customers around a little longer? Christ. We do need to make some money around here, you know. Shit, if you can't stretch a cocktail hour on a Friday of all nights, I don't know what you can do." He shoved one of the empty barstools toward the bar so hard it almost toppled.

"If you're going to ask for special treatment, I think you could at least make a decent effort at your job. Is that too much to ask? If you can't keep your mind on your job, don't bother coming in. Now, try not to fuck up the rest of the night, okay?"

Thomas glared at Jimmy, who'd been waiting to order drinks, and at Zorro, who had quickly melted over to the front door. An uncomfortable silence settled over the bar after Thomas stalked downstairs.

He'd broken one of the first rules of running a restaurant. You didn't yell at the staff in front of customers. Shouting a coarsely phrased tirade in front of people trying to relax over drinks and dinner was not done. Bad form. Embarrassed everybody: the customers, the boss, the other help, and particularly the person you harangued. Thomas should have known better. She suspected he did.

"Old-fashioned, two red, Amstel, Rock, Smith. And you can batter a couple more martinis for me, too." Jimmy lowered his voice. "What got into the second son? My lord, but I've never seen him even begin to act like that. What special treatment? If he had any sense, he would thank you for ridding the place of that lot, which you didn't even do deliberately, probably. They undoubtedly would have monopolized your bar and scared away all the marginally decent types who might have spent some money here tonight.

"People in the dining room were looking like they did not plan to linger during the Mickey Mouse Republicans Club meeting. I've never seen Thomas lose it before. He was thoroughly pathetic and will feel horribly embarrassed in a few minutes. Wonder how he'll handle that."

She rotated the long spoon inside the martini shaker much harder than she'd done for the first round. "Quietly, I hope. Let it go, Jimmy. If I linger over this postmortem, I might have to go tell Thomas what I think about his yelling at me, a prospect which does not bode well for our future as coworkers. I really do not need to take shit from him too, you know. Let's hope I at least get some sympathy tips out of it." Jimmy stifled a retort with a regretful look and walked away to deliver his drinks.

She hadn't even begun to tell him about Butler's latest news. Her conversational agendas were becoming harder and harder to keep. She wondered if Jimmy would recognize Blueboy's name. She should have asked Butler if his princely suspect only cut women's hair. And skin.

Alan settled himself at the bar, oblivious to any strain in the atmosphere. After she served his drink and accepted his compliments on the color in her cheeks, he turned to Owen to talk about some hockey brawl.

Conversations gradually resumed up and down the bar as she refused to acknowledge the few pitying glances she received. She eavesdropped on Owen and Alan, hoping Owen wouldn't mention the scene Alan had missed. The last thing she needed right now was for Alan to grow indignant with Thomas. Alan might find defending her honor a full time job these days.

She had just finished washing all the beer mugs dirtied by the problematic crowd when Zorro called her down to the service station.

"My, Rose, what do you do to inspire such devotion? You have only been behind the bar less than one hour and already that man you do not want to speak with has called you three times. The last call was about ten minutes ago, or perhaps a little longer. Who counts minutes when passion is involved?" Zorro took a cherry out of the servers' garnish tray.

"Also, there have been more hang-ups on the phone than I would expect to be normal. Do not worry, I will not allow this person to reach you over the phone here tonight. I am happy to protect you from such a suitor. You must just do your work. Put your mind to making your customers happy. That is the only thing that need concern you here tonight." He tossed the stem from the first cherry onto the bar and took another.

"And, Rose, if it is not saying too much, allow me to apologize for Thomas for the bursting out he just did to you. Some pressures must be bothering him. I see him on the phone half the night already. What can we say? It is not like him to yell in that way. He never makes such noises. Something must be eating at him. To be so loud was out of control. Please, forget it. He would want you to." Zorro rolled a third cherry around in his mouth for so long she feared he might attempt the stem-tying trick.

"Thanks, Zorro. Thanks a lot. And—"

"Rose, do not thank me. You can trade me a favor instead of thanking me. The favor I would like is for you to tell me your secret."

"My secret?" Which one could he possibly know about?

"Yes, how it is that you enslave someone to you so powerfully. This man, whoever he is, sounds very upset not to be able to talk to you, as if he is missing something he needs to live. Like he is under your spell. You must be a very special lover."

He actually winked before walking over to seat the couple who had waited by the host's stand while he teased her.

Zorro either assumed his promotion insured her friendship or had been reading some very New Age management guides. Not for him the distance of authority. Maybe he respected her more now in her new role as femme fatale. He might be waiting for her to request more favors, batting her eyelashes while making her coy appeals.

She'd prefer to give him tips on restaurant management instead of on enslaving lovers. Joking or not, the man whose quasi girlfriend had been murdered exhibited terrible taste by asking that question. Even if the clandestine girlfriend hadn't been the affair of the century and the boyfriend was really a cover story.

Unless it was the girlfriend who was the real cover story.

Chapter Twenty-seven

Flash. Flash. If life were the cartoon it mimicked lately, little light bulbs would be sketching themselves in the air above her head.

Long silences. Moans and groans. Lots of time in the office behind locked doors. Unexplained visits. Unsolicited alibis. Undeserved promotions. Doors that took too long to unlock. And don't forget a propensity for office sex.

The "1812 Overture" should play to accompany this burst of mental light. She hadn't imagined the moan tonight. Thomas claimed a girlfriend no one had ever seen. Thomas promoted Zorro when Ben wanted to fire him. Thomas knew things only Zorro could have told him. Thomas lost his temper uncharacteristically when Zorro stood too close to someone else.

Thomas had raised his voice two times tonight.

"To be so loud was out of control." She'd heard it from the one who should know. But not the one who should tell.

Zorro didn't limit his favors to Susan. Zorro had decided sleeping with people he worked with was such a good idea that he'd try sleeping with people he worked for too. Unless he'd worked his way down, instead of up, the corporate ladder. Or maybe he'd straddled both ends simultaneously. Of the ladder.

Hire a skywriter. Thomas and Zorro were lovers. Secret lovers. She had walked in on them twice without recognizing it, although she'd known something was odd in the office the other night.

Maybe Thomas' temper tantrum hadn't been inspired by jealousy. He might have thought she'd understood earlier, overestimating her deductive skills and misinterpreting her emphasis on the very personal nature of the favor she wanted.

Thomas and Zorro had known she would return to the office within minutes for her bank. Why hadn't they waited until she was safely upstairs? Why was the hallway dark? Why was Zorro now friendlier? Why had he snuck such strong clues into his apologies for the boss? Had he known what he was suggesting? Why couldn't she have gotten herself a job in a nice, reasonable, safe, restaurant where drinks and food were the only commodities being traded? Like the commissary for Sesame Street?

If Zorro and Susan were lovers, and Zorro and Thomas were lovers, Susan and Thomas shared a connection stronger than the one between bartender and boss. She remembered Jimmy saying Zorro and Susan had only dared their little romps in the office when Thomas was working. Perhaps Zorro hadn't really worried about Thomas discovering them. Having Thomas know what was going on was part of the fun for at least two of the threesome. The question she didn't want to consider was which two. Or just how long this triangle had lasted.

Rose worried at the puzzle while she made drinks and small talk for a busy bar. The crowd now doubled up at the bar was a more pleasant and more profitable mix than the earlier herd of young yuppies. She wished Thomas would venture upstairs to see them.

She wondered what could keep Thomas holed up in the office for so long on this busy Friday night. It wasn't like him to miss coming upstairs at least once or twice every hour to monitor the evening's progress. No matter what kind of confidence he might have in his staff, or in his new general manager, he should still check on things himself occasionally. It was as if Thomas were hiding out in the office.

Maybe he was down there answering the phone. She'd been unnaturally sensitive to its ring for the first few hours tonight, when Zorro had exacerbated her sensitivity by waving from the host's stand and pointing to the phone at what she assumed was the thwarted voice of her fan. But for the last hour or so, Zorro had been too busy seating people and cruising the dining room to answer the phone. She certainly wasn't picking it up. Nobody in the kitchen would have the time to answer now. So Thomas must be answering.

And maybe doing more than answering. She remembered what Zorro had said before about Thomas being on the phone most of the early evening. There were two lines on each of the restaurant's phones. Maybe Thomas also liked to make a lot of calls. What if Thomas thought muffling his voice and scaring people was fun? Even if she didn't answer the calls, knowing that they continued kept her fearful. Thomas would have to disguise his voice if Zorro were answering the phone. Unless of course this charade had a larger cast than most parlor games.

She tried to check this fantasy by remembering when or how often she'd heard the phone ring tonight, but had no clear idea if the phone had actually rung outside of her imagination in the last hour. It didn't seem like a good question to ask anybody.

If Thomas had been playing phone games before, he wasn't now. It was hard to talk normally with someone your thoughts had just accused.

"Well, it's good to see we've gotten some business again, Rose. Nice work. I need some air, so I think I'll walk over to Sheridan Square and get the early paper. Do you need anything? Zorro looks busy; you can tell him where I went. I shouldn't be gone very long at all. See you in a few."

Breezy was a new tone for Thomas. She'd heard it done better.

Rose didn't have time to reply before he walked away from the bar and out the door. Another first for him tonight: she'd never seen him leave the restaurant when it was busy, as if it made any difference if he hid out downstairs or left the premises entirely. She didn't know how he'd seen that Zorro was busy: her quick scan of the restaurant failed to locate the new general manager. Maybe the two men were just psychically attuned.

For that matter, maybe she'd misinterpreted Zorro's earlier wild gesticulations toward the phone each time he answered it. He could just as easily have been signaling that the calls had nothing to do with her as warning that her caller persisted.

So much remained open to interpretation. She needed to know so very much more. She needed to know too much more to figure it all out now. A bar three-deep in drinkers and talkers was not Holmes' study. She'd look almost as stupid puffing a pipe as she undoubtedly did standing still and silently staring at a perfectly ordinary closed door.

Rose shook herself back into high bartending mode, dispensing drinks and wisecracks with a slightly frantic air she hoped would be lost in the crowd. Better manic than morose. It was probably a chapter heading in some bartender's guide. They didn't call that show "Cheers" for nothing.

She hoped she hadn't sounded too cheerful in her good night to Alan, who was leaving unusually early for a Friday night. He claimed to be fighting off a cold, and she hoped her sympathy didn't sound gushed. She'd forgotten to ask him why he hadn't returned as promised last night and wondered if the oversight, ill health, or the crowded bar had made him unusually quiet tonight. It was probably a quite normal combination of the three factors. She didn't have to attribute mysterious motives to everyone.

Zorro didn't approach the bar or surface in the dining room after Thomas had left, so she couldn't tell him about the boss' absence. Nonetheless, he somehow managed to position himself at the door seconds before Thomas returned an hour later. Zorro welcomed the boss back with the attitude of someone who'd confidently controlled the restaurant all along.

Rose managed her own welcoming smile when Thomas handed her an early edition of Saturday's *Times*. She took the paper as a peace offering: it was far too meager an edition to consider a bribe.

Thomas was smiling. Zorro was smiling. Rose was smiling. Most of the customers were smiling, at least occasionally. What a cozy group it was. Such a lovely job.

The evening could well have ended on the note of ersatz warmth, too. The last hour of the night had created an uncanny model of restaurant efficiency and cheer. Satisfied customers departed with the flattering tinge of regret that flattered a restaurant; employees cleaned and counted tips with the special enthusiasm that signaled a lucrative night's end, and a contented owner added up figures that promised healthy profits.

Jimmy had told her earlier he'd need to leave the second he'd finished work, something about needing to have a conciliatory talk with his roommate, who would be waiting impatiently at home, "as if every minute after four o'clock heralded the Apocalypse."

So. It could have been nervousness at finding herself leaving the darkened restaurant with only Thomas and Zorro. Or worrying if her silence on the walk down the windy, dark, street seemed suspicious. Or even some mad urge to end the long, cold wait for a cab with a warm note, after the two men had insisted they wouldn't leave her alone on the dark corner.

She hadn't imagined how it would sound until she'd said it. The words, by themselves, were innocuous enough, and there was nothing particularly suggestive about her delivery. Her tone had been light. But clambering into a taxi while talking out of a face half frozen by the wind hadn't produced the most thoughtful of remarks.

"Well, guess there's no point in asking if anybody wants to share my cab. I remember the two of you go the same way and take the same cab. You two enjoy the rest of the night, now. See you both tomorrow. Good night." Rose told the driver her address, too anxious to bother with directions for the quickest route.

She imagined continuing her conversation with Thomas and Zorro, "Of course, I won't see the two of you together until after you've spent a night and probably half the day writhing around in some furtive bed in forbidden, secret passion. The kind of passion that could destroy your worlds if the word got out, although why the secret should be so damning in this day and age I've yet to figure, unless you want to confess to the murders here and now?

"And the word will get out, because, I, Rose Leary, am about to announce it to the world at large. I know your secret and I must share it. With everyone."

She might as well have yelled those words while the cabdriver waited for a green light in front of the two men, although her window remained closed against the wind, her lips hadn't moved, and the cabdriver, who'd acknowledged everything else she'd said in his cab, gave no sign whatsoever of hearing the threat. But then, she hadn't heard the words either, because she knew she hadn't spoken them out loud.

But Thomas had heard them. The look on his face swore to it. Her harmless pleasantries had screamed a different subtext to him. Threats were in the ears of the beholder. And the parting words she'd chosen to speak had allowed just enough interpretation to suggest far more than she'd meant. Thomas' expression announced that her farewell had not stopped at certain insinuating suggestions. He'd heard her words move into bold threats.

And yet Rose was the one who felt quite distinctly menaced. She knew she was in trouble.

She called herself the stupidest woman in the world. Bravado was for boys. A thoughtless quip might have moved her to the top of the endangered species list. It would be her own fault if she personally and tragically proved Butler and his Blueboy theory wrong. Posthumous proof wouldn't do a damn thing for her ego, either. Stupid. Stupid. Stupid.

Ignoring all the cabdriver's efforts at conversation, she sat silently for the rest of the ride home. It wasn't right for someone who considered words her life to use them suicidally. Sticks and stones can break my bones, but words can never— It didn't even rhyme.

Hurt me?

Chapter Twenty-eight

At least tonight's driver kept his promise to wait until she'd reached her door before he drove away. As if to remind her of My World, the foyer light had burned out again. Rose scanned the empty hallway through the foyer door as she groped for the lock. When she'd managed to unlock the door, a peculiar fragrance haunted the lobby. It smelled as if spectral Avon ladies drenched in strong floral cologne crowded the area. When she stepped into the hallway, her footsteps released more of the gift shoppe scent. The cloying smell grew thicker. Her foyer and hallway smelled like a maiden aunt's parlor.

Rose closed the second door tightly and then peered back into the entrance. A horrible crooked swathe started at her mailbox, slithered down the wall to the floor, snuck under the door into the hallway, and continued winding up the stairs like a bloody trail. The crazy track was red, several faded shades of red, and looked desiccated and insubstantial. She saw buds that had once belonged to miniature roses and petals that once had bloomed. The stuff gave absolutely no resistance under her feet but crumbled under her weight with tiny sighs that released more horrid flowery scent.

The mess on the wall and on the floor was rose potpourri. Somebody had either thrown or poured it over strong glue. The flowers' smell disguised the glue's chemical odors as thoroughly as the lavish potpourri layer hid the invisible glue. A closer look at her mailbox showed that its door had been sprung open and the box itself stuffed with the dried mess.

It might have looked pretty somewhere else.

But it didn't, not here, not in her hallway, not with her decorated mailbox eliminating any hope that the tribute might have been intended for a neighbor. The smell sickened her.

She should tell someone. Right away. God only knew what might wait outside her apartment door. After vainly straining her ears to hear any possible late-night revelry in the building, she absolutely refused to wake any of her neighbors after four in the morning, even on a weekend. All the decent bars had closed, while the nearest phone booth was two deserted and suddenly threatening blocks away. The creep could lurk around any corner. She couldn't imagine what any friend she called could do to help, besides commiserate. Sympathy wasn't safety.

That left the police.

"Hello, 911? Some mean man left dried flowers all over my hallway. He meant it for me, because he left them in my mailbox, too. Could you send someone right over, so that it won't smell so sweet in here?"

Sure, two patrol cars for the entire precinct, an hour after the bars closed on a Friday: they'd screech over here in seconds flat.

Or there was always Frank. Rousing Detective Butler

from his bed would guarantee his sympathy. He could yell at her for ruining fingerprints they both knew the creep was too smart to leave, and which the detective wouldn't consider that important anyhow. After he'd accused her of having too much to say on the situation herself, he'd try to convince her potpourri had never killed anyone.

She didn't need him to tell her that, not really. It was, in its miserable way, true. The dried flowers were not immediately life-threatening. Wanting to gag at their scent was not the same as being strangled. Flowers weren't blood, although the creep's symbolic gestures were becoming both more sophisticated and more direct.

Rose didn't want to stand here any longer, exposed to attack from all sides, even if her little flower boy had probably left long ago. The smartest thing to do was to get herself safely upstairs and into her apartment. She couldn't believe that he waited inside her apartment. Her hallway and mailbox locks were simple enough to spring, but he couldn't have gotten through her apartment locks so easily. And there was no way he could have broken in without leaving a mark.

If she saw anything, the slightest little incongruity, a smidgen out of the ordinary, she wouldn't go inside. No, then she would force herself to wake a neighbor and call the police, although probably not Butler at home. He'd doubtless appear with a nuclear warhead this time, overreacting even to a threat he swore didn't exist.

She told herself she'd seen the worst already. Nothing

more alarming waited for her to discover it.

She just had to walk up the stairs now. At least strong lights illuminated them. And there weren't a lot of blind corners on the landings, not if you crept up, pausing to lean precariously out over the banister to glimpse the next flight up. Taking deep, slow, breaths to fill your lungs with adequate air in case you needed to scream seemed a sensible precaution. She envied anyone in a basement apartment tonight.

He could keep his red carpet treatment. Following a path of fragrant dried flowers didn't ease her ascent. She carefully avoided stepping on the trail all the way up the stairs. But she couldn't escape touching it when she arrived at her apartment. A large, freeform puddle of petals stood like a scabby welcome mat outside her door.

Her artist hadn't stopped there. Not one to end a project below eye level, he'd finished with an echo of his opening flourish. The potpourri continued up her door, over her locks, and covered her doorknob. This final touch created an artistic statement with more meaning than the artist had intended. His magic seal covered her locks and doorknob in such a thick layer that Rose knew he couldn't be waiting inside.

Still wearing her gloves, Rose gingerly inserted her key and turned her top lock, wincing as she forced the point of the key to pierce the layer of dried glue and withered flowers. The bottom lock was less difficult. When she grasped the doorknob to open the door, she tried to ignore the dry whispers of the petals as her hand smashed through them to the knob.

She couldn't really mourn the poor blooms. They'd died long before she touched them.

Thank God he didn't get in. He probably hadn't even tried the door. She skittered from room to room, checking the apartment and cursing her paranoia as she did. An unexamined apartment wasn't worth living in. That little ritual over, she had one more chore to perform before settling down to solve everything.

Her machine was blinking like brake lights on the L.A. freeway. She didn't have the extra strength required to ignore its signals. Bracing herself, she pushed playback.

A trio of beeps, surprising nobody.

Butler was sorry about their little scene today. The thing was, why couldn't she just be happy that the guy was caught and she was safe now? He didn't know what it would take to convince her, but he would call her back tomorrow and try anyway.

Five beeps this time. Guess who.

Marie knew she'd be at work, but thought a nice dose of sisterly love would make a fine thing to return home to. Everybody missed her and why didn't she plan on coming for Easter, if not sooner? They could color eggs with the nieces.

Only one beep. Had he run out of quarters?

Catherine swore if they didn't have brunch one day this weekend, she'd know Rose had decided to drop her from her list of friends forever, meaning Catherine would spend the rest of her life wandering around with an irreparably damaged ego as a result. The guilt would give Rose wrinkles. Catherine meant it.

Great, he'd found change. Four beeps proved it.

Her ex-husband wanted to know what to do about last year's taxes. They'd had joint income for a few months, and the accountant said they should all three sit down and talk. His accountant, but she could get her own if she wanted. He'd always had impeccable timing.

And then, the call she'd been waiting for. The beeps and the hallway decoration hadn't satisfied all of tonight's communicative urges. The time, risk, and effort invested in the potpourri had warned her he'd crave further self-expression tonight. She'd expected he'd break his previous pattern and leave a recorded message. More muffled than ever, his voice also sounded more inhuman.

"Not all dead things smell so good, Rose. Dead love stinks. It smells worse than you can imagine. But kisses smell sweet, Rose. Sweeter than flowers. Everything should be sweet for us, Rose. Let it all be sweet, Rose. Breathe deep now. Nighty-night."

She'd jumped when he told her to breathe deep. Only a few minutes ago, her fear of meeting him had inspired her to do just that. No way for him to know that, however. None.

Focus on the phone calls. Fine. The detective insisted on his errors, her family offered love, her friends felt ignored, and her ex-husband sounded like a jerk. Oh, some maniac also wanted to have her, sex, and death all together in a merry threesome. Same old same old.

She should determine when he'd done his decorating project. The glue had completely hardened, but most glues these days dried immediately. No footsteps disturbed the potpourri path, but its creator wouldn't have wanted to mar his work. She couldn't tell if anyone else had walked in the hallway or on the stairs since her decorator had finished his work. Forty people could have walked up the stairs without stepping on the flowers, or she could have been the very first to admire his crafts skills. A guess that he'd finished his project within the last couple of hours didn't qualify as precise forensics.

Rose didn't need his schedule to see this as a new and bolder step for the creep. No matter what time he'd been strewing his little petals, someone in the building could have interrupted him. What could he have done, or said, if that had happened? She didn't know if it would seem worse if he'd prepared an explanation he considered plausible, or if he hadn't worried about needing one. No fun choosing between cocky and careless.

He went a little further each day. The pace was picking up.

The luxury of a leisurely investigation, if it had ever existed at all, had now vanished from the realm of possibilities. She had to focus. It had to end.

She'd made the obligatory written copy of his message,

a superfluous move since the machine had taped his distorted voice. Old habits died hard. She didn't anticipate finding a bonus of new information in tonight's words. His code didn't need a secret ring for this message. The biggest question was whether he'd made the call before or after his decorating spree. She'd bet after, but timing wasn't the burning issue here.

She put the transcription away and resisted the temptation to play his message again. It had nothing good to tell her. Only a masochist would consider, even momentarily, putting the tape into her deck and listening to him in stereo. No. She'd rather listen to heavy metal music or synthesizer polkas.

Mustering all her willpower and praying for concentration to follow, Rose settled down in her window chair. Diane's note still seemed the best clue she had, and she knew it had more to tell her. She tried to remember the note's exact words.

"Bad things." "You could know somebody all of your life and still not know everything." "Your own brother." What else had the note said? She hadn't totally trusted her memory for years, probably not since she'd blown out its best cells on grammar school catechism bees.

She found one of the copies she'd made of Diane's words. Butler had the original. He shouldn't have taken it. Or else he should have taken the whole thing more seriously. God damn him anyway.

"Your own brother." Susan had sex with the same

man Thomas did, often in Thomas' own office. Susan was brutally killed and her body was abused.

Diane had started to write a note pointing blame at Thomas. Diane had also argued with and vaguely threatened Zorro. Then Diane was killed and also raped. Thomas sent Rose on the errand that discovered Diane's corpse.

Thomas could have faked his alibis with tricky phone work and Zorro's lies.

Thomas knew Rose's phone number and her work schedule. He could have made those repulsive calls, even the ones she'd received at work. My World's phone had two lines. His trip for the paper tonight might have given him time enough to decorate her hallway. Oh God, what if he'd liked being involved in Susan and Zorro's affair? Who knew what offers Diane might have received or refused? What if Thomas liked casting his bartenders in the doomed-girl roles in his menages?

He must understand he needed to be more careful now. To a crazy person, crank calls could sound careful. Dead flowers could seem demure.

Thomas had looked at her with cold, mean, hatred tonight. Dead flowers and creepy calls were effusive compliments compared to that look. His glare had burned up any invitation she might ever have received. Her dance card was scorched.

She'd never favored the gothic, but she could sense her faith in herself as a judge of character wisping away over these mental moors. She'd liked Thomas when she first met him. She'd even thought he looked like a romantic hero. Rose watched her judgment drown at the bottom of a murky pool, her clothes weighed down by voluminous clothes with thick books in the pockets. She might not have the time for a proper mourning period.

Thomas could be the caller.

Thomas could be the killer.

Thomas thought she knew all about him, and Zorro, and God only knew what else.

Pleading ignorance and confusion wouldn't help her life expectancy. She couldn't expect leniency. The precedents weren't good.

Her case against Thomas was beginning to look airtight. All she had to do now was disprove alibis good enough for the New York Police Department and establish her interpretation of a crumpled note and a dirty look. Butler would buy it immediately. Right after he took out the mortgage on the Williamsburg Bridge. Fixed rate. No warranties.

Despite her confidence in her ability to talk herself into or out of anything, Rose didn't know whom to talk to next. Butler would scoff, Jimmy would shriek, and Thomas, well, Thomas might slash. Nor could she imagine going to Ben to reveal her suspicions about his brother. Blood was thicker.

And nobody else could do anything. Familial or friendly sympathy couldn't change a damn thing. She didn't want to expose anyone she loved to this madman's games.

She needed hard proof now. Harder than phones, flowers, or notes from beyond. Rock hard. Solid material. Hard enough to sell what no one wanted to buy. The stuff that screams were made of.

Would everyone believe her if her hallway held a path of blood instead of symbols? No. There would be no blood in her hallway. Ever. Perish the thought, not the thinker. Please.

Rose bruised her knuckles knocking on the chair's wooden arm.

Chapter Twenty-nine

Early Saturday evening, Rose raised her sore hand to knock on the office door as if she knew this door hid the tiger, not the lady. She didn't feel particularly relieved when Zorro's voice sang out permission to enter and actually cleared her throat loudly before turning the door handle. She'd play voyeur somewhere else, thanks.

"Ah, Rose. Good evening, and you do look lovely on this night, as always. Some day you must tell me about all your favorite stores. But, I am sorry, I cannot chat with you now. The entire restaurant is in my hands tonight. I have much to do. Please, count." He handed her the bank and returned to shuffling the day waiter's checks.

"Thanks, Zorro. Just one quick question before I start counting, okay?" She continued before he could refuse, "Where is Thomas? Isn't he working tonight?" She'd feel better if she knew where all the players were.

"To answer that question properly would take more time than I can spare, Rose. Let me say in brief that I do not know the location of Thomas. Early this afternoon, he told me on the phone that he was on his way here. And the day staff said he arrived before two and worked for a while. But then he must have left, although no one saw him walk out. He must have departed, because he is no longer here. Nobody knows when he left." Zorro looked at his large gold watch, twisting his wrist so that she couldn't avoid noticing the gaudy timepiece.

"Thomas was certainly gone when I arrived here at 5:30. Another good thing is that he expected me and felt the freedom to leave My World for me to manage. I am sure he will call to tell us where he is and when he will return. Do not worry, you will not have to answer the phone tonight either. I remember, you see."

He pointed to her bank, "But still, Thomas loves to surprise. So I think we should also surprise him by having the restaurant run even more perfect than usual when he returns. I cannot leave the office until you are ready to go upstairs also."

She smiled apologetically, counted her bank, and wondered who had taught Zorro the definition of brief. It was easier than wondering where Thomas had gone this time.

Rose stepped behind a full bar, with all the customers drinking like Prohibition would start within the hour. Between serving drinks, listening to pathetic ethnic jokes from three college students, and setting up for the night, it took her almost half an hour to notice that Laura hadn't pulled the liquor to replace the bottles Rose had emptied last night.

And neither the owner or his new general manager had troubled to remind Laura, an oversight like starting a long drive without checking the gas gauge. Rose had gone through over twenty bottles last night, and it looked as if Laura had drained several more today. After only a cursory check, Rose could already see that she needed more house vodka, Dewars, and Jack Daniels. So many missing bottles left the bar severely understocked. Tonight's inventory was full of holes.

Stocking the bar during a busy cocktail-hour rush would be awkward, but better than trying to shelve all the bottles in the middle of a Saturday night's action. Nothing would be as bad as reaching for bottles that weren't there, which would definitely happen later if she didn't get her supplies in now. Not wanting to make a new pull-list from the empty spaces on the shelves and in the backup cabinets, Rose felt more relief than annoyance when she found last night's list taped to the register. She'd have to remember tomorrow to ask Laura how the list had returned to the bar without the replacement bottles.

First she had to ask Zorro to pull more than two dozen bottles of liquor from the storeroom downstairs. She knew he'd order a busboy to carry the bottles up the stairs, and she resolved to tip the kid heavily for the extra work. It took five minutes to spot Zorro sitting and reading a menu at a table far back in the dining room, and another five before he acknowledged her waves and sauntered up to the bar.

She explained the situation, apologized for having to bother him, and handed him the pull-list.

He handed it right back.

"Rose, I cannot possibly leave the dining room now. There are several things I must be looking at. You will have to get the liquor yourself, although of course you must not carry the heavy bottles. Julio can carry them. It will give him a chance to strut his macho little muscles."

"But—"

"Do not waste your breath worrying about your bar. Believe me, I can watch over your bar while I also check on the important things in the dining room. A manager must know how to perform several duties at once. Now, go quickly. I will send Julio down to you very soon."

He handed her a heavy ring of keys, singling out the one with a yellow paper dot as the key to the liquor room. All of the other keys on the ring were color coded, too. Restaurant management, Romper Room style.

She saw that arguing with him would get her nowhere but into some rocky area of challenging his new authority. She still didn't want him using the bar register while she pulled liquor downstairs. Given her weak faith in his mathematical abilities, she was damned if she wanted to cover any mistakes he might make with her cash. She asked Zorro not to step behind the bar unless he absolutely had to, warning him of a mysterious gunk by the register certain to ruin his "gorgeous silk shirt." Flattering anything so brightly orange seemed like complimenting a chemical sunset.

The liquor room was past the office, at the end where the hall turned and led to more storage areas and the back door.

She struggled with the key for a minute, then opened

the door. The room was long and narrow, with cases of beer stacked waist-high and rough shelves holding well liquors on the walls near the door. More shelves, further back on both sides, held wines and brand liquors. A makeshift desk of two table bases supporting a large rectangle of plywood sat in the far right corner, under still more shelves. The desk held clumsily stacked boxes of straws, bevnaps, and stirrers, with other boxes scattered below the table.

Tonight, it also held Thomas' head and the upper part of his body. He sat slumped over the desk with his arms surrounding his head like someone whose catnap had grown into leonine sleep. An empty bottle of Amaretto lay on its side by his right elbow. Glops of the thick liquid puddled on the desk and onto the floor, filling the room with a strong fruity smell. Tonight had better be the end of National Sweet Smells Week.

Rose knocked on the doorjamb and called Thomas' name. He didn't stir. She stepped into the room, assuming he'd passed out after drinking too much.

At least he didn't snore. She didn't want to disturb this drunken stupor, but he'd passed out directly below three shelves she needed to reach. Waiting for him to wake up on his own might leave her standing here until closing time. In Hawaii.

She moved directly behind Thomas, leaned down, and yelled into his ear. Her breath ruffled his shiny hair. From this vantage point, she could see that Thomas and the empty Amaretto bottle were not the only things on the table. A piece of yellow legal paper stuck out from under Thomas' left elbow. A few words were scrawled in block letters.

FUCKING FUCKED ME

Knowing what a stupid move it was, Rose gently tugged on the paper until it slid out from under the heavy elbow. The message ended in *UP*. "Fucking fucked me up"?

It wasn't the most eloquent of confessionals, but she'd never thought of Amaretto as inspirational. Score another one for the Leary judgment: Thomas hadn't seemed like a maudlin and self-pitying drunk. No wonder he'd gotten so plastered. If she wrote like that, she'd want oblivion too.

This probably called for ice water in the face. Her own cleverly phrased letter of resignation would be simpler.

Dear Thomas,
I am sorry I had to wake you from
your drunken and irresponsible stupor
this evening. Finding you that way
was particularly painful for me after
last night, when I discovered your
illicit affair with our new manager
and came to the conclusion that you
* like to kill girls. It is with great regret*

Sleeping men didn't read. She braced herself in case he woke up punching, grabbed a handful of his shiny black hair, and tugged. His head didn't move. She pulled harder.

His head stayed on the desk.

Rose spotted something else on the floor next to the table—another empty bottle—a small, opaque, brownish plastic bottle with a white label. The kind you got from the drugstore but that never contained vitamins. The kind of bottle you hated to see empty anywhere near someone who seemed too soundly asleep. Sleeping pills, sweet liqueurs, and silence didn't promise a great prognosis. The note started to assume a new character.

Still, it might not be too late for a stomach pump. Hesitating for only the second it took to tell herself she didn't know for certain that Thomas was the killer, she began yelling for help as she started to lift his head.

Nobody answered. His head didn't move. It wouldn't move at all. It stayed stuck to the desk. She tugged harder.

It stayed stuck.

She yelled as loud as she could and used all her strength to lift Thomas' head. It came up with a ripping noise. What looked like part of the tabletop came with it.

Thomas appeared to be wearing a new kind of mask. The mask covered his mouth, and his nose, and most of his eyes. But it didn't have any holes. He could not possibly be breathing. His face was glued to a piece of shiny cardboard not much bigger than an index card. His face was sealed shut. Some of the Amaretto had seeped under the cardboard, enough to dry into a temporary fixative that had briefly stuck the mask thing to the desk.

Once she recognized the glue board, she didn't try

to pull the piece of cardboard off Thomas' face. The thick glue bonding the cardboard to Thomas' still features was so strong it would rip his skin before its hold broke.

Exterminators used glue boards to kill mice and rats. They stuck the cardboard pieces, glue side up, along the floors and walls and left them as traps. Sometimes the rodents were just immobilized in the glue, waiting to die of either starvation or more direct intervention. Other times, the exterminator added poison on top of the glue, and the end was quicker.

Between the Amaretto and the empty bottle of sleeping pills, Thomas probably hadn't needed any extra poison

Rose spotted three more glue boards at the edge of the table next to the shelves. He must have shoved this one forward on the table when he knocked the boxes around. The other boards were mercifully unoccupied, and Rose refused to speculate on the exact sequence of events that had landed Thomas' face on this one.

Twice in one week was too damned much. Only someone whose early education had been in the pale hands of chaste women in long black robes would entertain, even momentarily, a guilty fear that her bad thoughts were to blame. Calling someone a murderer was not murder. Not at all.

This wasn't exactly murder, either. Suicide was technically different, although the end result was the same. A dead person.

And Thomas was inarguably dead. Not even a Jesuit could dispute it.

So she'd called him a bastard, and a creep, and had even auditioned him for the worst villain's role. That didn't mean he should end up dead with his face all mashed into rat poison and his body sloppily anointed with a teenager's idea of a sophisticated drink. Nobody should. Particularly someone who hadn't confessed to any crimes first.

Rose hated recognizing how inadequately she'd described finding a body in her novels before this. None of the scenes she'd written had created the chill that threatened to paralyze her right now. She wouldn't need notes to remember this feeling.

Rose put Thomas' head down as gently as her shaking hands could manage, left the room, and started slowly toward the stairs. Her yells had obviously not pierced the jukebox's loud shield. Calling for help from the liquor room had been like screaming in a soundproof cell.

She wondered how long it would take Butler to arrive. She tried very hard not to cry this time. Somebody had to keep some shreds of dignity around here.

Refusing to cry beat wondering why.

Chapter Thirty

Rose stopped and turned around at the foot of the stairs. Zorro's enormous key ring should include the office key. Four colors later, she stepped into the office. She picked up the phone, dialed the precinct, and told the man who answered what she had to say. She asked him to tell the officers answering the call to use the rear delivery entrance. He agreed that uniformed men storming through a crowded restaurant wouldn't help anybody's investigation, or reputation. Then she asked him to find Detective Frank Butler and make sure he came soon.

Rose found Laura's home number on the staff list above the phone, dialed it, and asked her to hurry back to work. She didn't offer any explanation, but Laura heard the urgency in her voice and promised to return right away.

The second line's light started to flash just as she said good-bye. Rose answered the call before the first ring. Butler, finally. He asked if she'd sworn herself to destroying any dinner he might ever enjoy for the rest of his life. Her laughter drowned out his sputtering questions for a full minute before she could reply.

"It's a restaurant, Frank. The crime scene is a restaurant. We can feed you here. We have lots of food. And lots of booze, bottles and bottles and bottles of booze. Hurry over, you'll like it here."

"What do you mean, 'crime scene?' I thought you told

the desk guy suicide."

"I didn't use that word. I described what I found and he chose his own professional term. Anyway, isn't a suicide still a crime scene? Isn't it still a crime to kill yourself? A capital crime?" She bit her lower lip until it bled to choke back another attack of laughter.

"Why don't you just get here, Frank? We can argue in person, okay?" Rose hung up the phone and struggled to compose herself. Uncontrollable comedic attacks weren't any better than crying. Hysterical didn't sound like a compliment once you'd stopped telling jokes.

She prayed Zorro would hear the phone ring upstairs. She dialed the restaurant's main number and waited for him to pick up. He answered on the sixth ring.

"Zorro, it's Rose. You have to trust me for a minute here. Put Jimmy behind the bar, have Ellen cover the door, and meet me downstairs. It's an emergency." She hung up on him, too. His footsteps marched down the hall moments later.

"What the fuck, Rose? How dare you let yourself into our office? Thomas will become most angry when he hears of this. I will not blame him. I do not promise that your job will continue to exist after this. What are you doing in here? And how do you think to give me orders?" Zorro's face didn't show as much anger as his words. Nor did his face collapse in sorrow when she told him what she'd found.

Four loud bangs on the delivery door interrupted her

explanation, followed by the sound of voices approaching in the hallway. That door should have stayed locked during business hours.

"The cops are here. I'll stay downstairs, not that they'll give me much choice. Laura's coming in to take care of the bar. We'll be all right, Zorro."

"No, we will not be all right, not with Thomas dead. You act like a wise woman, Rose, but you speak like a fool. It is all very terrible. I must see Thomas. I think I must see him before the police crash in on his last rest." Tragedy took its time reaching Zorro; his tone sounded more annoyed than sorrowful.

"You don't want to see him. It's ugly. It's too late, anyway. The police won't let you in there now." She knew she wouldn't return to the liquor room tonight.

"They cannot stop me. I will see him if I choose." He shoved her out of his way as he rushed out of the office. Two of the cops stopped him a few yards down the hall. She heard the drone of questions begin.

They'd start with her very soon.

Somebody had to call Ben and Joe Victors. She'd rather answer every question posed by every officer in all five boroughs than make those calls.

"Hi, Frank, has anyone called the family yet? Somebody has to tell them. Whose job is it, anyway?" Her thoughts had summoned Butler. Clap if you believe in Tinkerbell.

"Good evening, Ms. Leary. They're both on their

way down right now. Thank you for suggesting the call, however. The bottom of your left shoe must feel sticky. You left a terrific little footprint in that mess on the floor. What all did you touch in there?"

Butler's smile looked like the most familiar thing in the office. He closed the door, motioned her back into Ben's chair, and sat himself on the desk's edge. He leaned forward expectantly. "Here we go again, Rose. Tell me everything. Please. You're good at this, remember?"

Oh God, time for the question waltz again. Rose fought a sickening sense of deja vu. She'd already done this routine; once had been quite enough, thank you. Closing her eyes didn't make Butler disappear. She'd tried that already too.

"Frank, I don't want to know how to do this. Being an experienced corpse finder is not on my life goals list. Honestly, it's not."

She started her sorry story and told him everything she could remember, knowing even as she spoke that it wouldn't be enough. He somehow contented himself with raising one eyebrow when she described Thomas' note and reading his final word, even though of course she'd had no idea at the time that it was his last word. Words.

"I mean, really, what kind of suicide note is that? 'Fucking fucked me up.' These are Thomas' last words to the world? It doesn't seem right. It's too, I don't know, too coarse for him. Not his style. Something about it feels so odd." She rocked her left foot on the floor.

She'd worry about her shoe later. "I know I wasn't the one supposed to find him, either. Only Zorro should have been able to get into the liquor room tonight. I'm surprised he had the key, now that I think about it. But why would Thomas want his lover to find his dead body? Even if guilt over the murders had finally gotten to him, why would Thomas want Zorro to see him like that?"

She hurried with her own questions before Butler could start his, "Wait, Frank, don't say it. I admit it—I really do sound stupid now, don't I? I have proof the guy slashed and brutalized two women, so why do I think it weird he doesn't worry about sparing his boyfriend's feelings? Maybe Thomas knew Zorro better than we do. That was not a man overcome by grief I just saw. Forget it, I don't even want to speculate anymore about the dynamics of that affair. Aren't you glad this is finally finished, Frank?"

Glad did not appear to be Butler's primary emotion.

"Good Christ Almighty, Rose, what are you talking about now? What guilt? What lover? What murders? What proof?"

He lowered his voice, "Don't bother to answer. I know all about it now. The real reason you work nights is so you can watch all the worst soaps all day long. You watch them, and you read trashy books. Then you stroll over to your desk and create cockamamie stories. These wild assertions and accusations, to you they probably seem normal. Nothing odd about them at all, unless it's the lack of commercials. Calm down now. You only have to tell me about what you actually saw tonight. In real life, I mean. So let's start again."

"You don't have a clue what I write, Frank. I don't watch soaps and I rarely read trash, except of course for on airplanes and in certain moods. Who are you, anyhow, the cultural critic for *The Post*? And I'm supposed to be the one who clutches at straws? Your pride just can't admit how wrong you were, can it? Poor Blueboy is about to lose his big Butler bargain special: three convictions for the price of one. You are the most—"

Loud roars interrupted her tirade. A wild creature stomped down the hall, bellowing in rage and sorrow. Butler opened the office door, and they could see three husky young cops failing to halt Joe Victor's movement down the hall. The cops could have halted an avalanche or hushed a hurricane with less effort. The man wanted to see his dead son's body. Joe looked ready to kill anyone who insisted on blocking his way.

Rose had never liked Butler as much as she did at the moment when he barked out the order to let Joe through. He planted himself squarely in front of the grieving man.

"I'm sorry for your loss, Mr. Victors, real sorry. I'll make sure they let you in to see your son, but you have to give me your word you won't touch anything in there. My men still have work to do."

Joe scrutinized Butler, then nodded his agreement. Butler stepped aside, calling to the cops in the liquor room to get out, take a five-minute break, let the man's father have a moment in there. The hall filled with grumbling men as Joe headed into the almost empty liquor room, with Butler three steps behind him.

Rose refused to watch. She couldn't escape hearing Joe's broken moans and prayers. His mourning's elemental power overwhelmed every other sound.

They walked out of the liquor room, and Joe looked around the hallway and back toward the storage areas. He stared at Butler.

"Here?"

"No, we have to look here, too."

"Outside?"

Butler thought a moment, then nodded his head.

Joe walked to the open delivery door and stepped into the alley, which sloped down from street level. He grabbed the first of the large metal garbage cans lining one side of the passage. He hurled it fifteen feet up the alley, where it crashed and rolled. Then he picked up the next can and threw it. There were nine cans. He made them all thunder.

When he'd finished with the cans, Joe returned to the door and sat on an empty milk crate, with his hands supporting his head in a silence more brutal than his rampage.

Ben finally appeared twenty minutes later. Framed in the doorway at the far end of the hall, he stood motionless for a minute, as if fearful that stepping into the hallway would shatter the air itself. Rose watched him ignore everyone as he walked down the hallway. He stopped outside the liquor room to absorb the tableau under the photographer's garish lights. He shook his head, his face set into its own hardened mask.

Then Ben approached his father. He knelt beside the older man and put his arms around him. They clutched each other. Ben pulled his father to his feet, keeping his arms in a strong circle around Joe.

Joe's voice didn't waver, "He was our baby. Our baby is gone now."

"I know, Pop, I know. Come with me. I'll take you home; the family will be there. Aunt Theresa is calling everyone already. I'll come back here for a little while, then I'll stay with you tonight. It's enough of this place. Nothing more you can do here. Basta."

Ben had walked his father almost to the stairs while he spoke. He left the older man standing there alone for a minute and hurried back to Butler and Rose.

"This fucking place is closed for the night. We should show some respect for the dead. I won't have people eating and drinking up there while my brother lies dead down here. I want all the customers out within the next ten minutes. Anybody wants to talk about it, tell them they can wait until I get back and talk to me."

He shook his head when she asked if she could help, "Jimmy is shutting his mouth and taking care of business for a change. He'll have the place emptied real soon. Zorro thinks he's helping. I got too much on my mind to bother with him right now."

He patted her cheek. "Jesus, Rosie, you okay? I'm sorry you had to see that. Zorro should have gotten the booze himself. I don't know what the hell went on here today. I see you later, all right?" He pinched her cheek like a sad old uncle before he went to take his father home.

Butler ushered her back into the office and pointed at Ben's chair again. He took the deep breath she recognized as the prelude to a question barrage but exhaled fast and loud when the phone rang. He answered before she could reach the phone.

The concentration on his face and the grunts he kept feeding the phone told Rose the call was police business. He asked the "sir" on the other end if he was sure and made him repeat some description three times. Then he hung up the phone and straightened his shoulders as if he'd heard the firing squad cocking their rifles.

"Sit down, Rose. Don't argue again, just sit down. That was one of my colleagues, calling from Thomas' apartment, which we gave a little once-over just to see if anything interesting turned up. With his brother's permission, so forget about whatever Gestapo spiel you were probably composing."

He paused for a full minute, "I guess I have to tell you this, but you better keep it quiet until I tell you it goes public. You gotta swear that."

She nodded solemnly.

"God only knows why I'm trusting you with this. Anyway, they looked in the wastebasket in Thomas' bedroom. Inside the basket was a shitload of empty, neatly creased condom packets. Packets folded precisely into fours."

He mimed folding a square. "Rose, you know those folded rubber packets that you thought were so important, the ones I thought you'd developed some kind of fetish for? I guess you were right about them. Shit, you clocked this whole crazy mess. The wastebasket next to Thomas' bed was full of your precious clues. Fourteen of them, all folded the same way, all mixed in with old newspapers and shirt cardboards. Same brand, same batch, same fold."

Butler opened his hands as if waiting for a gift. "You got it, Rose. It wasn't Blueboy. Thomas was the killer." He didn't look pleased at his news.

"I'd already figured that out last night, Frank. I was probably going to call and tell you about it tonight, not that you would have believed me. Thomas' note makes more sense now. Fucking did fuck him up. Completely. At least he had eclectic tastes." She hoped Butler wouldn't start lecturing her on the delay.

His tone sounded more like a prayer than a lecture, "So, you were right. Thank God he decided to kill himself next, instead of, instead of, um, somebody else."

"Me, Frank? You can say it now, now that I'm safe." She caught him with her own unwavering look. He met it.

"Yeah, Rose, instead of killing you. I think that's something to thank God for. Or at least I did a second ago, until the sound of your voice kept interrupting my humble prayers." He didn't stop studying her face.

"Thanks for telling me. And thanks for everything else you tried to do." She didn't know why his scrutiny didn't bother her this time.

"Who says I'm finished trying?" He waited to see her reaction.

She felt too grateful at finally feeling safe to worry about what he meant. An enormous release flooded her, dissolving all her questions. The killings would stop now. It was over. Over. Over. Over.

Chapter Thirty-one

Two hours later, Rose stared at her answering machine in sick disbelief. She couldn't have received twenty-eight normal phone calls on a Saturday night. Her machine had miscounted. Perhaps her resentment had broken it. Must have. She could not have gotten this many calls. Could not.

She pushed play, then listened to the beeps of twenty-eight hang-ups. Her friends and family knew she worked Saturday nights. No one would expect to find her at home. Even her creepy caller knew her work schedule. But how could he know she'd arrive home hours earlier than usual tonight?

Wait a minute. The caller didn't know anything anymore. He couldn't have made the calls, either, with or without automatic redial. He probably hadn't placed all the calls as soon as she'd left her apartment. Then only a little more than an hour had elapsed between when she left home and when she found Thomas. That timeframe seemed irrelevant anyway, since the corpse hadn't suggested death had closely preceded discovery. Some cooling time had elapsed in there.

Even Butler agreed with her now. Thomas was the killer, and Thomas was the caller, and Thomas was dead.

Dead guys don't dial.

There were no hotlines from hell, and these were not calls from the great beyond. Thomas hadn't made these calls. Someone else had obsessively dialed her number. The creepy caller didn't die.

She couldn't expect any mercy.

It really hadn't ended yet.

Rose couldn't stay in her quiet apartment with such nasty thoughts her only company. Before they'd left work, Jimmy had said he would take advantage of the early night to meet a friend for a late dinner at the Lion's Head. Worn out from the shock of finding Thomas' body, she'd refused his invitation to join them. The four hours she'd spent this afternoon cleaning the potpourri mess from her hallway and door had also argued with her muscles and increased her fatigue.

Twenty-eight hang-ups gave her a second wind.

She turned the machine off, unwilling to return home later to further proof of her caller's devotion. She flicked on three more lights, grabbed her coat, and ran down the stairs. Walking on West Fourth Street all the way over to Christopher without once looking over her shoulder ranked as a major accomplishment tonight.

The Lion's Head was jammed. She recognized several people who'd been at My World earlier sitting at the bar among the Head's regulars. She waved quick hellos to a few friends but squirmed her way back to the dining room without stopping. Jimmy and his friend sat at the prized table under the window. Jimmy's handsome friend looked oddly familiar.

"Rose, what a pleasant surprise. You know Chuck,

don't you? Sit down, we just ordered, what do you want to drink? I'm so glad you came instead of sitting home all alone worrying or whatever you do there these days. What luck, I've been wanting you two to get a chance to talk for ages now, if I could ever coordinate the timing.

"Now Chuck's shift just ended, and you and I are having a kind of half-holiday, courtesy of Thomas the departed. I mean, honestly, what a terrible, tacky, way to die. I'm surprised at him. I really am." Chuck had shaken her hand when Jimmy introduced them but waited for Jimmy to finish before he spoke.

Jimmy didn't give Chuck the chance to talk, "I know I'm gibbering like a snotty queen, so don't either of you bother to mention it. I just can't deal any better right now with somebody's committing suicide like that. I can't help it. Rat poison and Amaretto? Give the devil his due, like cyanide and champagne at the least. Do not go grossly into that good night. Sorry about that, but at least I admit my limitations."

It wasn't until she offered a rueful smile while burly, blushing Chuck told her how glad he was to see her again that Rose remembered where she'd seen his face. He'd been one of the uniformed cops trying to block Joe's progress down the hall earlier tonight. Since then, he'd traded his uniform for a big brown ski sweater and jeans. His blush acknowledged her recognition, but he still didn't speak.

"So look, Rose. Chuck is probably going to kill me, and you have to promise not to make any public announcements about this, but I think it's only fair you should know. I want you to relax finally and not feel threatened anymore." Chuck looked worried, but Jimmy rattled on before he could interrupt.

"Thomas was the killer. They found absolute proof of it in his apartment. Do you remember me telling you about a queerly folded rubber package near where they found Susan's corpse? Actually, Chuck told me about that. But, anyway, someone supposedly spotted another package, folded the same way, in Diane's hallway the day she was found. Clue-a-rama, or coincidence?"

She didn't venture a guess.

"Right, well, guess what they found liberally strewn through Thomas' boudoir garbage? Nothing but scads of his very own little signature folded rubber packages. Yes, Virginia, there is a serial killer. Do you believe it? We should have been doubting Thomas all along. I knew he was peculiar, but this goes way beyond even my low opinion of the man."

Jimmy grabbed a wine glass from the unoccupied table to their left, "Chuck, just stop looking like that. Rose knows how to keep her mouth shut. Thomas was also tormenting her with scary phone calls, so it's only fair to put her mind at rest now. She's far too special to be tortured any longer. I mean it. Order some more calamari or something and cheer up."

Jimmy's smug tone tested her discretion. She didn't have to worry about breaking her promise to Butler now.

"I knew about that already. I heard Detective Butler get the phone call from Thomas' apartment." The look on Chuck's face when she mentioned Butler's name said he regretted not hoarding his own classified information. Confiding secrets to Jimmy didn't indicate tremendous character judgment; trusting his silence was like wearing a lace muffler to warm your throat.

Her own judgment looked better now. She'd never completely believed Jimmy's claim that eavesdropping had provided all his information about Susan's death. Only Jimmy would call the merciless pumping for information Chuck must have succumbed to eavesdropping.

Chuck ordered another bottle of Zinfandel and food for himself and Jimmy. They'd stopped insisting she order something to eat when she said her appetite was in mourning for Thomas.

"So, what did Butler have to say about all this?" Jimmy would never fill a customer's wine glass so full.

"Basically, he, uh, thanked God seven or eight times. It was like a prayer meeting in there for a while."

Of course, few of Jimmy's customers drained their wine glasses as quickly and appreciatively as she had just done.

"Honey, you should have told him to go ahead and make it a novena." Jimmy took the pepper mill from the nearby service station and dusted the plate of fried calamari the waitress delivered. He dunked a choice group of tentacles into the aioli and nibbled the longest strand first.

"I don't think Butler could manage to stay on speaking terms even with God for nine days, Jimmy." She didn't think her line had warranted laughter as deep and long as Chuck's. Then again, she wouldn't want to work for Frank herself.

While Chuck's laughter sounded more playful than hostile, it still forced Rose into a decision. She wouldn't tell Jimmy and Butler's nice young subordinate about her continuing phone calls now. Not until she'd told Butler first. It was only fair. He deserved that much, didn't he?

Once she had one topic to avoid, every substitute threatened to lure her into newly forbidden territory, too. The weather, for instance, reminded her of the last big snowstorm, and how she'd spent that evening, and what she suddenly needed to tell the man she'd spent most of it with. If she didn't talk herself, she'd have to listen to Jimmy, who seemed determined to exhaust every snippet of knowledge or speculation about Thomas' death. Sitting through his postmortem was out of the question; she'd rather sit at home counting beeps.

She drained her glass in an unladylike gulp.

"Jimmy, Chuck, you'll have to excuse me. I'm even more tired than I realized, and this wine hit me harder than it should. I need my bed. So, I'm going to grab the paper and go home and collapse. Sorry. We'll have to do this again soon, on a night that begins more happily."

"But Rose, I really wanted you and Chuck to have a chance to talk. He's a writer too."

Her heart sank.

"Really, what do you write, Chuck?"

"Poetry, kind of lyrical haiku, except they're longer. Would you like to hear a couple?" Chuck had found his voice.

"God, I'd love to, but we're going to have to put a rain check on that too. Next time, though. I'll look forward to it." She stood and motioned to the rising Chuck to remain seated.

"Don't get up, both of you stay where you are. I'm only a few blocks away and lots of people will still be out. Your entrees aren't even here yet."

Jimmy licked aioli off his fingers. "Now, just because Thomas is dead and nobody's after you anymore, don't get too bold. It's still New York, you know."

"Yeah, Jimmy, I know. See you tomorrow night, and you real soon, I hope, Chuck."

She took a cab home, tipping the driver more than the meter charge. Upstairs, she unplugged the phone, opened a bottle of better Zinfandel, and used the first glass to wash down a handful of tryptophan. It would be a long while before she'd ever want to think about taking any harsher sleep potion. She took the entire Sunday *Times* to bed with her, barricading her mind from frightening thoughts with its weight. She was down to the second section of *Real Estate* and two hours past dawn before she fell asleep.

She slept the deep, sound sleep that makes waking seem the dream.

Chapter Thirty-two

Walking into My World Sunday evening reactivated the nightmare. Jimmy stood behind the bar, looking as if someone had forced him to work at a bowling alley wearing a polyester uniform with his name misspelled on his chest.

He answered her quizzical look, "Zorro—catch and absorb that—Zorro fired Laura today. She didn't show him the proper respect. He is the new general manager. He told me so. What strains my poor credulity even more, so did Ben, who must be totally unhinged by grief to promote a person he dislikes so. Any brilliant explanations for all of this? Please, put my fevered mind to rest. Working here is starting to feel like taking street drugs."

She shrugged, "I knew Thomas planned to promote Zorro, but I figured that scheme was probably history now. Ben likes Laura too much to let Zorro fire her. He also despises Zorro even more than he likes Laura. It doesn't make any better sense to me than it does to you."

She tried to edge her way down to the office, but Jimmy wouldn't end the conversation so readily. He was a hard guy to cut short.

"Well, I think I might actually envy Laura quite soon. Wait until you see it—Zorro parading around like he's supreme manager of the universe, not inexplicably in charge of some little Village dive. It would be funny if it didn't threaten to hurt our pocketbooks. And sanity. I'm telling you, Rose, the death of Thomas did not end this story. New and crazier verses are being written every day. We're entering into the third and terrible testament here."

"Hush, Jimmy, it'll be all right. I'll get behind the bar quickly so you can return to the dining room. Tables and chairs are obviously better for your mental health. Let me get my bank, then I'll help you close out the bar register." It worked, even though she'd thought her reassurances sounded blatantly false.

She stopped in the women's room before going into the office, so she could hurry straight upstairs once she'd counted her bank. She wanted to start behind the bar as soon as she could, before Jimmy started telling the next stranger who walked in how peculiar things were getting.

No time for phone calls now. She'd avoided looking at—forget plugging in—her phone all day, but she'd had half-promised herself to call Butler from the restaurant's pay phone before her shift started. Informing the detective her calls hadn't stopped could wait a few more hours. It wasn't as if he'd proven himself especially effective at stopping the harassment.

What would he do, tell her she was imagining them too? Extol the glories of tapped wires? Tracking the man down on a Sunday evening implied an urgency she refused to admit. Let the detective have his day of rest. Maybe it would inspire the caller to emulation.

She stopped about three feet away from the partially open office door when she heard Ben's voice.

"There's a line, Zorro. There's a line past which even you can't push me. Enough about my brother now. Fucking enough. God help me, but you've won your promotion and your piece of the profits. So now you're going to have a change of heart about Laura. You're going to pick up this phone, call her to apologize, and ask her to please come back to work here. If she says no, you're going to beg. Tell her about stress or some damn thing. And you're never going to fire anybody I hired again, got it?"

Ben's voice rode over Zorro's attempts to answer, "We'll call you the manager and you can play Mr. Important if it gets you off. But, Zorro, don't start taking it serious. Try real hard to keep your mouth shut around me from here on in. You got what you wanted, so shut the fuck up now. Or I'll make sure you don't talk anymore. Ever, you sick bastard." Nothing in Ben's voice would encourage any sane person to challenge him.

Zorro didn't sound threatened. "Ben, please, you must not attempt to frighten me with empty threats. What would your father think if he heard such speech? If I had to tell him the things you say and other things that I know of?

"His heart is breaking because one of his sons killed women. Would he feel any better if the other son killed men? Or if he knew that his son killed the first woman so she could never sleep with his boyfriend again? One son a queer swish, and both sons murderers? The poor old man, I wonder if his heart could take it. I think there has been enough murdering at this restaurant for a while, Ben."

Now Zorro's voice drowned out Ben's reply. "Just to make things easy again for the poor staff, however, I will allow Laura to come back and will give her the chance to fix her attitude. We must excuse grief, I suppose. It will be beneficial for the morals—I mean morale—of the restaurant. I want everyone to see that I can be very easy to work for when things are done right."

Ben cursed loud enough to cover the soft sounds she made as she crept back to the hallway door, inched it open, and slammed it shut.

"Ben? Zorro? Is anyone down in the office? It's Rose, and I need my bank. Hello?"

Zorro answered, telling her not to stand on ceremony, but to come right in. Both men smiled stiffly when she walked into the office. Ben gave her the seat in front of his desk. Zorro sat in Thomas' chair as if he'd owned the position for years. His name should be etched on the door next.

She counted her bank in record time and rushed upstairs to an empty but very clean bar. Jimmy was darting around the quiet dining room before she'd put her money in the register. Neither one of them needed to hurry.

Few New Yorkers chose to drink or eat in a place whose owner had given it the ultimate bad review. Thomas' suicide, aided by the tabloid's gleefully naming him the Restaurant Ripper, had quarantined My World. This third death had tarnished the glitter of whatever fascination the first two had provided. She'd never seen business this bad here.

The regulars who did come in seemed to order their drinks surreptitiously, unwilling to call attention to their presence. Several people asked to go downstairs to pay their respects to Ben. He was taking his own turn at hiding out in the office all night.

Rose envied him the opportunity to spend the evening in the office, instead of watching Zorro's first official night of management. The new general manager assumed airs too lofty for Windows on the World and acted as condescending to the few customers as he did to the staff. Nothing about his behavior boosted either business or morale. Divas had debuted at the Met with less fanfare. And more modesty.

Ben wouldn't be the only one damaged by Zorro's blackmail. The entire restaurant would suffer right along with him.

The best thing about Sunday night was its end, a closing certainly not delayed by any lingering customers. Zorro made too much of counting her bank, taking thirty minutes to do the work of five. Ben didn't bother to disguise his impatience.

Zorro finally finished stacking coins, "Perhaps, Ben, you would like to leave early tonight? Rose and I can put the restaurant to bed, as Thomas always called closing."

Ben slammed his hand down on the desk hard enough to bounce the coins onto the floor. "Don't you ever talk about my brother again, you fuck. His name don't go in your mouth, got it?"

Zorro traced his lips with his forefinger slowly before he answered, "Whatever you request, Ben. Would you like me to get down on my knees now and, um, pick up the money from our floor? Or would it please you more to watch Rose do it?"

Rose rolled her chair away from the desk, as far away from the two men as she could move in the crowded room.

Ben grimaced when he saw her move, then stood slowly. "Clean up the mess yourself for once in your life, Zorro. Rose and I will wait in the hall. With the door open."

She followed Ben into the hall silently. "Sorry again, Rose. Wherever that bastard is from, I wish he'd go back there. His story changes every day. But I know it's a bad one. Too bad Tommy didn't listen to me."

When Zorro finally finished, Ben deposited the cash in the safe, put on his coat, and stood waiting outside the office door. He followed Rose and Zorro upstairs.

"Don't you just love our restaurant when it's deserted and dark like this, Rose? It feels like our own private world, do you not think?" Zorro didn't wait for her answer. "Now, Ben, let me kill the final lights for you."

Ben ignored Zorro. He double-checked the lock on the front door, pushing on the door with more force than the chore required. Zorro hummed as the three of them walked to the corner. Rose didn't think she'd ever waited so long for a cab.

Zorro stepped in front of her when a cab finally arrived, "You will not mind if I take this first taxi, I hope. I have a late date, you know. Life, after all, must continue."

Small talk seemed impossible as she and Ben waited in the wind for another cab. She was just about ready to suggest she'd rather walk when one appeared.

Ben opened the door and handed the driver a folded bill. "Watch her into the door, buddy. Night, Rose."

"Ben, you'll freeze out here. Let's share the cab, please."

"No, hon, I need the walk tonight. Maybe the wind will cool me down." She'd never heard his voice so flat before. His forced smile worried her. She suspected that Ben's sorrow mourned more than his brother's death.

She tried to ignore the fear she'd felt while watching Ben struggle for control tonight.

But who controlled Ben?

Chapter Thirty-three

"Talk to me, Rose, talk to me, please."

She'd heard it twelve times before noon Monday. Creepo was right on top of the new week. Getting a strong start on it. Bolder than beeps, his plea still didn't make her want to talk. She'd grown so sick of hearing him that she'd finally turned off the machine and unplugged her phone again.

The phone stayed disconnected all day Monday, all day Tuesday, and most of Wednesday. She'd plugged it in only to make duty calls to everyone who'd worry if her machine didn't answer. Her explanation, not open to discussion, was that she just wanted a few days' peace after all the frenzy at My World. Wouldn't you know her machine would pick this week to need a trip to the repair shop? Damn.

Going incommunicado was a feeble attempt to recreate the relief of thinking her caller dead. Her efforts to feel grateful that her caller wasn't the killer felt almost as satisfying as making an appointment to have your teeth cleaned. Or a grammar school lecture by Mr. Policeman, who had always vehemently forbidden talking to strangers.

She didn't reach Butler at his office. She'd been good about trying to call him at different times and even included notice of her malfunctioning phone machine in the messages. He shouldn't worry or attempt any unwanted rescue missions if he couldn't reach her.

He'd probably assume she was calling to congratulate him on a well-solved case. You'd think a detective would work in his office once in what amounted to almost three working days. Thomas couldn't have been the only villain he stalked.

She'd squandered the two days away from My World in her apartment, leaving home only for an hour's walk each day. She spent hours and hours writing descriptions and summaries of the last two weeks, vainly searching her scribbles for some elusive explanation.

Then she made lists of everyone she knew, trying to see if any name in her acquaintance would work as the creepy caller's identity. His monologues resisted attribution to anyone she recognized. When she wasn't writing, she slept or flipped nervously through the thirty dollars' worth of fashion magazines she'd bought Monday.

Something more than the continuation of her calls, and the impossibility of identifying their maker, bothered Rose. Something elusive. She tried to isolate its source, suspecting that it originated at My World.

Around and around and around. Over and over and over again.

Thomas could have felt so jealous of Zorro and Susan that he'd murdered Susan and then killed Diane, either considering her another rival or protecting himself against her threat to tell Ben, and maybe others, about his affair with Zorro. Or maybe Thomas had decided he liked killing, enjoyed the act itself. Leave the explanation for the postmortem rapes to the pathology shrinks, who could also determine what anachronisms had made concealing his homosexuality so deathly essential.

Zorro's promotion made better sense when coupled with his affair with the boss. So did Zorro's attitudes, and his daring in flaunting sex with Susan, and his little drug games, and even his ghastly incompetence. Nothing mattered as much as the relationship between the two men.

Fashionable as it would be to assign the drug issue a central role in the story, My World wouldn't turn into a major distribution center no matter how hard she tried to imagine it. None of the signs were there. Drugs had merely made a bad thing worse. His affair with Zorro started Thomas sliding down the crazy chute; drugs had only smoothed the descent. Whee.

Next Rose struggled to understand why Ben acquiesced to Zorro's blackmail. Discovering Thomas had been gay as well as homicidal might pain Joe Victors. She suspected learning his surviving son had paid hush money to buy his ignorance would be a harsher blow. Ben underestimated his father's strength.

Maybe cocaine did arrogantly refuse to remain an anonymous bit player even in this drama. The shit clamored for a larger role. Rose could imagine Zorro threatening to implicate Ben in drug dealing at the restaurant, but he'd have a hard time bluffing his empty threat. While Ben might have given in to blackmail, he was not yet a broken man.

So something didn't gel in her mind. So what. Life was not a colorful molded dessert suspending fruit cocktail. Characters in real life didn't always behave the way her author's mind would have dictated. She was living this story, not writing it.

The case was solved. She should stop looking for trouble.

Trouble, and a quiet phone.

The killer and the caller were different men. Ergo, the caller wasn't a killer. The odds that the caller was harmless were as long as the interstate. So why didn't she feel relieved?

Her caller's persistence naturally worried her, and that distress fostered nagging suspicions. His persistence couldn't last forever. She would just outwait him, tormenting herself with pointless speculations about an already closed case while she waited. It passed the time and didn't tempt her to spend as much money as the ads in the magazines.

Idle thoughts were also keeping her away from her novel. If the murders were over, why couldn't she write?

Chapter Thirty-four

Rose returned to the real world at six o'clock Wednesday. Daring fate, she reactivated her phone machine before leaving the apartment. If the calls persisted, and if the sun came up again tomorrow, she'd find a more powerful way to cope than faking a game with a fixed score. She'd think of something. Or someone.

Ben sounded gruff when he gave her tonight's money, but Ben had sounded gruff since the first day she met him. Time to stop looking for layered meanings in everyone and everything.

The onus of Thomas' death had already worn off in the city of short memory. The restaurant had a good crowd for this early hour. Rose hoped it would get much busier, too busy to worry.

A woman with frizzed white-blonde hair and bold black eyes wanted Rose to tell her all about the murders and the suicide, too. She was a sociology student and thought it would be useful to her career to know all the details. After several attempts to deflect the woman's curiosity failed, Rose finally told her to go buy some textbooks, with pictures if necessary. The woman finished her spritzer and left. Thomas would have yelled at Rose again if he'd seen her lose yet another customer. Oh.

Alan came in with a young man she'd never seen before, sat as close to the service end of the bar as possible, and ordered his usual and whatever the kid wanted.

The kid wanted a Long Island Ice Tea. A Long Island Ice Tea consisted of a full shot of every clear liquor on the speed rack. That meant vodka, gin, rum, tequila, and triple sec, all in one glass, with splashes of coke and lemon to fake its namesake's taste. Rose asked for i.d.

"Rose, please, this is my guest. Rose, meet Ricardo. Ricardo, Rose. Ricardo works for me, for my company. He's old enough to work hard. He's got two kids, for Christ's sake, Rosie. I don't drink with children. We just call him the kid at work because he has so much energy."

Ricardo looked as chagrined by Alan's explanation as he had by her request. She could now see lines no kid knew around his eyes. He scowled as he pulled out his wallet.

"It's okay, Ricardo. Forget the i.d., but I'd love to see a picture of your kids. You know how tough they're getting about underage these days. They have us checking anybody who doesn't use a cane." That got a big smile, a shot of two adorable little girls, and a quick glance at the adjacent driver's license with Ricardo's legal age of twenty-six. They looked younger every day.

Good: her apologetic approached mollified Alan, Ricardo's macho disappeared into his proud fatherhood, and she wouldn't answer any summonses tonight. There were no problems; there were only solutions.

Ricardo made a wonderful addition to her bar, because he kept Alan occupied. The two men drank fast as they discussed the power structure at their job. Alan assumed a fatherly executive air the younger man could probably see through as quickly as he finished his drinks.

Long Island embraced Ricardo. He'd held up fine through three of the concoctions, but the fourth had begun to tell. He had mentioned living nearby in Chelsea, and she'd ascertained early that he wasn't driving. So she'd given him the fourth drink.

Rose got busy at the other end of the bar and then with orders for the dining room. She didn't notice when Alan left. His newspaper and money remained next to his half-full glass, so it took her a while to realize he wasn't just downstairs.

"Where'd Alan go, Ricardo?"

"Back to the office to get something. That guy, man, he's always givin' people things. I think this present, I think it is for you."

"Oh, that's nice." She didn't want to lug another unwanted roast home. Maybe she could sell it to Ben real cheap or trade it in for chocolate mousse.

"Alan, yeah, man, he's a strange one. Crazy sense of humor, too. Loves to give funny things, make people laugh and be all surprised. At work, he don't always act so funny, but now him and me are friends, you know? Like, prob'ly he'll get me a raise soon. Working in that office, with the money, his connections are good. And the favors I did him was no big thing. Took me two minutes the first time, maybe ten the second. Easy way to make a little extra money, 'cause he say he wants to pay, even for a favor."

Ricardo's speech slurred.

His eyes had started to glaze. Alan had better get back soon and put the kid in a cab. No more Ice Teas, not tonight. She wanted to distract him from emptying his last drink too quickly.

"So, Alan likes to give funny presents, huh? Like what?"

"I shouldn' tell you."

"Listen, Ricardo, Alan gives me things all the time. Flowers, a roast, stuff like that. Tell me what other kind of things he likes to give, the funny ones, I mean."

"You got it, lady, flowers is it. But I never seen anybody give his girlfriend the kind of flowers Alan likes to give his woman. Even if it is supposed to make her laugh and remind her of some old joke the two of them have together, I still think it's crazy. Weird stuff, I tell you."

"What's so weird about flowers?" And who was Alan's girlfriend? Since when?

He lowered his voice, "Hey, you tell me, you think dead flowers is normal?"

"Dead flowers? You mean they weren't real fresh, right, Ricardo?"

"No, I mean they was dead. Dead like gone. All ugly and dried out."

Rose felt a little dizzy, "So, what did his girlfriend say when she got them? Maybe she likes them that way. Maybe it is their secret joke."

"I wouldn't know. All I do is deliver the stuff. I never

hand them directly to her. See, that's why Alan needs me to do the favor. He leaves stuff for her when she's not there. And me, I know how to get into places to leave things, you know what I mean? Don't get the wrong idea—I don't do that stuff no more. But I still know how to get into a hallway. Most the buildings in this neighborhood is easy, anyway." He was starting to enjoy his tale.

She didn't give a damn if he were Willie Sutton. "What exactly did you leave for Alan and where did you leave it?"

She'd blown it.

Worry started to permeate Ricardo's drunken bragging, "Hey, lady, what you gettin' so serious for? Damn, I'm puttin' myself in trouble. The deal was I don't tell anybody. Alan gonna have a fit. You don't have to tell him, right?"

She backpedaled like a circus clown. "Hey, Ricardo, no sweat. I just think it's funny. Alan's girlfriend is a friend of mine." Close.

"And I want to tease her a little, because she didn't tell me about his surprises. He'll never know. Girls stick together, you know? Anyway, tell me exactly what you gave her, and where she lives too, so I make sure I'm talking about the right person. I'd hate to start any trouble by mixing things up. If you don't want to tell me, I could always ask Alan about what all you did for him."

Desperate times called for desperate measures. Ricardo was a bright young lockpicker; he saw her veiled threat immediately.

"You promisin' me you ain't gonna let Alan know where you found this shit out?"

She wondered if she should cross her heart, "I swear."

"Okay, then dig this. The first time, I bring the chick a big bouquet of dead red roses. You know the kind that cost a whole lot, with the long stems? Man has to be crazy to spend all that money and then let the things sit around gettin' dead before he gives them to somebody. You know?"

She did indeed. "What else, and where?"

No sober person would have returned her pathetic attempt at an encouraging smile, but it seemed to work on Ricardo, "The second time was a real kick. You know that shit made up of dead flowers and perfume got the name like dope? Pot—pot something. I cracked up when I saw it on the bag.

"Anyways, the second time this woman must have split a gut laughin'. Alan got a wild idea, and I took care of it for him. This stuff made a little red carpet for this woman. From her mailbox, all the way down her hall, and up her stairs, and even onto the knob of her door. Like some kind of magic princess or something." Ricardo chuckled at the memory.

The answer to the question screeched through her brain. She asked it anyway, trying to buy herself a minute to think calmly, "So where was this building?"

"Eleventh and Fourth Streets, on the corner. Crazy corner, too, those streets meeting like that. Remember, Alan can't know I told you any of this." Ricardo looked at her with the first worry she'd seen on his face.

"He won't hear it from me."

No, not from her. From the Angel of Death, maybe. From the last face he ever saw. Hovering above him during his long, slow, excruciatingly painful death.

Rose had to decide how to handle this right now. Alan himself was walking in the door. She felt as if she might levitate with an anger that small weights of relief couldn't ground.

Alan. It was Alan. The creepy caller, the giver of dead flowers, the donor of dead meat. Alan—silly, stupid, harmless, ridiculous, pathetic Alan.

The miserable bastard had managed to terrorize her for day after horrid day after horrid day. He'd invested himself with the violence around him, frightening her with vicarious threats. She had been frightened by Alan. Very frightened.

She couldn't face him across the bar. She waved to Ben in the dining room and told him she absolutely had to go to the women's immediately. Then she ran downstairs, after giving Alan the most appealing look she could manage. It was hard to do come-hither when you wanted to kill.

Alan never required much encouragement. Her look was more than he needed. He followed her down the stairs whistling.

Chapter Thirty-five

Rose filled her lungs with air, but she didn't yell. She grabbed Alan by the shoulders, shoved him against the wall, and hissed a deadly monotone. "Okay, my secret admirer, you don't have to beg anymore. I'm going to talk to you."

He stopped squirming, the most resistance he'd offered.

"I recognized your voice. Finally, I recognized your voice. I also found out there's a pay phone right on the corner by your office, a phone that always has a lot of traffic noise in the background." It was a wild guess, an attempt to keep her promise to Ricardo. A successful attempt. Alan looked terrified. She loved it.

"And the flowers, Alan, the flowers got a little old. Flowers here, flowers there, on the stair, everywhere. Couldn't you have tried something a little more creative? Herbs are nice. You should have tried a bouquet garni, Alan, put a little spice in it." She took another deep breath. Hysteria was history.

He stood dead still, face completely pale, looking at her in total terror. This might not have been the way he'd imagined she'd talk to him.

She couldn't stop, "Tell me, what did you think was going to happen? Did you think I would return your affections? Think I would hear your sick little 'nighty night' so many times I'd get hypnotized into liking it? Familiarity, even when you try to be mysterious about it, it does breed contempt, Alan. And contempt would be heaven compared to how I feel about you."

He looked like a worm pinned to a collector's board. "Rose, I didn't mean anything bad. Honest. I thought you'd like being courted that way. All I wanted—"

"You thought I'd like it?"

They had probably heard that one upstairs. She was losing control fast. Deep breathing, keep it cool. Let him hang himself.

"It was only a few phone calls and some flowers. Please don't act like I tried to hurt you. The last thing in the world I would ever do is try to hurt my little Rosie. Hurting you would be hurting myself." Greasy little tears were forming in his vile, frightened, eyes.

She heard footsteps pounding down the stairs and looked up to see Owen jumping down the final three steps.

Alan yelled at the interruption, "Get away, you stupid snapper. I'm talking to Rose alone, the way we both want it."

He continued in a softer tone, "Rosie, I never loved a woman the way I love you. My other phone friends were nothing compared to you. You and me were the best."

That did it.

"Right, Alan, you and me. You and me. Like this."

She stepped back, remembered every bar brawl she'd ever watched, and hauled off the fiercest right she could manage. He crumpled when her fist smashed into his chin. All he did was crumple.

"Owen, give me a quarter, and take this sniveling coward into the men's room. Don't let it get too far."

He did as she'd asked, with Alan following his leading arm like a shadow. She dialed the precinct with her left hand.

"Hello. This is Rose Leary, calling from My World. What can you do to someone who's been harassing and threatening women over the phone and contracting break-ins to their buildings?"

The voice on the other end asked her to hold, and she stood impatiently listening to an odd series of hisses and crackles on the line. Ben would be furious if she didn't get upstairs soon." Rose, it's Frank. You okay?"

"What are you doing on this call? I didn't ask for you." She didn't need his questions now.

"They had orders to patch your call through to me, whenever it came in. I'm not in the city, so the connection sucks. What's going on?"

"I'm fine, and I have a surprise for you. Thomas didn't make those calls. They didn't stop when he died. A customer here made them. I should have figured it out before. He's right here, actually. I mean very close. Somebody's putting cold water on his face right now." Her hand wouldn't mind getting near some ice in the immediate future, either.

"Why cold water?"

"Because I just hit him as hard as I could, Frank. But

we can talk about my pugilistic powers some other time, please." She'd never heard Butler laugh so loudly. The good sound carried clearly over the terrible connection.

"Stop it, Frank. I have to make this quick."

His laughter doubled.

She spoke over it, "I'm not the only one. He said he's done this to other women. And he finally left messages, so you guys can do voiceprints or whatever that technological trick is. What now, Frank?"

"Shit. Listen, Rose, I can't get there tonight. I'm sorrier than I can say, but even if I started driving now it would be too long before I got there."

"Where are you, Frank?"

He ignored the question. "But this is what I'm going to do. I'm sending a couple of guys over to take this jerk in. Don't worry, they'll use the downstairs entrance again. I'll be in the office waiting to talk to you by the time you wake up tomorrow. So call me from a phone that works, please. We'll take care of your friend, don't worry."

"Frank, I don't have anything to worry about anymore. Get it? I'm really in the clear this time. I am a happy and safe woman, Frank. With a sore hand."

He laughed again before they hung up.

Owen had been leaning in the men's room doorway, listening to her.

"You can explain it all later, Rose, but I heard the basics. I'll keep Mr. Alan quiet down here, refraining with great difficulty from hurting him myself, until some other men come to take him for a little ride. Dirtbag."

"Owen, you're terrific. I owe you. Now I should explain this to Ben without anybody else catching on."

"Go ahead, Champ."

The good thing about undemonstrative men was their cool in a crisis. Ben understood the gist of her whispered information very quickly, muttering that he'd never liked the little bastard anyway. He asked if she wouldn't rather have him take care of Alan himself. She decided it was safest not to explore that offer and reassured him she had everything under control. She went back behind a bar now missing Ricardo. She'd kept her promise to him, too.

Five minutes later, Ben told her to run downstairs for a minute. Chuck and another uniformed officer had arrived. They arrested Alan quietly. He started babbling his confession before the last syllable of Miranda subsided.

At the end of her shift, Rose went to the precinct and filed her complaint. Alan had already volunteered the names of three other women he'd tried the same tricks with. Two of them wanted to press their own charges. Rose left the station in what seemed record time.

Chuck offered to walk her home. She refused. He insisted. She refused again, telling him she wanted to enjoy her new feeling of unharassed, unthreatened, unbeatable freedom.

He insisted again.

She refused. She'd walk straight across Bleecker. It was only a few blocks.

He said Butler would put him on tunnel duty if he didn't see her safely home.

She agreed, on the condition that he walk on the other side of the street. Nothing personal, but she needed to enjoy this alone, silly as it might seem.

She reveled in her emancipation all the way home. Lyrical haiku would have killed the mood.

Chapter Thirty-six

When she looked out the window in the morning, the sky's dirty elephant grey squashed any hope of blue. Sheets of icy rain squalled against her windows, shrieking in the wind. Lowering clouds had stolen two thirds of her view. She thought it all looked glorious, the most beautiful morning she'd ever seen. Only a philistine fool would call this late February storm bleak or dismal. Its brutal beauty sang a special glory, if one could only hear it. She pitied anyone unable to appreciate the wonders of the gorgeous day. If Chuck were here, he could recite all the poems he chose. She'd appreciate every one. Every extra counted syllable.

Something about the dull grey light particularly flattered her phone. She'd never fully appreciated the economy and grace of its design or the gaiety of its cheery red. Her splendid machine would trill only with welcome calls. Marvelous invention, the telephone. She couldn't imagine a day without its happy ring.

Even her calendar looked promising. With the terrible fear gone, the forty-three days she had left to finish her book seemed more than generous. She couldn't wait to get back to her real work.

Today demanded celebration. Rose put down the cup of coffee she'd started sipping, walked to the kitchen, and clambered onto a kitchen chair to reach her cappuccino machine on top of a cabinet. It was one of the few wedding presents she'd salvaged. She stored it as inaccessibly as possible to frustrate caffeine mania but still hauled the contraption down monthly to burnish it until the copper shone with a rich gleam.

She hummed as she took milk from the fridge and two pains au chocolat from the freezer. A glorious celebration breakfast. Lee Bailey should do a book: *Meals to Relish When Your Life and Sanity Are No Longer Threatened.*

She was fortifying herself before her one o'clock appointment with Butler at the precinct, although she hoped he'd choose her alternate suggestion that they meet at her apartment. Her perceptions of the day as beautiful hadn't blinded her to the point where she actually needed to immerse herself in it. He was out and about already, anyway. His shoes were already ruined. They could tie up any loose ends better here than at that dreary precinct house. Home ground might even provide her with the moral fiber to resist gloating. More than was fair.

The foam from Rose's second cappuccino had vanished along with the crumbs from both pastries. She had started to make her third, and absolutely final, coffee when her buzzer rang. Butler should have shown the courtesy of calling before coming so early, but disappointment in his breaching etiquette was like regretting acne as a sign of youth.

She pushed the button on her intercom box and requested the caller's identity.

Squawk. Crackle. Screech. Syllables disappeared into impossible static. Her building's intercom system worked about as often as a homely young model did. Her visitor must be Butler; nobody else would wander around making unannounced visits in this storm. Poor man, how sad to have to worry about murderers still. She wondered if Butler drank cappuccino as she buzzed him in.

Suddenly Rose had a terrible thought. What if it weren't Butler? What if Alan had decided to retaliate for her punch yesterday? Maybe jail had taught him about direct action, and about attacks more intimate than phone calls. A vengeful Alan could be climbing her stairs right now.

She ran to the phone, dialed the precinct, and asked for Butler. The deskman told her he'd left the office. That news didn't guarantee he was the person climbing her stairs. Rose dignified her tone, identified herself as Alan's lawyer, and asked where she could reach her client.

She felt absolutely no sympathy at hearing Alan's behavior had become so bizarre overnight that they'd sent him to Bellevue for observation. Nothing she could do about it if his own mind decided to punish him before the courts had their chance.

Butler should have informed her of this new development. She'd ask him why he hadn't mentioned it as soon as she let him in.

She was pulling the brush through her hair when he rapped a knock significantly gentler than he'd used on his last visit. She tucked in the white silk blouse she'd substituted for her old sweater as she reached the door.

Wait, this was still New York and she still hadn't reverted to innocence. Rose couldn't believe she'd almost unlocked her door solely on the assumption that Detective Frank Butler graced its other side.

She peered through her peephole and swapped one disbelief for another. Zorro stood on the other side of the door, beaming at the peephole and waggling a bottle of Cristal that protruded from a brown paper sack.

Zorro was here, outside her door, waiting for her to welcome him into her apartment. He might ruin a good bottle of champagne while he waited.

It wasn't a party for one anymore. Zorro already knew she was home and ready for company. Rose couldn't think of a single excuse to keep him out. Why alienate the new boss? She'd let him in, force down a little champagne, and then explain she had to meet an officer at the station house. It wasn't the sort of excuse people disputed, particularly not people in Zorro's position.

Guessing why he'd come would leave her holding the doorknob until the metal disintegrated and the Cristal went flat. She quickly dismissed the idea that he might want to move his blackmail to her. What could he want, fifty pages a month?

Zorro wore jeans and a black turtleneck under a black overcoat. It was the first time she'd seen him wear any pants not made of leather.

"Ah, Rose. Good morning, almost afternoon. I hope you will forgive the intrusion. Your line was engaged when I tried to reach you. This is a spur of the moment call, to tell you all the truth. I had to do business at the bank around the corner. It is too miserable outside to head back to the restaurant so soon. A manager's hours are long ones, no? But, we must break up the toiling with little islands of relaxation now and then." Zorro hung his coat carefully over a kitchen chair.

"Forgive me, but I heard of your problem with Alan and the brave way in which you solved it last night. I felt I must congratulate you. You are as brave as you are beautiful. Do not, even for one moment, think that you must apologize for asking me to intercept his calls to you at work by telling a falsehood. The stress on you must have been very bad, so the lie is forgiven."

He flourished the bottle. "Remember I once promised we would drink champagne together? It is time now, I think, to put sorrow behind us and celebrate whatever we can. So, shall we drink this humble bottle together? Perhaps it will brighten up this ugly morning."

Cancel savoring the strange beauty of the day; she wouldn't debate weather appreciation with her new boss. Rose agreed with him, mentioning how sorry she was her appointment with Detective Butler would force them to rush. Zorro said he never minded drinking fast.

She'd drink his champagne pleasantly, only scratching around the edges of his boldness if it seemed safe.

Zorro was not the kind of guy you sat at the kitchen table with. She ushered him into the living room and went back to the kitchen for champagne flutes. He'd left the bottle and the bag on the kitchen table. The bag had been carefully smoothed and folded.

He'd folded the bag very neatly. It was in such precise sections, it looked perfect, like an illustration of proper folding techniques. She'd never had the patience to fold anything that carefully in her life.

Perfect folds. Precise folds. Perfect fool.

Take two men. Add sex. Find contraceptive packages. Then blithely subtract one of the men? Jesus Christ, they'd all been doing equations with half the factors missing. There wasn't a single thing in God's sweet world to prove the folded rubber packets found in Thomas's bedroom had belonged to him and not to his lover. Zorro.

The crazy parts all scrambled together. They fell into a perfect line, a precise line. A fold. Of foil. Zorro. Oh no.

The little intruder nagging and twitching around the back stairs and bottom floor of her mind this week finally identified himself as a loitering suspicion that they'd blamed the wrong man for the murders. The dead can't defend themselves, and the accused's lover certainly didn't care about defending his beloved's reputation.

Not at all. Losing profits from blackmail was a bigger sacrifice than he cared to make, thank you. The only thing Zorro would defend was the opportunity to continue profiting from his little venture. He'd had to invest too heavily entering the market to sell short now.

Diane hadn't worried about sitting around the kitchen table with Zorro. Ugly precedent.

Three points for Nancy Drew. Ten more if she survived this encounter for the next three minutes, forget generations.

Still, she had no firm reason to assume Zorro had come here to kill her. That might push his luck too far. She was lucky she'd mentioned her date with Butler so soon. Zorro had no cause to want to kill her. She hadn't given him any reason to suspect she knew a thing. Not for her the notes threatening exposure. No, not at all.

She shouldn't feel so frightened. She might be reading far too much into this visit. It was perfectly possible that it was in fact a friendly visit.

Rose couldn't wait to see Butler.

She put the bottle of Cristal and a white linen napkin on a tray. She was reaching into the cabinet for flutes when she heard Zorro's footsteps behind her.

Chapter Thirty-seven

"Is everything all right, Rose? Having trouble opening the bottle? I have just been sitting by your window, looking out at the rain and wind."

"No, Zorro, everything's fine. I'm just dusting off these flutes. Haven't had champagne for a while, so I wanted to make them sparkle again before I poured." She tried hard to arrange her face into a smile before she turned around.

Rose looked at the cappuccino machine on the drainboard in front of her, hoping to check her expression reflected on its side. The angle didn't work.

Instead, she saw a distorted reflection of Zorro standing in the doorway. He looked very small, as if he were miles instead of yards away. Zorro's tiny little hands were not empty. He was holding two tiny little things. One of the things Zorro held was the legal pad she'd written all her descriptions of the My World affair on.

He hadn't been looking out of the window; he'd been reading. Reading all her descriptions, suppositions, and accusations. She hadn't wanted him to see that. Maybe she could still talk her way out of this, telling him it was the outline for a story, and she just used real names sometimes. Right.

She squinted into the copper as if it held her future, trying to identify the second tiny thing in Zorro's hands. Short future. Zorro had a switchblade. He was raising it now. And moving toward her. It wasn't a friendly visit anymore.

Rose tightened her grip on the stem of the flute she still held. She slammed the glass against the side of the sink, twirled around, and slashed in Zorro's direction.

She had the advantage of surprise. He stepped back out of her reach, but not before she gashed his right arm just above the elbow. The cut looked about four inches long and bled enough to suggest she'd gone deep.

He switched the blade to his left hand. She prayed he wasn't ambidextrous as she feinted with the flute, trying desperately to force him further into the center of the kitchen. She needed more room to maneuver.

Now that he'd moved closer, she could see tell-tale white rimming his nostrils. His grossly enlarged pupils shouted cocaine—lots of cocaine. Zorro's look of shock changed slowly into a lopsided smile.

"Ah, Rose, I always feared you might be too smart for your own good, although putting your thoughts in writing was not too clever. I never thought you would be as stupid as Diane. But I do admire your courage. You have no experience in fighting, and your weapon is a crystal stem that may shatter at any moment. And my wound is only on the surface. You cannot win." His voice assumed a hypnotic tone.

"Put it down, Rose. Put down your poor little weapon, and we will talk. We will look into each other's eyes and talk together. I did not come here to hurt you. I came in friendship. Finding these pages upset me, but nothing bad has to happen here. Two smart people can always reach some agreement, or so I have found. We can talk together until we come to our own agreement."

He edged almost imperceptibly closer to her with each of his calm, intentionally soothing words.

She slid along the wall to his right, inching her own way out of the corner. Zorro was not Rasputin. His tranquilizing tone and his steady gaze wouldn't work. The last place she would look was at his eyes. Although she knew reasoning with him would be howling into the void, she could talk as well as he could. Better.

"Forget it, Zorro. You'll kill me the minute I put my weapon down. Just like you killed Susan and Diane. Sorry, I'm not falling for the trick. You'll have to come up with something better."

They stood five feet apart, each grasping a weapon. She told herself a crystal flute with the bowl broken off so jagged shards pointed up from the stem was not necessarily inferior to an undoubtedly cheap switchblade knife. Zorro tried to ignore the pain of his cut; Rose tried to ignore the impossibility of what she was doing.

She hadn't trained for this. She always closed her eyes when these scenes came on in the movies. She didn't know the steps to this dance.

But Zorro did. He'd had lots of practice.

Nightmares weren't this bad.

Nightmares didn't try to slash your flesh.

Zorro lunged at her, knife raised. The distance between them vanished. She looked up to see the knife slashing down. It caught her in a long but shallow cut across her right breast. Blood blossomed on her chest as she ducked and twisted while Zorro raised the knife again. The knife landed in her shoulder, three inches of its vicious blade buried.

It was the advantage she'd prayed for.

The knife was buried in the doubled-up shoulder pads under her blouse. Only its very tip pierced her skin, just enough pain to tell her what had happened. The pads must have slowed the blade's descent as they absorbed most of the power of its thrust.

Rose groaned pitifully as she slumped further down and saw the expression on Zorro's face change. He looked ecstatic, thrilled at the blood and by seeing his knife disappear into her. He wasn't discriminating enough now to discern that something other than flesh had absorbed his blade. He didn't question why a bony shoulder had felt so soft.

He stood over her, slowly preparing to take the knife out of her shoulder. He didn't look as if he wanted to rush. His fever didn't waste itself by speeding through the good parts.

Rose looked up at him, putting a poster child's pleading into her eyes. She'd slid halfway down to a sitting position now.

"Zorro, please." She wanted to get herself into the

optimum posture and slumped down a little more.

"Beg away, bitch. I might do you differently. You are the kind of bitch who suffers better with knowledge. You can feel the knife while you hear my story."

She tried to look as if the knife caused her great pain. He smiled when she grimaced.

"Thomas had already killed Susan, out of his stupid jealousy. You see, I seduced the man out of boredom and to get myself an easy job. Then he goes to such lengths. Afterwards, he weeps, telling me of his sin as if I am the priest he once tried to be. Getting caught loving a man stopped that career, also. He was such a poor frightened man. I had to clean up his mess. Taking his money was so simple." Zorro's smile widened as he bragged.

"All I got to do was move Susan's body around and fuck her coldness. Stupid Thomas thought he had made her death look like a robbery. But I used my copy of his keys and put her in the back to confuse everyone and make them wonder about Ben."

Keep him talking. Gather your strength.

"It must have been easy for you, Zorro. You were smarter than all the rest of them, weren't you? Even smart enough to engineer alibis. Did you make money off letting someone impersonate you on vacation, or was that just to give you and Thomas a chance to spend more time together?"

He didn't answer with more than a nod, as if deviating from his story might lose his momentum. "Then Diane was too easy. So stupid, with her little threats to run to Ben and her eagerness to have her ugly earring back. I hate sloppy people. Her floor needed mopping even before I entered. Still, the knife loved Diane so much that I had to honor it. So I fucked her cold, too." He watched her slump down even further.

"I think you will be different, Rose. I think the knife and I will enjoy you together. Just a few more cuts to make you lie more still. And then the big cuts and the fucking. I think they will share you, like Thomas and Susan shared me. But you will not be in charge, and I, I was always in charge. I am a man of power." He reached into his jeans and pocketed something she couldn't see.

"Yes, I will try something new with you. You will die a happy woman, looking into my eyes. I have given you information, so that all your questions will not haunt me. I have no need for more ghosts. For every giving, there is a taking. And the knife and I will take you at the same time. It will be my gift."

He stood over her, gloating in anticipation of the pleasures to come. In a minute, he would raise the knife out of her shoulder. His hands were already tensing.

Rose took the deepest breath she could and tightened her grip on her weapon. She thrust up between his legs with all her force, driving her crystal spear into him.

Rose ended Zorro's future as a rapist.

Chapter Thirty-eight

No rest for the weary. Rose had just finished tying Zorro's hands behind his back with two extension cords when she heard another knock.

Zorro had passed out after his Grade B movie scream at her attack. She still didn't take any chances. She'd pulled his switchblade out of her shoulder and put it on top of the refrigerator, out of his reach. She hadn't dared remove her weapon from his wound. She worked quickly, anxious to call 911 and see Zorro removed from her home. The wound shouldn't be fatal to the rest of him.

She probably couldn't avoid a trip to the precinct sometime today. There were worse things to see in your future.

She walked to the door and peered through the peephole. Her overwhelming sense of delight at seeing Butler on the other side amazed her. She wanted to open the door and hurl herself into his arms. Stress was famous for eliciting outlandish and abnormal reactions.

Instead, Rose turned off the overhead light, edged around to the far side of the door, patted her hair and opened the door just wide enough for Butler to see her but not into the kitchen behind her.

Better to break it all to him gently. Somehow.

Butler howled with laughter. "Jesus, Rose. You really are too much. Sickest sense of humor I've ever seen. I'm including my own here. You're worse than I am, and a lot of people wouldn't believe that could happen in this world. I love it, I gotta tell you. I love it."

"Love what, Frank?" Someone must have slipped drugs into her espresso beans. She couldn't be hearing this. The man who was supposed to be her bastion of control was gibbering like a hyperactive kid at Baskin Robbins. Last night she'd punched a man. She'd emasculated another within the last hour. Now just the sight of her totally unhinged a hardened detective. She was beginning to feel truly dangerous. It beat in danger.

"I love the fact that you should go to all this trouble just to break my balls, Rose. I didn't embarrass myself enough the last time I burst in here, you're gonna remind me of it. How could you be so sure I'd come by, though? Not even you would have walked outside looking like that, would you? Hope the tomato sauce doesn't stain that nice blouse. Doesn't it feel kind of sticky in your hair?"

He thought. He actually thought. Dim lighting didn't begin to excuse it.

"It's not sauce this time, Frank. And I'm not breaking your balls, although it turns out to be quite a skill with me."

She stepped back, pulling the door wide open. He looked from her face to the bloody scene in the kitchen. His face sobered and he reached for her.

Frank pulled Rose to him. He held her tightly for a minute. Then he pushed her away just far enough to give himself room to rip the buttons off her blouse. As the little pearlescent buttons scattered all over the bloody kitchen floor, Rose fell back weakly against his supporting arm. She felt as if all the strength she'd saved had flown away with the buttons. The expression on his face as he stared at her breasts frightened her.

"Not bad."

"What?" She bolted indignantly out of her ripped-bodice swoon. There really was no rest for the weary. Life was insult upon insult upon insult. She wouldn't take this one, though, not from him and not now. She found a small reserve of strength.

"How dare you take advantage of my weakened, injured, momentarily distraught condition? How dare you? And who the fuck do you think you are, anyway? Did I request your appraisal? Why don't you call 911 instead of leching around here like some ridiculous stud? We have a man here with a pretty serious injury, in case you hadn't noticed. Just because I had to hurt him to defend myself doesn't mean I want him to die on my kitchen floor. I can think of better prospects for that role right now."

Zorro moaned as if on cue. Butler barely glanced at him before looking at her again.

"Your cut, Rose. It isn't bad. You won't even have a scar, thank God. Calm down, now. If I hadn't taken a look, how would I have known how many stretchers to tell the emergency people to bring? Why don't you relax now? Please. You should lie down. Quiet. We'll press a nice clean towel to your cut while you do." He opened drawers until he found a dishtowel and handed it to her. She held it gingerly against her cut, as much for modesty as first aid. She wished he hadn't picked a linen one.

He'd left the kitchen to call for help, but returned within seconds. "Hold it with more pressure than that, for God's sake. The idea is to stop any bleeding, not blot it like a powder puff. I'll do what I can for this guy until they get here, but you shouldn't be in the room. We'll have plenty of time to talk later. Wouldn't you like to lie down now, Rose?"

She shook her head. Although his voice had calmed her, she wanted to stay where she could see him. Both of them.

She'd embarrassed herself by casting Butler as a *Playboy* editor. His interest had been purely professional. She didn't leave the room but discovered that sinking into a kitchen chair felt enormously better than standing up.

Rose wanted Butler to understand, to know everything. It suddenly mattered terribly to her that he tell her it was all right. She needed to hear the words. Soon.

"He did it, Frank, he confessed. But, he didn't do all of the first one. I mean, Thomas killed her, but Zorro moved her around and raped her. And Zorro did Diane, all of it. The earring did matter, Frank. It was how he got in. And the rubber mattered even more. I knew it had to." She pressed the napkin against herself harder.

"They faked all the alibis. I think Zorro knew how to use all the phone company's special features real well. See, Frank, I'm not crazy. I knew it wasn't finished before. I did, didn't I, Frank?" Zorro still hadn't moved.

"Will he live, Frank?"

"Longer than he deserves, Rose. Remind me never to get you real mad at me again, okay? You do know how to make a man's life not worth living if you want to, don't you?"

"It was my only chance. He was going to kill me. I knew too much, and he found out I did. So he was going to kill me, Frank. Frank, he really wanted to kill me. And then he was going to rape me, just like he did the others. He told me all about it. About how he was going to kill me, and rape me, and—"

She stood up, needing to see Butler's eyes while she talked. "So I stopped him, Frank. I shut him up. I had to."

"You did, Rose. You had to. And you did what you had to. It's all right. Everything is all right. We don't have to worry anymore." He was holding her gently again, careful to keep the towel over her cut.

She leaned into him. "Frank, don't you mean I don't have to worry anymore? Like you always say, no matter what terrible thing is about to happen?"

"Goddamnit, Rose, I said we. Because I meant we. Do. Not. Have. To. Worry. Anymore. At least not about this creep, anyway. Are you really going to question every little word I say forever? What is it, it bothers you so much to hear somebody else talking that you try to pretend they don't know how to do it right? Somebody ever wants to get you as badly as you got Zorro, they'd aim for your tongue. It's probably indestructible anyway."

She closed her eyes.

"That's more like it, Frank. Now you sound like the man I love."

"What did you say?"

"I said you sounded like the man I love, Frank. Whatever man I might eventually, someday, love, that's how he'll sound. From that, we must deduce that he sounds like that now, too. That's what I meant. Don't worry, Frank. That's all I meant."

"It's still the nicest thing you've ever said to me, Rose."

"So far, Frank. Maybe I've been saving the good stuff."

"For what, the end of the world?"

"No, the end of the worry."

"How long were you going to save it? The worries don't end, Rose; they change. A man could die waiting for a kind word from you."

"You said it, Frank. I didn't. This time, I'm not saying a thing. Not a word, not a syllable, not a phoneme. My lips are sealed."

"Why the sudden silence, Rose? Afraid you can't find any words that aren't insulting anywhere in your huge vocabulary?"

"No, that's not it at all. But Zorro might wake up at any minute and I wouldn't want him gossiping all over his prison about the passionate embrace we're about to share. The next thing you know, he'll be telling all the criminals we're having an affair. We both have reputations to consider here, Frank. I think I may even be in shock. So, the smartest thing for us to do in this situation is not to talk anymore. Not another word."

Butler didn't argue.

About the Author

Maureen Anne Jennings has worn the hats of a journalist, copywriter, editor, publishing consultant, media relations manager, book festival director, and Fillmore East staffer. She owns more than 100 hats, not all of them work related.

Her short fiction has appeared in the anthologies *Traveler's Tales Italy, Cartwheels on the Faultline*, and *Saltwater Sweetwater*, as well as in various periodicals.

After the obligatory waitressing in college, she squandered a few years behind the bar at various dives in lower Manhattan. She also owned and operated a pub in northern California. Be careful what you write about.

She graduated from Fordham University summa cum laude in comparative literature and still reads as many novels as she possibly can. Words are her life.

Connect

Email: toughprose@gmail.com
Twitter: @toughprose, @maureenjennings
Facebook: Tough Prose Press, Maureen Jennings
LinkedIn: Maureen Anne Jennings
Google+: +Maureen Jennings,
          +Tough Prose Press
Web: ToughProse.com

Some new platform, coming soon.

Made in the USA
San Bernardino, CA
12 October 2014